The ENEMY at HOME

C. M. CONNEY

Published by
Ace Lyon Books
August
2018

Published by
Ace Lyon Books
Acelyonbooks.com
First Edition
Cover Design by S. M. Savoy
C. M. Conney The Enemy at Home

ISBN 978-1-947122-24-6
ISBN-10: 1-947122-24-X

Other Books by *C. M. Conney*

The Real Deal (A ST9 thriller)

Take the Shot (A ST9 thriller)

Moon Caught (Paranormal Romance)

This book was inspired by the heroic volunteers who risked and lost their lives serving on the front lines in the medical field.

While the setting of the book is real, the characters are all fictional although more than a few VADs and QAIMNS died in the war. Official numbers are debated, especially among the volunteer forces where poor records were kept.

During the Battle of the Bulge, the German's surprised the Allies and overran the lines, causing the medical personnel to retreat under fire, including the women who had so bravely volunteered. Their sacrifices remain mostly unrecognized and are a testament to the truly inspirational heroism of the English nurses. I like to think some had as happy an ending as my fictional characters, Brook and Jack.

C. M. Conney

Table of Contents

The ENEMY At HOME

Jack Leaves Home

May 1940

"Don't cry, Marie," Jack said, putting his arms around her and patting her back.

Marie pulled away and lifted her apron to wipe her eyes. "How can you go? You've only been home a day."

"Where are you going?" Jack's brother, Edwin, asked as he entered and held out his hat.

Marie bobbed her head and accepted it. She helped Edwin remove his coat as she said, "Master Jack is joining up. Tell him that's ridiculous."

"*I* will speak with my brother. Inform Agnes I won't be here for dinner."

"I'll be fine, Marie," Jack said and gave her another quick hug.

She sniffled and hugged him hard.

He closed his eyes and rested his cheek against her graying hair.

Edwin made an annoyed sound and tapped his foot.

"Don't let him bully you," Jack whispered.

"Don't you be worrying about me." Marie pulled away and used her apron to wipe her face again. "The mister won't you let go. I'll see that your room is properly aired, and you'll stay home as you should. Going away to school is bad enough, but this..." She tsked and patted his cheek before scurrying away.

Jack gazed after her, smiling fondly, glad his father had her company although it likely hurt him as it did Jack to see the resemblance to his mother. He pushed his memories away and turned to face his brother.

"Don't waste your breath. I'm going."

"I suppose it's for the best, although you'll devastate the old man. Have you spoken with Phips? In eight months, you'll be twenty-one and need to put someone else in charge of Sylvan if you won't be here to take over."

"I was hoping you'd do it? Dad can hand it over to you instead of me until I get back."

Edwin frowned and straightened his cuffs. "The running of the company is no small job."

Jack glanced at his brother's shaking hands and sighed hard. His brother's bland expression gave nothing away, but it was obvious Jack's news had upset him too, despite the fact that it had been Edwin's idea in the first place that he join up.

Edwin was the one who'd spoken of a young man's duty to country when he'd last come home. And Jack had agreed it was cowardly to hide behind wealth as the children of Edwin's friends did to avoid service. He laid a hand on his brother's arm.

"I'll be fine. You can run Sylvan as you see fit until I return. I'll go speak with Phips and Groger today. My allowance is enough. You can keep the profits while you're running it."

His brother made a face and stepped away.

Jack rolled his eyes and released his brother's arm. His brother hated talk of money and displays of affection. He thought them both crass.

"Don't be such a fuddy-duddy!" Jack called over his shoulder as he headed to the door. "And take care of Marie and the old man.

Jack stood on the parquet floor, trying not to feel like he was five years old and being called in for a scolding. Warm sunlight streamed through the open French doors behind his father's double-wide mahogany desk.

Built for two, Jack could almost see his mother's ghost in her usual spot across from his father. Soft spring breezes wafted a hint of roses to him. Roses she'd planted and cared for herself. Everything about this house held memories of his mother. She'd designed every detail with loving attention.

He tore his gaze from her empty seat and

glared at his father. Not because he was angry, but because he didn't want his father to notice the sad glance at his mother's empty seat and be reminded of his loss.

"Dad, I'm going!"

"You can't go! I need you here. Calm down and we can talk about this."

Immaculate in his pinstripe suit, his father's once brown hair had turned snow white since the accident four years ago that had killed Jack's mother and sister. The lines in his face deepened as he gazed at his son.

Jack ran his hand through his short, brown hair and scowled. His father licked his lips and traced his fingertips over the open folder before him. The nervous gesture made Jack feel bad. His father loved him and was worried.

"Look, Dad," he said in a softer voice. "I'll be drafted in a few years anyway."

"Son, you're only twenty." His father drew in a deep breath, obviously searching for patience. "Sylvan is vital to the war effort. You won't be drafted if you're managing it. Why join now? America has no part in the war..."

"Buttons," Jack scoffed and rolled his eyes. "I'm not making buttons. We both know it's just a matter of time before America joins the fight. I'm joining now, and when we do go overseas, I can make a real difference."

"Buttons are crucial. Not glamorous, but important. I'm getting on in years and need you."

Jack cut him off. "You have Edwin. He'll be more than happy to run Sylvan too."

"Sylvan is yours. Your mother worked hard to get that company going."

"I know."

The hurt in his father's voice made him wince. But if his father had his way, he'd be wrapped in cotton and kept on a shrine to his mother's memory.

"I love Mom and Janice, but it isn't fair to expect me to give up my life for them."

"I'm trying to save your fool life!" his father snapped. He half rose and leaned over the desk, bracing himself on his hands. "War isn't glorious or an adventure. It's dangerous!"

"I know that!"

The two men glared at each other a moment.

His father straightened and held out his empty hands. "Son, please, just finish college first, and we'll talk about this again when you graduate."

"I already told them I won't be back until this war is over. Dad, I'm sorry, but I'm going and not for an adventure."

A twinge of guilt roughened Jack's voice. He did think it would be exciting to see Europe and be involved in the fight for freedom. He looked forward to getting away from his brother's increasingly annoying criticisms and lectures on running the company.

"I really believe we need to help our allies now, before it's too late." *That wasn't even a lie,* he told himself. He did believe the Nazis were a danger. *It didn't matter that by joining I'm avoiding working in the family's business,* he told himself firmly.

"You're all I have left," his father said in a broken voice and rose his hands to cover his face.

Jack stood stricken, not knowing what to say. His mother's and sister's deaths had devastated his father, leaving him a shell of the man he used to be. He never laughed or smiled now. The once welcoming house seemed cold and lonely, and Jack hated it. He'd been happy to go to off to school, and maybe been a bit wild, but he missed the parties and crowds of his youth. He missed his father's booming laugh and his sister's giggle. Most of all, he missed his mother's quiet smile and the soft look in her eye when she gazed at them.

"Dad, they're arresting and separating families. Innocent people. If we do nothing and they succeed in pushing passed their borders, they'll try here next. You now they will. We need to stop them."

"I'm not arguing the Nazis need to be stopped, but you can help more here— at home!"

Jack threw his hands in the air and spun away. "The enemy is there, not here! I'm not making buttons!" he called over his shoulder as he slammed from the room.

Brook Leaves for Europe

May 1940

Brook's father, Doctor Eugene Taylor, was a man used to getting his own way, and Brook knew this would be a difficult talk.

"You'll stay here, and that's the end of it. You'll get your degree and work right here in England. How can you even think of joining?"

Brook glanced at her mother, Lillian, for support, but she stood at Eugene's elbow and scowled, nodding agreement with everything he said.

Her father's secretary, Marilynn, poked her head into the office and gave Brook a small, encouraging smile but said nothing.

Brook had been coming to this office and working with her father since she could walk. He'd taught her everything she knew and had encouraged her to get her nursing degree and now her doctorate. Marilynn was a good friend and understood Brook's need to help. She closed the door, leaving them alone. The muted sounds of her father's crowded waiting room faded with the closing doors.

"Dad, they need surgical nurses, and they need them overseas, not here. I'm young but well trained. Let me join the nursing corps, and I can make a real difference."

"Absolutely not!" Lillian snapped and released Eugene's arm.

She shook her head so hard her still vibrant dark hair swung loose from the knot on her neck. She absently tucked it back into a neat bun as she spoke.

"Your father is right. That's no place for a young woman. Why anything could happen to you. We forbid it, Brook."

"Mother—"

Her mother took a deep breath and clasped Eugene's hand in both of hers. "We agree the need is dire, but you can help right here at home. We've discussed this and decided that even the Voluntary Aid Detachment is too dangerous. No, you'll stay home and finish your schooling."

Eugene disengaged his hands from his wife's grasp and absently patted them. "Queen Alexandra's Imperial Military Nursing Service is much too dangerous. You'll be a doctor, Brook not a VAD, or a QAIMNS," her father said as he stepped forward and hugged her quickly. "I love your kind heart, and I realize the nurses are dangerously understaffed, but I can't let you go,

Brook. It's simply much too dangerous. You can finish your medical degree and work with me right here in London. We need surgical nurses too, and when you're a fully qualified doctor, we'll hang your shingle beside mine. Your mother and I love you and want you safe."

Brook hugged her father hard a moment before hugging her mother. She'd known they would forbid her joining, but she was legally an adult. Guilt formed a lump in her throat.

"I waited to finish this year of school, but I can't wait any longer. I'm going to join up today." She held up her hand as her father opened his mouth. "As a VAD, but I'll go where they send me. Gloria tells me the training is quick because the need is so urgent. I won't be able to complete my degree right now."

Tears filled her mother's eyes, making the lump in Brook's throat grow.

"I'll be careful, Mum, but they need me."

Her mother pressed her lips together and shook her head.

"You will not! I forbid it, Brook," her father said. He glared as he gathered a stack of files and strode from the room.

Marilynn entered and lifted an eyebrow.

Lillian waited until the door closed behind him before saying, "Keep money on you and stay in camp with the other nurses. As proud as I am of our young men, they can act wild—"

"She'll be fine," Marilynn said and took Lillian's hand. "Brook has a good head on her shoulders. She won't put herself in compromising situations."

Brook grinned ruefully.

Lillian narrowed her eyes, placing her hands on her hips. "I expect you to remember you're a lady and behave in all ways appropriately. War isn't an excuse to act immorally."

Brook hugged them both. Guilt deepened her voice when she spoke. "I'll make you proud."

She hurried from the room before they could see her tears.

Her mother thought the VADs remained in England, but she knew they served on the front lines. Her best friend, Gloria, wrote her weekly, and the stories she told chilled Brook. England's young men needed help. Help she could give. Her father would be angry when she left, but he'd forgive her.

On the street, she glanced back at the hospital. Since war had been declared last September, the hospital bustled with activity. A hushed air overlay the entire city. Laughter held a hysterical edge and tears seemed to linger in everyone's eyes.

England was worried and hunkering down for a fight. Sandbags lined the streets and shades covered the windows. Airplanes overhead set off sirens and panicked running to the nearest shelter. Her father was wrong thinking she'd be safe here. Nowhere was safe from the German Reich. The Nazis had declared war on the world.

Jack at War

Four Years Later
NOVEMBER 1944

Jack let his rucksack fall to the snow and removed his helmet to tighten his scarf. The khaki wool around his ears made hearing difficult, but all he could hear anyway was Frank and Henry bickering. Most of the men in his platoon plodded down the narrow dirt lane without speaking.

He snatched up his rucksack and shrugged it on, awkward in his thick gloves.

"Hey, buddy, you dropped your bedroll." The new guy, John, handed him the tightly tied blanket wrapped in ripped canvas as Jack nodded his thanks.

"Requisition a new pack. Yours is holier than Jesus."

"That's his lucky pack," Frank said and slapped Jack's shoulder. "He'd have been dead ten times over without it. There's a story for every damned bullet hole. Hey, remember back in Paris, when that guy tried to pop you while you were sleeping?" Frank said as he fished a cigarette from a mangled pack in his top pocket and lit up. He inhaled deeply, the smoke mingling with the frosty air they exhaled.

"Bloke thought Jack's pack was his head and released a full clip into it. Shot the hell outa his helmet." Frank snickered and nudged Jack with his elbow. "Tell John about that time in Amiens when you stopped to take a piss—"

Jack let the words wash over him. Frank would keep telling stories until they stopped for the night or the lieutenant made him shut up.

The memories Frank thought were so funny Jack found terrifying. He clearly remembered the sound the machine gun had made as it had shredded his bedroll. Those bullets had been meant for him, and it was just dumb luck he'd gotten up minutes before, leaving his helmet atop his pack.

His pack was lucky, he thought and hitched it higher on his back. He'd been shot twice, both bullets slowed by his pack and ending up mere flesh wounds that didn't even require a visit to the doctor. Their medic had patched him up, and he was able to stay with his squad.

And he liked these guys. Too much maybe. It was easier not to know them, not to care. He was sick of this war and this place. He was sick of mud and snow and being cold, hungry, and dirty. Warm rooms and clean beds seemed like a dream. He couldn't remember the last time he'd eaten hot food or taken a shower. June and his discharge seemed like a million years away.

His life had become a series of long walks interspersed with violence and the death of friends. At another time, he'd have enjoyed these Belgian forests and quaint towns, but there was no enjoyment left in his life. He really wished Frank would shut the hell up.

Frank's laughter and John's questions made it hard to remain in the mindless state where you didn't notice the pain in your feet and shoulders or the ache in your legs from walking all day.

"Button it down!" Walt called over his shoulder. "Intel has this next section of road defended."

"Yes, sir, Lieutenant," Frank said and stuffed the red rag he used to clean the Thompson machine gun he carried into his pocket.

Jack eyed the gun enviously but didn't envy Frank having to lug that beast around. Only four men in the platoon carried machine guns. Frank kept his gun in pristine condition. He caressed the gun lovingly and spent as much time cleaning it as he did talking.

Jack unlimbered his Springfield rifle and stripped off his gloves. All around him his platoon did the same. The talk died down, and they tried to step quietly. In Jack's experience, intel was usually a day or two behind. Walt knew that too though and would compensate. He'd warn them before they walked into the shit.

Walt had a knack for sensing when it was about to hit the fan. The entire platoon kept one eye on him and dropped as one when he lifted his fisted hand ten minutes later.

"Hawkins, take Trenton and James and ease through the trees there and see what we got," Walt whispered. "Pryor, Michelson, and Adams, you three, go left."

Walt was still sending his men into position when Jack led his small squad forward into the left-hand trees. Heavy vehicles chugged along somewhere in front of them. Men spoke but were too far away for Jack to make out the language.

Jack crouched and darted from tree-to-tree, his eyes scanning for movement, or dislodged greenery and dirt. They rarely ran into traps, but it had happened. He bit back a laugh. His pack had saved him from a trap too. He'd thrown it to a base of a tree where he'd intended to bed down, and it had blown fifty feet. It had survived with only a small scorch mark and a stain from the can of beans that had exploded to show for it.

His shoulders relaxed, and he straightened as they drew closer. The men before them spoke English. Just to be safe, he remained low until he laid eyes on them, but he knew they were his guys.

"Michelson, head back and tell Walt. I'll see if I can find an officer," Jack said.

Michelson gave him a two-finger salute, and he and Adams ran back to their platoon.

"American!" Jack called as he exited the woods holding his gun over his head. "The Twenty-eighth, Platoon L, here. Anyone got word from Dutch?"

Men walking beside and riding in the trucks paused to stare. Some nodded greetings, but most went about their business as if he wasn't there.

A tall, thin man, marching with a group of his fellows, gave him a friendly smile and spit a wad of tobacco juice into the muck covering the road. "Sure, Mack, the bird's back in the nest but our lieutenant has the latest." He cupped his hands around his mouth and bellowed, "Peters, Walter's group is coming in!"

A brawny man who'd been sitting on the open tailgate of a fully loaded truck jumped down, ran over, and offered his hand. Jack shook his hand and eyed his worn uniform. Stains marred the elbows and knees like his. But unlike his, this man's pack bulged with supplies. Jack eyed it enviously. He was down to his last can of beans and had eaten half-raw rabbit two nights in a row now.

"Good news for you," Peters said in a thick Jersey accent. "I got orders to send you in for resupply, and this road is clear all the way back. You'll be eatin' hot tonight, boy." Peters slapped his shoulder and nodded to the trucks. "We're headed to Bastogne to dig in. Got orders to support the port there in Antwerp. There's a big push coming. We'll have these shitheads cleared up in no time."

Jack nodded noncommittally. He'd heard that too many times to count. The big push sounded dire though. Usually, the officers called for, 'little skirmishes, or, a small dust-up,' and that meant Jack and his buddies would be deep in the shit for days.

Walt joined them, and Jack wandered off while the two officers talked. His platoon gathered around, most, like Jack, taking out their last can of beans and squatting on the side of the road to eat it.

He'd have liked to sit, but the light snow had been churned to mud and having a cold, wet ass wasn't on his list of things to do. He used his finger to scrape the side of the can clean, then crushed and stowed the empty can in his pack before standing to take a quick head count.

"All thirty accounted for, sir," he said when Walt joined him.

"Let's double time this, boys. Word is we're getting resupplied and might even get Christmas off. I don't know about you, but a shower and bed are all I want for Christmas."

The men laughed and joked, full of good cheer at the prospect of a few days rest and real food. Jack smiled too but what he wanted was home. He wanted to see women and children smiling instead of starving and begging for food. He wanted to sleep an entire night without worrying someone was going to shoot at him.

Walt slapped him on the shoulder. "Let's go. Pryor, lead us out."

"Yes, sir," Jack said with forced enthusiasm and put some extra oomph in his step.

The men fell in and followed with a firm stride. Jack peered over his shoulder and smiled. By damn, he was proud to serve with these men. They marched on the edge of the road, wearing their ragged clothes and carrying empty packs with their heads high and their steps firm.

Walt called out a cadence, and soon all the men were yelling their marching song. Pride straightened Jack's spine as the men in the trucks saluted Walt. When the last truck had disappeared in the distance, Walt let the song fade, but the glow of pride remained until they reached the outskirts of Wiltz.

This must have been a nice place once, Jack thought sadly as they strode up the muddy dirt road. Tents now filled the fields on both sides of the street and crude fortifications had been built across the once-green fields. Barbed wire surrounded the machine guns and cannons that now lined the street and sandbags edged trenches, empty now but waiting like graves. Jack turned his gaze away.

Someone on the trucks had called in their imminent arrival because tents and hot food waited for them.

"Pryor, see about replacing our radio and hand in our requisitions, then you're off duty with the rest of the men on a three-day pass."

Jack saluted and jogged away. Three days of sleep and hot food. It sounded like Heaven.

A blaring siren worked its way into Jack's dream. The dancehall on second street back in Pennsylvania morphed into the Parisian whore house where he'd spent his last leave over eight months ago. The girl in his arms spun out of his embrace on the music. He knew her name was Josie, she was the last girl he'd danced with back home, but her face remained a shadow.

A sharp rattle of gunfire mixed with the music, and Josie began unbuttoning her shirt, but he couldn't concentrate, the siren wouldn't be ignored.

When he opened his eyes, a clanging bell had been added to the air-raid siren. All around him men grumbled and stamped their feet into boots. The dream refused to fade. He'd been serious about Josie and crushed when he received the letter breaking it off, and now he couldn't picture her face.

"Should've fucking knowed," Frank complained as he stood and stretched. "One fucking day."

"Better than none," John said.

Jack had to bite back his laugh when Henry punched him.

"Hey," John said all indignant.

"Knock it off," Jack pulled Frank away before he could hit John too although he wanted to punch him also.

"Fucking new guys," Frank muttered.

Jack slapped Frank's shoulder and grabbed his gun right as Walt ran in.

"Leave the weapons but shake a leg. Grab your macks; it's raining out there. Our field hospital was hit, and they're rushing them here.

"Pryor, take five men and get down the west road. Assist in the triage. The rest of you are with me. The trucks have jammed up in the mud, and we're going to hump those poor sods to the hospital."

The men quit grumbling and ran after Walt. Jack didn't have to ask for volunteers or assign anyone. His usual crew ran out the door behind him. Cold rain trickled over the brim of his rain gear and across his face. Wind grabbed the oiled canvas and whipped it, letting the rain soak the front of his trousers.

All around them, men yelled questions and instructions their voices loud to be heard over the screams and moans of the injured and the wind tossed rain.

"Looks like they let an idiot drive," Frank said in harsh disapproval.

Jack had to agree. Some idiot had managed to slide sideways and tip himself over, blocking the entire road. Injured men sat on the ground, most sporting new bleeding wounds and older bandaged limbs. Another truck had rammed the first and a third had tried to avoid the two and ended up on its nose in a foxhole on the left. Men had been flung from the back of that truck, landing in the barbed wire surrounding the fox hole. Most of the screaming came from them.

"There'll be a kit in the truck," Jack said and headed to the closest cab, slipping on his gloves as he ran.

"Stop moving!" a man yelled in a voice tight with pain. "They'll cut us out just stop struggling, you're making it worse."

Previously injured men, wearing patient gowns, not the thick, wool uniform that offered Jack some protection as he reached into the wire and began cutting, were tangled in the heavy wire. Other soldiers had arrived and begun cutting them loose. Curses and cut-off screams rent the night air.

"I got him," a man said at his shoulder as Jack fumbled one handed with the cutters, trying to support the man's legs as he freed them so they wouldn't tangle in the uncut strands beneath him.

He glanced at the older man beside him, nodded, and continued to cut, ignoring the barbs that cut into his hands and arms as best he could. The two of them lifted the man out and went back for another. When he laid the second one down, a woman leaned over the first man. Soaked brown hair straggled over her cheek and she clutched her dark-blue coat closed with one hand.

"How bad?" the older man asked.

Jack turned to peer through the dark, but it appeared as if all the men trapped in the wire had been freed. He turned back in time to see the nurse hand the man a shred of white cloth.

"Tie it on his right hand." She stood and cupped her hands around her mouth. "Take the ones with the white cloth on their wrists first." She squatted again and brushed at the blood dripping down her cheek with one hand as she spoke. "You're going to be fine, soldier."

She glanced at the older man and nodded reassuringly but spoke to the man on the ground. "The scratches are mostly shallow, and I don't think you'll lose your sight. No, don't try to open your eyes." She yanked off the white, veil-like hat on her head and ripped it apart. With gentle hands, she wrapped the man's eyes.

"My mates." The man struggled to rise, and the nurse pressed him back down.

"Do what the nurse says, soldier," the older man said, and with a slight shock, Jack realized he stood beside Dutch himself.

"We'll take care of them." The general patted the injured man's shoulder and rose. "They're all out. You did good."

"You need to stay still or you're going to ruin all my hard work," the nurse added.

"Birdie?" The man on the ground said the name hopefully.

"Yes. You can trust me. I swear you won't be blind, and you'll hardly be scared at all. I'm more worried about the stiches you broke. You just lay still until they come for you."

Her patient moaned, and her lips tightened. She smoothed his hair and gathered her skirt to rise.

"You'll see me tomorrow," she said in parting and ran to the next man.

Jack waved his arm to gather his squad. Everyone saluted the general before running after the nurse.

"Jesus," John said and crossed himself as they came up on the wreck laying sideways across the road.

Dead men strapped into stretchers littered the ground. Wounded men lay in the mud, the lucky ones covered by ponchos or bedrolls. Blood darkened the puddles. Something had exploded, taking parts of men with it. Luckily mud and rain mostly obscured the chunks spread across the ground.

Jack averted his eyes from the grisly sight and bent to help an injured man adjust the thin piece of tarp over an unconscious man on the ground. At least Jack hoped he was unconscious and not already dead.

"This one, sergeant."

Jack turned to the light soprano voice and

bile rose in his throat. A woman shouldn't be in the midst of this horror. Two men shouldered past him and picked up the man she'd indicated as she crawled through the mud to the next man.

"Can someone give me a hand here?"

Jack crouched beside her.

The woman spoke without looking at him, her hands busy in the chest cavity of the man before them. "Hold the belt on his leg tight. Release it every three minutes for ten seconds. Make sure whoever moves him keeps the pressure on. "

Jack gripped the tourniquet she'd placed on the man's leg. "Frank, take my poncho and rig something over this guy. What do you need, ma'am?"

"A towel or shirt or something. Here, can you hold this?" She glanced at him quickly as she handed him a bloody suture kit. Blood still trickled from a cut on her scalp and her eye was beginning to blacken. Something had scrapped her cheek, leaving a rough, red patch, but she had the prettiest blue eyes he'd ever seen.

"Fuck," she snapped, and he snorted with laughter, surprised by the foul word from her. With her English accent, she sounded refined and delicate, but she continued to mutter swears as blood spurted between her fingers.

Frank handed the nurse his mack. She took it absently and folded it into a crude pad, pulled out a piece of metal from the man's chest, and pressed the material to the wound. He and John stood over them, stretching out John's poncho to block the rain from the woman's bowed head. She worked quickly, her fingers deep in the man's chest again.

"What have we got here, nurse?" a man asked. He leaned over Jack, his once white coat was now stained and soaked. Rain had flattened his hair and trickled in rivulets into his soaked clothing.

"Metal post from the truck nicked the artery, doc. He's got another bleeder in the leg. I got this one stitched, but it's rough."

"Can you clamp the leg?"

"I think so." The man by the wheel there has a crushed pelvis and his buddy isn't going to make it. He might be dead already. There's a four-inch-deep gash along the back of his skull and his arm was torn off. I used a tourniquet but..."

"Save the ones we can."

"Yes, sir," she said in a tight, trembling voice.

"You're doing fine."

The nurse bit her lip and nodded.

Jack glared about him. This girl didn't belong here in the mud and filth. She should be in a drawing room sipping tea. Not here surrounded by violence, cold and scared and heartsick.

"Okay, when I say, release the belt." She shook out her hands and leaned closer. In her hand, she clasped a small clamp. He didn't know how she could see anything what with the spirting blood and rain and the three men looming over her, but she sat back on her heels a minute later and patted his hand.

"Hold this just like I've got it. "

He gingerly took the small scissor-like handles from her.

Cold rain sluiced across his side as she crawled away. He hadn't even realized her body heat was warming him but now that she was gone, he missed her presence.

"You're going to be just fine," she said to the next man as she examined the bleeding gash on his leg. "How's the head? You still see me okay?"

"I be fine, Birdie. Take care of me mate."

She smoothed his hair and patted his cheek before crawling to the next man. "Looks like you wanted to go home, huh?" she said as she gently moved the man's hand from his chest. "This feels worse than it is. Try to take slow, shallow breaths. I can help you, and you're going to be just fine.

As she spoke, she fumbled in a black bag hanging from her side, removing a clear vial of liquid and filling a needle that she injected into the man's shoulder.

The man she'd just checked tried to sit but gave up. He groaned, clutched his ribs, and laid back in the mud. "What's wrong with him?"

"He has absolutely no sense of humor."

The groaner laughed as the man she worked on wheezed out a chuckle. She patted his hand and turned to his friend.

"Tony has a punctured lung and maybe a few broken ribs to add to his broken leg and bullet wounds from yesterday." As she spoke she withdrew a package of gauze from her bag.

Jack watched doubtfully. Between the rain and blood, the gauze seemed pointless to him. She seemed to think so too because she let it flutter away, keeping only the thick waxed packaging that she turned inside out and pressed to the man's chest.

"Sorry, I know it hurts, but it'll be better soon. Take shallow, slow breaths. That's right." She continued to speak encouragingly as she used her free hand to check his pulse.

"Can one of you hold this down?"

"I got it," John said and hurried over.

The nurse pushed herself up and ran through the rain to the next clump of men. The three men leaning over the two on the ground made way for her.

Four men ran up carrying stretchers. Jack rose slowly to his feet, trying to keep the clamp in his hands from moving. One of the stretcher carriers glanced at the wound and winced but brought out a thick roll of surgical tape.

"Hold him steady for a minute and I'll tie that down."

The orderly carefully took the clamp and packed gauze around it, then used half a roll of tape trying to get it to stay. Jack removed his poncho and tucked it around the injured man who still hadn't regained consciousness.

"Okay, lift him nice and easy on three," the orderly said.

Jack helped lift the man and took the stretcher poles so the orderly could oversee the wounds.

Jack held the tape, reading the orderly's name off his uniform "Will he make it, Burns?" Jack asked as they hurried to the hospital as fast as they could through the sleeting rain.

"Maybe. Can't say." Burns waved down an approaching ambulance. "Surgery for this one, STAT."

Jack helped load the man into the back of the ambulance and then ran back to the wreck. The girl was still triaging patients while Frank held his poncho over her in a futile attempt to block the rain.

"What can I do?" Jack asked.

"Get the lung guy to the hospital next, then this guy. Tell the doc or an orderly that guy" – she gestured with her chin to a man lying on his side clutching his leg— "has a compound fracture but it was a clean break. I'm worried about infection. He needs to get somewhere warm and dry pronto."

She waved a hand through the air and brushed at the mud splattered on her face. The mud smeared with the blood on her hand but the water trickling down her cheeks washed it off.

Her lips were blue with cold, he noted and stood closer, using his body to block the wind.

He followed her to the next three men, holding her kit and following her directions, only leaving her side to inform the stretcher bearers on who to take first and pass on her instructions.

Men continued to arrive and carry the wounded away and the noise and confusion abated. He glanced around but didn't see the general.

The doctor returned and examined the next patient with her. "You'll be fine," the doctor said to the man at their feet. "You got a good whack, but your stiches held up. Hang in there for a few more minutes, and we'll get you warm and dry." When he finished speaking, he used the flashlight in his hand to check the nurse's eyes, grabbing her chin with one hand as she turned away.

"I'm fine," she said.

"You need to go get warm and into some dry clothes." He furrowed his brow and pursed his lips. His gaze lit on Jack, and he smiled slightly. "Escort the nurse to the tents behind the mess tent. There should be an empty one there. The rest of the nurses will be along tomorrow."

Jack nodded he understood, but the doctor's attention was already on the nurse again. "This should've been an easy duty. I'm sorry for your sake but happy for theirs you were along. These men can thank you later for their lives. Clean up and get some rest. We can handle this from here." He traced the dark circle beneath her eye and skimmed the edged of her bruised cheek with his thumb. "Volunteers like you are making all the difference. If you ever need a job..." he trailed off and stood, offering her a hand to help her to her feet.

She stood and watched uncertainly as the last men were removed from the scene.

"I'll catch up," Jack said to Frank when he hesitated.

Frank nodded and ran off after the last wounded.

"Miss?"

She glanced at him and smiled ruefully. Mud covered her skirt and pulled at her boots with a sucking sound as she stepped forward. She hesitated at the back of the truck and Jack was surprised to realize she was crying. Rain hid the tears that trailed down her pale cheeks, but her sniffling and eye rubbing gave her away. Her cheeks pinkened when she turned to him.

"Sorry, it's stupid but I don't want to go back in there. Will there be clothes or anything in the tents?"

"Your gear is still on the truck?"

She grabbed his shoulder and pulled him back as he stepped forward.

"Don't— Please. Can we just go?"

"Yes. I'll have someone bring your bag. I can scrounge you something to wear and maybe a cup of tea?"

"Tea would be lovely," she said wistfully.

Shivers racked her hard by the time they

reached the tents. He wasn't much warmer and wished he had a coat to offer her. He'd stood as close as he could, trying to block some of the wind and now sleeting rain, but she was soaked through.

"Leave your wet clothes by the door," he said as he held the door for her.

Canvas nailed to wooden frames formed these tents. Like the one he was staying in this one had a wood floor and cots placed every four feet. He flicked the switch to the right of the door and the bare bulb dangling in the center of the room lit. He handed her a blanket from the foot of the bed and went to see if he could get the small pot stove going. Without the other women's body heat, the stove would do little but even a little was better than nothing.

To his relief, someone had already laid kindling and the stove started right up. He held his hands to the flame a moment to ensure the stovepipe drew correctly before turning back to her.

Her elbows were pinned by her wet jacket, and she strained futilely to free her arms. He burst into laughter and rushed to help her.

"Here. Let me help," he said and grabbed the end of the sleeve.

Her form-fitting, blue jacket had gotten stuck halfway down her arms, and she thrashed silently trying to make the soaked material release her. She giggled while he yanked.

"We might have to cut this off," he said.

Her clothing was soaked through and bunching up on her arms as he tried to pull.

"Let me try to pull the sleeves down first," he said as he forced his fingers up the tight sleeve.

She obligingly stood still while he tugged with her clothing. Blood had left pink stains across her white shirt, and he hoped none of it was hers. Beneath her shirt, she wore something lacy over her full, high breasts. The lace showed clearly through her soaked shirt. He averted his gaze from the stiff nipples poking the soaked material.

She barely came to his chin, and he bet his pack was heavier than her. A fine tremor racked her, and he could hear her teeth chatter. He tugged her closer to the stove, standing so close to her, he could see the faint line of freckles crossing her nose and feel the warmth of her body. The intimacy of the moment felt odd. Just standing beside her felt odd, but he liked it.

The jacket finally came loose with a sound like paper tearing.

"Hope I didn't rip it," he muttered.

She laughed again and rubbed at her arms. Her fingers fumbled at the small buttons of her cuffs. By her red face, he knew she was getting angry.

"Here let me." He undid her black tie and the tiny buttons on her collar and cuffs. He wanted to help her with the others but the red in her face had grown to alarming proportions, and he thought she was holding her breath.

He snatched her jacket from the floor where he'd dropped it and placed it and her tie on the back of the only chair in the room.

"Lots of blankets," he said as he gazed at the unmade beds. A gray wool blanket sat at the end of each green cot. "The men's showers are on the opposite side of the mess tent, but... I have no idea where the women's showers are. I could bring you some warm water to wash up in," he offered.

"I have enough water, thank you." She grimaced as she wrung out her hair. "I'll shower tomorrow. I'm so tired I could sleep for a week."

He picked up a blanket and laid it over her shoulders. Water still dripped from her hair and down the side of her cheek. He began removing her hair pins and rubbing the freed strands with the blanket. She sighed softly and leaned closer.

He wished she was his. More than anything he wanted to pull her even closer, to drop her wet clothing on the floor and tuck her against his body until her shivering stopped. He'd love to see a smile light her beautiful eyes and hear her laugh. She tensed as his hands stilled in her hair. He cleared his throat and stepped away.

"I'll bring you something to eat and wear." He gazed around the empty tent and frowned. "Are you sure you'll be okay here?"

"Where else can I go?"

The questioned stumped him. He didn't even

know if there was a hotel in this town. He'd spent the last day repairing his gear and sleeping, not traveling farther than the showers and mess tent.

"I'll assign a guard outside. Rest easy in here."

"Thank you. You've been very kind."

He wanted to stay and talk with her, to pretend this was an ordinary night at home. The sweet lilt of her voice sounded like he imagined a great lady would sound as she invited you in for tea and scones. If he closed his eyes, he could picture her in a lace dress with her hair loose around her shoulders, the sun streaming through crystal windows highlighting the thick brown strands of her hair.

He winced. Her hair was currently sopping and his mooning over her was keeping her shivering before him.

A blush heated his cheeks as he inclined his head and hurried from the tent. He ran all the way to his tent and grabbed his last clean pair of pants, and then stole John's clean shirt and socks.

John entered as he was rummaging through Frank's pack.

"Borrowed a shirt and took your clean socks for the nurse. Who has a clean sweatshirt?"

"Hawkins. All his stuff is clean." As he spoke, John headed to Hawkins' bunk where he helped himself to a sweatshirt.

Jack stripped off his wet clothing and

grinned at John who handed him Hawkins' clean clothes.

"Set a watch rotation outside her tent," Jack said, his voice muffled by the shirt he was pulling over his head. "She's alone in there, and while I don't think our boys will give her a hard time, it's better not to take chances."

"Yes, sir."

Jack stuffed his purloined clothing into his pack and ran out the door. A light snow had replaced the rain. Flakes settled on his bare head and shoulders but didn't chill like the rain had. Despite the hour, the mess tent was crowded. Frank hailed him and waved him to a table by the door.

"Can't stay. Need to bring the nurse some tea and food."

A man with a bandaged head and a gray blanket around his shoulders rose. "Birdie saved our asses. Again. Let the man through."

Jack smiled to himself as the men made way and offered chocolates and cigarettes for her. He declined but thanked them.

"She made quite the impression," Walt said as he wrapped a ham sandwich in a paper napkin. He added an apple and three cookies and handed the food to Jack who accepted a canteen from the cook before taking the food from Walt.

"I set a guard on her," Jack said.

"Good idea."

"Her kit is still on the truck."

"I'll see to it." Walt rose a hand and beckoned Jones over while he spoke. "Take her the food. Word has it she's been up since yesterday. She's a surgical nurse and they sent her along so she could rest up for tomorrow."

Jack snorted.

"I guess they expected some, ahh, relapses from moving them."

"If the goddamn Germans would just respect the damned red crosses, we wouldn't have to move the injured until they were well enough. We're losing more men that way."

Walt lightly slapped his shoulder. "Preaching to the choir, son. Don't keep her waiting."

Jack eased through the crowd with the food clutched to his chest beneath his coat. Back outside, the snow had picked up, *or maybe it was the wind,* he thought hopefully. He didn't look forward to trudging through a foot of snow. He knocked on the door post but got no answer.

"She hasn't made a peep," John said. He leaned against the wall with his rifle on his back.

"Go back to bed. I'll stay until the next guy shows."

John gave him a two-finger salute and jogged away.

Jack smiled slightly. It occurred to him that the girl had distracted him utterly from missing his sleep, something he'd have sworn impossible a day ago.

She'd left the lights on, he noted as he

opened the door.

The single bulb cast wavering shadows over the room. She's also taken his advice and spread out all the blankets, laying on a thick stack with another stack over her.

She was sound asleep, one slim arm atop the covers, the rest of her buried beneath the blankets. He winced. The blankets were rough wool and sure to scratch her skin.

"Ma'am," he whispered.

She moaned lightly and thrashed beneath the covers. He placed the food on the floor and felt her forehead.

"Ma'am," he said again louder.

Her arm flailed as if pushing something away and she stirred, then sat with a sharp cry. She'd left her hair down and damp strands straggled around her bare shoulders. She clutched the blanket to her chest and took deep gasping breaths as if he'd frightened the wits out of her.

"Sorry. I didn't mean to scare you. I brought you clothes and food."

"You didn't. It was a dream. A nightmare." She rose trembling hands to her face. The blanket slipped, exposing the tops of her breasts, and he was instantly aroused and then angry with himself. She wasn't here to be ogled by a stranger. She'd come and risked her life to help those wounded in battle. And he was an ass for taking advantage, inadvertently or not.

He shook out a blanket, tucked it around her

shoulders, and gathered her hair. Firelight flickered on the dark strands and glinted in the water droplets on her skin. He began combing her hair with his fingers and rubbing it with the blanket.

"You're freezing," he murmured as he rubbed her back. He was shocked when she began to cry and clutched him.

"It's okay. You're safe. You're safe," he repeated, knowing he lied but not knowing what else to say.

She pushed away a moment latter and rubbed her eyes, leaving her hand cupped over the injured one as if it hurt.

"Sorry." Embarrassment laced her mumbled apology.

"The clothes won't fit, but they'll be warmer than nothing and the blankets are scratchy. They're clean," he added in a cajoling voice.

She dropped her hand and hiked the blanket up, offering him a shy smile. "Thank you. You've been very kind.

"Tea and food as promised." He gestured to the food he'd brought and stood.

A lost expression crossed her face and her anxious gaze traveled the empty room.

"We're right outside," he said as reassuringly as he could.

Instead of comforting her, the words upset her. Tears again sprang to her eyes, and she turned her back. "Could you stay for a bit? Just a few minutes... If you'll turn your back, I'll change quick, and we can share the tea."

"I can stay."

He sounded breathless to himself, and he wondered what she thought of him. He couldn't think of anything he'd rather do than have tea with her. He wished they could have tea at restaurant at home. He'd take her for a walk in the park, or maybe take her sled riding. It was winter after all, and they could drink hot chocolate and eat cookies and sit beneath a soft blanket, a red one, and put their feet to the fire.

She cleared her throat and he started and hurriedly turned away.

"I was just thinking, I wish we met somewhere nicer, somewhere warmer."

A piece of her clothing hit the floor with a wet splat. A lump formed in his throat and he rubbed his hands together hard.

"Warmer would be amazing," she said wistfully. "And quiet. I miss the quiet the most."

"I miss hot food. I dream about roast beef and potatoes."

"Mmm, Yorkshire pudding. My mum makes the best pudding."

The longing in her voice made him sad. She should have all good things.

"This damned war," he muttered.

"My father didn't want me to come." Her breath caught, and she made a soft, unhappy sound. "I'm decent— I guess."

She'd said it so doubtfully, he glanced over

his shoulder.

"Just a bit big," he lied and knelt to roll his pants up.

She held the waist tight and giggled. Her giggle made him smile. Time stopped when he met her eyes. His heart began to pound. In another life, maybe he'd have knelt before her with a ring in his hand.

She smoothed his hair back and rested her warm palm on his cold cheek. For seconds they stared at each other without speaking.

"You're freezing too," she said breaking the spell that held him.

She was flustered, but he didn't know if he'd caused it or the situation had. Still holding her borrowed pants up, she handed him a blanket. He accepted it and tossed it over his shoulder, then dragged a cot closer to the stove. He gathered the food and sat on the cot. Men and machinery sounded muffled in the distance. It felt as if they were alone in the world.

She sat so close beside him, her shoulder brushed his. A faint smell of strawberries surrounded her mixed with an earthy scent.

Blood and rain, he thought ruefully, and handed her the thermos top to pour the tea, steadying her hand with his. He longed to leave his hand on hers, and again he wondered what she thought. He wanted to know everything about her, but she was exhausted and cold and likely in no mood for small talk.

They shared the sandwich in companionable

silence. He refilled her tea, letting his hand linger on hers. When she handed it back, she took his hand and leaned on his shoulder. Surprised, he glanced at her. Her eyes had closed, and she was already dozing.

"No, stay," she blurted when he stood.

The fear in her voice stiffened his spine and he wished he'd brought his gun.

"I'll stay as long as you want me." He rose and spread another blanket over her, then sat with his back to the wall and patted the cot beside him. She blushed but snuggled closer half-lying beside him.

"Sleep. You're safe here."

She relaxed against him and was asleep in minutes, a soft, warm weight against his chest. He smoothed the strands of her wet hair back and traced the shape of her face with his fingertips. Her black eye was visible and darkening. Only a small dab of mud remained beside her ear. The cut on her hairline had stopped bleeding, and he wondered if she were hurt anywhere else.

Frank opening the door woke him. He'd slid down, and she slept with her head on his shoulder and one leg over his.

"She was afraid to stay alone," Jack whispered.

"Uh huh." Frank smirked but tiptoed across the room to add wood to the stove. "I'll cover for you, but you better be back in your bunk before

Walt comes on duty here at oh-seven-hundred."

"Thanks, man."

Frank nodded and gave him one last envious glance as he flicked the light off and closed the door.

She murmured and snuggled closer. Her too big pants had slid down, and his hand rested on the bare skin of her lower back. The soft curve of her ass brushed his fingertips. It took willpower to resist the urge to caress her, to stop his hand from trailing the swell of her buttocks or the curve of her breasts. Warm and relaxed against him, he could explore her body while she slept but that would be a base betrayal, and he was still a gentleman.

A soft exhalation escaped him, and he withdrew his hand, placing it over the blankets to avoid temptation. He'd never been so comfortable in his life. He was warm and his stomach full, and she was relaxed, perfect in his arms.

"This must be what normal feels like," he whispered.

She murmured again and turned farther onto her side. On her stomach now, she lay with her face pressed against his side and one arm bent back awkwardly over his.

"You don't look at all comfortable now." He lifted and resettled her against his chest, putting both arms around her and tucking her head beneath his chin. Her hair was almost dry and curled around them in a tangled mass. Her warm breath sifted through his shirt, and he wished they were both naked. He wanted to feel her breasts against his chest and run his hands through her hair. He settled for wrapping a strand around his thumb and forefinger.

"I could love you," he whispered.

He was already half in love with her. The kind competence she'd shown, her musical voice and brilliant blue eyes had captured him.

The unfairness of it all threatened to choke him. His platoon headed out in another day, and he didn't even know her name. He'd go back on patrol, and she'd go wherever nurses went and then return to England. When this shit was all over, if he managed to live through it, he'd return to Pennsylvania and the job he'd run from at the family's factory.

"God, I was an idiot." He made a mental note to write his dad before they went back out. Life as a button maker sounded amazing to him now. Three meals a day and a warm bed at night with no one shooting at him sounded like Heaven. He ran his hand lightly over her back. To sleep with a woman and be able to relax and not have to worry she'd stab you while you slept was a miracle he'd never expected to live long enough to experience.

His first women in Wales had been practiced. A cold flirt, she'd finished with him in minutes and headed back to the bar, and he'd been too shy to ask her to stay like he'd wanted to. His second visit had been with a kinder woman. She'd laughed over his amazement when she'd had an orgasm. He hadn't known a woman could. He'd thought sex was something they endured for the sake of having children. But she'd enjoyed it and shown him how to use his fingers to give her pleasure and laughed again when he'd asked her how to with his cock.

He blushed as he remembered his embarrassment when she'd said there was no sure way, but he did just fine. She'd been sweet in a patronizing way, and he'd meant to go see her again before they shipped overseas but hadn't had time.

He'd gone to the whorehouse in Paris with his squad and been afraid to close his eyes. The fake laughs and sly smiles, the flirty lies that meant nothing, and the mercenary hands on his body had his hackles up the entire time he was there. He'd worried his date would reach for a gun or a knife if he let his guard down, and he'd left as soon as he finished.

"But you're a woman to trust, aren't you? A man could sleep easy with a woman like you."

He quieted when she stirred. He didn't want to wake her. Asleep in his arms was perfect, and he wished it were just the two of them and they had forever. He drifted to sleep to her soft breaths.

When he woke again, he knew it was almost seven. The clock in his head kept perfect time. A skill he'd developed in the way soldiers did so they could sleep deeply anywhere and wake when they needed to. A soldier who slept late too often, and missed his guard shifts, would find himself on all the shit details. Sleeping too deeply could get you killed. You never knew when the enemy would find you.

Reluctantly, he slid her to the side as he rose and covered her with another two blankets. The stove had gone out and it took him a few minutes to get it going. Walt poked his head in as he was feeding it.

"Chilly in here," he whispered and slapped his gloved hands together.

Jack nodded to the chair beside the door. "She doesn't like to be alone. Has nightmares."

Walt sat and stretched his feet out, resting his rifle across his lap. "I'll wait in here until she wakes. Go get some rest; we go back out tomorrow."

Jack saluted and headed to the KPX to buy John a pair of socks and Hawkins a sweatshirt.

Brook Wakes to a Fresh Perspective

Brook lay cocooned beneath the blankets still feeling his warmth. She'd heard them speaking and knew she should rise but lethargy grabbed her. The left side of her body ached. She'd be dead now if one of the men hadn't grabbed her and held her tight as the truck rolled. Instead, she'd escaped with minor bruises, and he'd gotten a truck strut through the leg. Unable to pry him loose from the corner they'd gotten wedged in, she'd left him bleeding in the truck.

These poor, brave boys who clutched their wounds and sent her away to help others. She'd never hated anyone before, but she hated these German soldiers who dropped bombs on hospitals and schools. Tears filled her eyes and trickled across her cheeks. Pain in her eye made her moan.

"Are you okay?" the man at the door asked in

a whisper.

"Yes. Bad dream. Sorry to disturb you."

She sat and clutched the covers tightly about her. They smelled of him, and she closed her eyes and breathed deeply.

"No problem at all. Shall I see about finding your kit?"

"Yes, please."

He rose and gave her a friendly bob of the head. Cold air rushed into the room when he exited, making her shiver. The cot creaked as she swung her legs to the side and she hated the emptiness of the room.

"I could love you too," she whispered to the crackling fire.

She glanced at her sodden skirt and debated rising to try to save the letter in the pocket, but she didn't want to save it. She didn't want to see the words, 'whereabouts unknown.' Her entire family had disappeared. Her home was destroyed, and she didn't know if they were alive or dead. She bowed her head and prayed for their safety.

"Maybe they got relocated again." The words seemed to echo in the empty tent. *Please, God let them be safe somewhere.*

She'd write again, this time to the war ministry. Her father would be working if he were alive, and her mother would be helping him, she was sure of that. Someone somewhere would know what had become of Doctor Eugene

Taylor. "Please, God, don't let them be dead."

The irony didn't escape her. Her father had worried over her volunteering and been adamant about her going overseas, but she was a trained surgical nurse and the most need was at the front lines. To many boys lost limbs or died because trained help was too far away, so she'd gone despite her parent's disapproval. And now her father was the one missing, her letters returned unopened, her enquires always ending in whereabouts unknown.

A distant gunshot made her flinch. While she wallowed, men died. With trembling fingers, she braided her hair and tucked it into a neat bun. Her boots were still wet, but she donned them anyway, jamming them on over the thick socks. Her borrowed pants sagged off her hips. She eyed her bloodied shirt and shrugged before ripping it apart and braiding it to make a belt.

Snow drifted down in fat flakes outside. She grabbed the arm of the first man who passed. "Hospital?"

"Two rows down and three left."

She nodded her thanks and ran through the snow, leaving him staring after her.

Warmth and an antiseptic smell encased her when she entered. She breathed deeply of the familiar scent. A man glanced up from a box he was sorting through.

"I'm a surgical nurse," she said before he could ask or order her away.

"Gowns behind you in the first cubby. Scrub

up. Operating theater three is in use, and they could use a hand. Doc's doing a tricky resection. They been at it for hours now."

She stepped through the doorway. Empty benches sat before wooden cubicles lining the walls. At the end of the room, two doorways were blocked by white curtains. She stepped through the white curtain on the left as he spoke and pulled on a white surgical gown over her clothes. Paper hats and masks sat above a metal sink, the source of the antiseptic smell. She tucked her hair beneath a hat and let a mask dangle beneath her chin as she scrubbed.

"We get a lot of new patients?" she called loudly to be heard over the running water.

He came to the door and leaned on the jamb. "A fair amount. Almost done with this lot though. I hear their gearing up for a big push. Get your rest while you can."

She jerked her chin in reply. Holding both hands before her, she used her butt to push through the other curtained doorway. Every field hospital was laid out exactly the same way. She found her way to the operating room with no problem. The surgeon glanced up when she entered but returned his attention to the patient before him.

"Curette," the doctor said and held out his hand.

The man hovering over the tray leaned closer. The doctor sighed hard. "The long one with the—"

Brook grasped the instrument and placed it in the doctor's hand. He nodded his thanks and continued his work. The man at the tray cleared his throat.

"Halstead," the doctor said.

She handed him the instrument and began rearranging the tray.

"Burns, take a break, the nurse has this," the doctor said.

"Sorry, sir." The man hovering over the tray said and gave Brook a sad, nervous head-bob.

"You did good. A little more training and you'll be a real asset here," the doctor said.

Burns nodded but his shoulders slumped as he left the room. Brook took the suction from the doctor and expertly cleaned the incision sight.

"Thank you, nurse..."

"Taylor, sir."

"Clamp."

She glanced at the door closing behind Burns and handed the doctor the clamp, then blotted his forehead. For two more hours, she handed him tools and assisted.

"I can close if you like," she offered when he straightened and bent backward with both hands pressed to his lower spine.

"Yes, thank you, and great work."

She didn't look up from the small, neat stiches she was applying. When she finished, she checked the patient's vitals again and then began gathering her instruments.

Burns stuck his head in the door. "The doc could use a hand in theater two. I can clean up."

She stripped off her dirty gown and gloves and ran to the changing room. The day passed in a blur, and by six she was exhausted again and starving. Her fellows had arrived, bringing with them the rest of the patients from the abandoned hospital. Men lay shoulder to shoulder on narrow pallets, filling the hospital corridors. Orderlies and nurses scurried among them.

"Brook," one of the nurses greeted, sounding relieved. Green eyes smiled at Brook from beneath a wild tangle of red hair.

"Lydia." Brook gave her a quick hug.

Lydia held her at arm's length and examined her with a critical eye as she said, "We'd heard your convoy got hit."

"Friendly fire. It panicked the driver and we wrecked. No gunshot casualties but lots of trauma."

"Most of our patients made the transition just fine." Lydia linked her arm in Brook's and pulled her away. "Whatever are you wearing?" She didn't wait for an answer but continued speaking. "Never mind. You can borrow something until your gear is replaced. The doctors have left for the night, and we're not to disturb them for anything less than a life or death emergency. Come take a break."

Brook allowed herself to be led to the now

crowded changing room. Women greeted her and laughed and talked amongst themselves. She waited for Lydia to strip off her gown and put on her outer clothes. A group of ten women headed to the mess hall together. Brook kept her eyes down when they entered. She hated the shocked silence followed by the too loud chatter as the men tried to talk to them. She understood their loneliness, but the attention made her uncomfortable.

Lydia squeezed her arm against her side and patted her hand, intercepting every man who attempted to speak with Brook with a bright laugh, easily turning the attention to herself. And she garnered quite a bit of attention with her curly red hair and bright green eyes. Taller than Brook, Lydia had long legs and a bigger bosom. Brook felt like a child beside her, more from the sophisticated way Lydia acted than their differing sizes.

Lydia accepted a cigarette and leaned close to let the man of her choice light it. *She'd picked a real handsome one*, Brook thought wistfully. She blushed and turned away when he caught her staring.

She peered around hoping to see J. Pryor. He was handsome too with kinder eyes and a sweeter smile. Lydia's choice had a cold look in his eye. Brook preferred the still sweet boys, not the hardened men who didn't seem to mind the killing.

She let the talk and laughter flow over her as

she gathered her plate and took a seat in the center of the women. More nurses joined them, QAIMNS and Army, not VADs like she was, the new arrivals all wore uniforms. The men still greeted them enthusiastically but toned it down.

Brook pushed her plate away, thoughts of her father making her ill. She could join Queen Alexandra's Imperial Nursing Service now. The uniform would afford her more discrete treatment from the men, and the pay would be better and hours easier. The only reason she hadn't was her father had been so set against it. Afraid he'd stop her, she'd gone without saying goodbye and now she might never see him again.

"Still no word from home?" Lydia asked, handing her the tea from her tray. "You English and your tea. Give me bloody coffee any day."

Brook laughed at Lydia's fake English accent as she knew Lydia wanted and sipped the tea. Lydia leaned closer and whispered. "You need a man. They make a great distraction."

Brook choked on her tea, making Lydia laugh. All around them men stopped to stare. Lydia winked at her and rose, slowly pulled on her gloves, her gaze traveling the men, landing on the handsome one who'd lit the cigarette for her. Brook blushed as Lydia smoothed her jacket, running her hands over her breasts, down her sides and over her ass.

Someone whistled, and men laughed but Lydia didn't break eye contact until she turned to head to the door.

"She won't be back tonight," Penny, the nurse on Brook's left, whispered.

Brook flicked a glance to the door in time to see Lydia's prey join her there. The two spoke with their heads close together and Lydia's laugh again silenced the men around them.

"She's a free spirit that one," the woman beside Penny said.

"She's going to catch something." The matron's sour tone stifled the giggles around Brook. "Best get to your beds— alone! We have a busy day tomorrow. Penny, check the rooster; I've slotted your crew in for morning and gave you two, night watches."

"Yes, ma'am," Penny said in a soft, respectful voice.

Brook glanced wistfully after Lydia before rising. She gathered Lydia's tray and returned them both before following Penny to their tent. A tent that remained half empty. Lydia wasn't the only volunteer to find company for the night.

While she'd been gone, someone had refolded the blankets and straightened the room. Her wet clothing had been removed and her bag placed at the foot of a cot. She picked up the blanket and sniffed it, but it smelt of damp wool, not J. Pryor. She wondered what the J were for— John, Joseph, James. Those names seemed too formal for him. He had a certain devilish light in his brown eyes. *Maybe he was a Johnny or Joey.*

"Oh, good, they found your kit," Penny said

happily, bringing Brook from her pointless musings.

Brook changed into the heavy flannel gown she slept in and carefully folded the borrowed clothes.

Maybe tomorrow I could look for him to return them, she thought in sudden excitement. Excitement that faded as she remembered his friend say they were going on patrol. She should've looked for him today. Tomorrow he'd be gone, and she'd never see him again.

The thought saddened her. She lay beneath her blanket and pictured his face behind her closed eyes. *Was that what normal felt like,*" she wondered. She'd heard him when he thought her asleep. It had almost disappointed her that he'd remained a gentleman.

I should've kissed him, she thought, suddenly angry with herself. *What would it have hurt? I might die tomorrow. This might be my only chance to learn what love feels like and I'm wasting it.* Beneath the covers, she trailed a hand over her breast. It didn't feel at all like the inadvertent brush of his hand that had filled her with heat and a longing she didn't have words for.

She'd shamelessly taken advantage of his kindness. For all she knew he was married with five kids. She smiled and turned over to clutch the thin pillow to her breast. He wasn't married. A man like him would wear his ring proudly. She doubted he was much older than her. Like her, he'd probably signed up the minute he finished school. She wondered what drew him, the thought of helping others or the glory of war most young men seemed to feel until they'd been here awhile. But by then, it was too late, and they were stuck here with no way out except death or injury so severe it got them sent home. A four-year sentence in Hell they voluntarily accepted.

She was still awake when Lydia returned an hour later. Flushed, with her shirt buttoned wrong, Lydia began undressing for bed. A low light still burned beside the door as it always did so those coming in or going out late for duty didn't wake the rest of them. The volunteers weren't as regimented as the official nurses. No one checked up on them, and they were free to spend their off hours however they wished.

Brook usually spent hers cleaning her clothing or writing letters home, but she took few hours off, preferring to spend her time here caring for the wounded. It seemed silly to her to waste time reading or chatting when men lay alone and in pain mere steps away. She'd rather read to them, and they seemed to enjoy it, smiling and hiding their pain when she sat beside them with a book.

She wrote letters for them, and read to them, and held their hands while they died. A sob caught in her throat.

"You okay, sweetie?" Lydia asked.

"Fine."

"Sorry, did I wake you?"

"No. I was awake worrying."

"Still no word from your family?"

Another sob made her voice shake. "Not yet."

"Jeffery works in the radio shack. Shall I ask him to send a message?"

Brook leaned on an elbow. "Yes, please. The last letter I received told me my father accepted a position at a camp in Barrow, and he warned me that security was tight, and he wouldn't be able to send letters with any frequency. I know they weren't killed in London, but it's been two years, and I haven't heard a word. I was thinking the hospital might know where my father is. I know the hospital itself is closed but they must have reopened somewhere. Everyone can't be dead."

To her embarrassment she began to cry.

"Oh, sweetie, I'm so sorry. We yanks forget your home is under attack too." Lydia sat beside her and stroked her hair until her crying stopped.

"You're among friends here. We'll help you find them," Penny said, surprising Brook who thought Penny sound asleep. "My husband works in personnel. He's stationed in Paris right now, but he has friends all over. I'll write him too. This war can't last forever. We'll be home with our families soon."

"Thank you. You've all been so good to me."

Lydia kissed her brow. "Get some rest." Her voice lightened, and she patted Brook's hip. "And find yourself a man."

Brook drifted to sleep as the women began a laughing argument over the merits of men.

Jack Gets Hurt

"Jack, you awake?" John whispered.

"I am now," Jack said crossly and unfairly.

He'd been awake, daydreaming of nurse Birdie and her beautiful blue eyes. He wondered if that was a last or first name. The friendly, familiar way the soldiers spoke to her made him think it a first name. Man, he wouldn't want her job. As scary and uncomfortable as his job was at least he didn't have to hear men cry for their mothers and wives. Or not much, he amended as the sound of a low sob traveled on the still night air.

"Can you give this letter to my girl? You know, in case—"

"Give it here," Jack said and extended his hand. He'd known John had been troubled the last few days. Not even Frank had gotten a laugh out of him. He settled the letter in his inside pocket beside the one he carried for Frank.

A smile crossed his face as he imagined the

woman who'd marry Frank. He bet she had round cheeks from laughing and laugh lines around her eyes, and she was probably plump. She'd have to be a great cook to keep up Frank's bulk. And his kids were probably annoying, pestering little devils with a million questions or maybe they were quiet, used to listening to their dad ramble on.

"If we don't make it—"

"You can't talk like that," Henry said. Talk like that will get you killed. This is nothing. We'll be up and over that hill by tomorrow."

A loud burst of artillery emphasized his words. To their left, machine gun fire was met by rifle shots. Up and down the line more shots rang out until the noise made distinguishing friend from foe impossible.

Jack peeked his head over the edge of his foxhole but still saw no one. He ducked and threw his arms over his head as a missile shrieked past and landed twenty feet to his right. The men there screamed and cursed.

"Tell her I love her, Jack," John shouted.

"You'll tell her yourself. Keep your head down and stay right behind me." He gave John a quick, encouraging grin. He remembered his first big engagement when he'd almost shit himself he'd been so scared. Now, he didn't worry over the mortars passing overhead or the distant screams and gunfire. All that mattered was this fox hole, these five men, and his mission.

He waited until the next round of gunfire faded and motioned his squad forward, running crouched over through the dirty snow. A broken wall lay before him. Starlight glittered on the snow, casting odd shadows. He hoped John wouldn't shoot at any and give them away. So far, they'd managed to cross this field without incident.

His pack bumped his back as he ran; he'd forgotten to tie the waist strap. A sharp rattle of gunfire drew his gaze to the left. He lifted his rifle and fired. His squad joined him, shooting at the bright sparks that showed where the enemy hid behind the low rock wall they ran toward. He didn't stop running.

Bullets kicked up dirt and snow around him, and he cursed as shrapnel ripped into his leg, stinging like a hundred bees.

Behind him, John mumbled a prayer but kept shooting and running. All five made it over the wall. Jack used his rifle like a club on the surprised man laying alongside the wall. John shot past his shoulder, the noise deafening.

This was the part Jack hated. They were behind enemy lines now and just as likely to be shot by their own men as the enemy. Panting hard, he reloaded his gun, then dropped to his chest and pulled himself forward on his elbows. The shallow trench behind the wall led both north and south. He headed north toward the sound of the machine gun. Henry would be watching their backs and Stan would be watching east. The wall blocked the west. The danger there was from their own troops.

Another sharp burst of gunfire warned him before he put his head around the corner. He gripped his rifle and got to his feet, staying crouched as low as he could, and leaned around the corner. A quick glance confirmed these were krauts, and he opened up.

Frank joined him, his bigger gun screaming in his ear. His squad ran past the dead on the ground and fired blindly on the next group.

When the smoke cleared, Jack was relieved to see they were enemies and they'd taken a machine gun nest. Frank laughed as he grabbed the handles of the big machine gun and turned it to face north along the wall. From this close, the bullets sounded like one continuous noise as if the air itself screamed, and they'd managed to catch the next entrenched gunners by surprise.

Jack couldn't hear them scream over the sound of the gun, but he saw them fall and blood spray. He slapped Frank's shoulder and ran passed him, cutting to the east to bypass the wire surrounding the gun and clambering up the mounded dirt, using one hand to brace himself. At the top, he dropped to his stomach and opened fire on the already dying men, ruthlessly suppressing any pity he might've had with memories of prisoners rescued in such emaciated states they didn't look human.

John slid down into the trench beside him

and nudged a corpse with his toe.

"Better them than us."

The ringing in his ears was still so loud Jack had to read his lips. He didn't answer. He was too busy swinging this gun around.

"Keep your head down!" he yelled and pulled John to his knees a second before a blast of automatic fire lit the night over their heads. "They know we're here now." Staying as low as he could, he pulled the trigger.

Men yelled as they raced to their position. Noise was breaking through the ringing in odd spurts of clarity and muffled gibberish.

"Americans," Jack bellowed. He kept yelling it until the first men leaped the wall.

They'd either heard him or realized he was friendly by his firing position. None shot at him anyway, for which he was grateful. His ears still rang, and he was sure he was yelling louder than he needed too as he grabbed the shoulder of a private and pointed south.

"Our men are behind us at the next gun. We're going back, and we'll clear south."

He grabbed John's arm and ran bent over back to the gun they'd just left. Henry waved them over the dirt embankment and signed that he'd seen a hostile group to the east. Jack slid down the mounded dirt and began reloading as he spoke.

"Frank, can you and Henry hold this if I take John, Stan, and Alfred?"

"Roger that. We got your back."

"I made out about fifteen, so two full squads at least," Henry said. He still faced away from them, watching their backs.

Jack didn't bother ask where. There was only one place they could be. A squat, stone barn six-hundred-yards away offered the only concealment beside the thin patches of trees spread intermittently across the field to the base of the rocky hill.

Jack led his group at a run to the nearest trees. Stumps beneath the snow made for tricky footing. Until recently this had been a forested slope, but now only thin, spindly trees remained. In the distance, a soft, red glow gave away the mortar teams position, but they still had a field to cross and a hill to climb to reach them. Jack didn't think they'd realized their outer defenses were breached yet though. The mortars still screamed over his head and landed behind the wall.

From the corner of his eye he spotted another team running to his right and lengthened his stride. More and more soldiers would be crossing the wall and the mortar teams would notice and change their aim. He crossed his fingers for Frank and the other men holding the big guns. He figured it'd take at least two shots for the mortar teams to change their sights and hit them. He hoped it would anyway and give the men time to run.

Ten feet from the trees, he yanked John to a

stop.

"Never run right to them. They'll block you just as good from a distance and it's likely to be booby trapped."

He pulled him down to his stomach as he spoke, hoping John could hear him over the ringing in his ears and began to crawl toward the barn, resisting the urge to duck his head. "Keep your eyes on the windows. Stan will be watching the flanks. He starts to shoot, that's when you look back. You'll get yourself and us killed if you don't trust us to do our jobs while you do yours. Keep your eyes on your assigned sector. Our lives depend on it."

He rose to his feet when he reached the edge of the trees and took a quick look around. About three hundred yards away, a group of their men was fired on by a group in the trees further down. Jack slapped John's arm down as he rose his gun.

"Forget it. Our mission is the mortars."

His eyes narrowed on the barn. It was both an obstacle and an asset. Crouched as low as he could get, he began to run to the barn. A mortar whistled overhead and landed behind him with a bone-jarring whoomph of sound and whoosh of air. Dirt and rocks flew into the air and cascaded over him doing nothing except making him run faster.

The near miss lightened his guilt though. Frank would know he was the next target and be taking cover. As he ran, he removed a grenade from his belt and pulled the pin. He lobbed it through the barn window, yelled, "Down!" and laughed when Frank's gun sounded behind him.

Trusting Frank not to shoot him, he jumped to his feet and ran across the front of the barn and threw another grenade inside the doorway. He kept running, not wanting to be shot by Frank when he shot at the men running from the building. He tossed his last grenade into the far window and scrambled in after it exploded.

The unfastened strap on his pack caught and yanked him to halt half inside the window. Three dead men lay right inside the door. Jack didn't know if his grenade or Frank's gun had caught them. Another two, obvious grenade deaths, lay in front of the far window as if they'd run but to slow to avoid the shrapnel that had shredded them. He let his gun slide to the floor to use both hands to jerk on his pack. Movement above him caught his eyes.

The kraut snarled as he rose his gun and took aim. Time slowed as Jack thrust on the wall with both hands, trying to pull himself in, cursing himself for letting his rifle fall. The man in the loft seemed to realize he was stuck and was taking his time to aim. Jack's pack ripped away right as the man in the loft shot. Bullets splintered the window frame, sharp splinters of wood grazing Jack's face as he fell to the floor. John shot the man and clambered in behind him as Jack reached for the gun he'd dropped.

Jack pointed to a small window in the now empty hayloft above them to the right. The man John had shot hung half off the wooden platform. Blood dripped down his arm and pattered to the floor, *in a sure to be nightmare inducing sound*, Jack thought with a guilty wince as he glanced at John's pale face. To Jack's knowledge this was John's first face-to-face kill and the first stayed with you.

"Pack saved your life again," John said admiringly.

Jack nodded acknowledgment and grinned ruefully. He thought it more likely his pack had saved John's life. If he'd gotten inside, the man would've shot at John; the overhang would've covered Jack.

"Get your back to a wall and watch these back windows. Shoot anyone who comes in. Give me ten minutes and come out that window there." Jack gestured with his chin to a wide window in the hayloft he assumed was used to bring in the hay.

Without waiting for an answer, he climbed back out the window right as Frank reached it. The men exchanged hard grins and darted around the side of the barn, leaving Henry crouched on the corner with his back to Stan.

Frank rounded the corner first, already firing the big gun. As Jack thought, the remaining men of the two squads crept along the back of the barn, half heading to them and half away.

Men screamed and clutched at wounds as they fell to the snow. Bullets whizzed past Jack's head and impacting the barn, spraying rock chips over him. Frank dropped to one knee, letting Jack fire over his head. In less than a minute all that remained were twitching corpses.

"It's clear!" Jack called for John's benefit. He hadn't heard any shots inside the barn, so doubted any of the men had climbed back in. The four who ran around to the right he could leave for Stan and Henry if they didn't continue running east and head to the trees.

He hated to leave loose enemies at their back, but their mission was the mortars.

John climbed out the window and dropped the eight feet to the ground, landing easily.

Jack wiped his sweating brow as he spoke. "We're going straight up. They'll have no angle on us until we reach the top. At the top, we'll reload and spread out to crest at the same time." He grinned when John handed him a string of grenades taken from the corpses in the barn.

"Great. Everyone throws two on my signal, and then we charge."

Gunshots, fired by the enemy hidden in the thin woods, peppered the hill around them as they ran up it. More and louder shots sounded behind them— American troops trying to hold back the men shooting at them.

My team isn't the only ones climbing the hill, he noted in satisfaction. Hunched shapes against the night-dark slope, only discernable as friends by the direction they faced, hurried up the hill, using their hands to pull themselves through the coarse brush and scrub that covered this hillside.

Jack was glad the hill was so steep. It gave them great cover. The mortars had ceased flying over their heads. The enemy had either run out or were running away. Both good news as far as Jack was concerned. His platoon had been fighting heavy for a week now. Someday, someone would name this battle, and dumb kids like he used to be would think it a glorious fight when as far as he was concerned it was stupid.

Who cared who owned this stinking hill? If it were up to him, he'd let them keep it.

Birdie's face flashed into his mind's eye and his teeth showed in a grimace. For her, he'd clear this hill and a hundred more like it. She deserved to live in a world not peopled by lunatics who thought themselves gods.

He'd seen enough of the death camps to know the Americans fought for more than the halt of illegal expansion. He reached the top of the hill and stopped to catch his breath and make sure his gun was fully loaded.

His team spread out, putting five feet between them. Jack clutched a grenade in both hands, held up three fingers, and began putting them down one-by-one.

The concussion of the ten grenades rattled his teeth. Dirt, rocks and debris better not examined to closely, rained around him as he stood and pulled himself over the lip with one hand. Bullets flew around him. Sharp whining bites of death that somehow miraculously missed him. He ignored everything, his sights set on the black carriage of the machine that sent the mortars over the fields and into his platoon. He ran forward and didn't realize he screamed until he tripped and went to swear and had no breath.

Armed men began firing at him or behind him, he wasn't sure which, the bullets whizzed over his head like a swarm of angry bees. He lifted his rifle, pulled back the lever, took careful aim and fired. He did that until his rifle clicked empty then rose and ran forward, letting his rifle swing from its strap and swung his pack in front of him. All around him men screamed and cursed, yelling directions and prayers in a confusing cacophony. He withdrew the shaped charge from his pack and slapped it on the mortar.

"Mission accomplished!" he snarled and ducked, covering his face with his arms as he ran away.

The explosion deafened him. Chunks of metal rained down in a hundred-yard radius. Men behind him cheered and another explosion rocked the hillside. He laughed as another sent more shrapnel into the sky. He was still laughing when a piece of sharp metal pinwheeled through the sky and slammed into the back of his head.

Brook Falls in Love

"Nurse Taylor!" Doctor Roberts called and gestured her over when she glanced up.

She finished taping the bandage on the stiches she'd put in her patient's chest and hurried over.

"We're getting overwhelmed. I know you haven't finished your schooling, but I've seen your work. I'm sending you to theater three. If you run into anything you can't handle, send him to theater two, but it'll be a long wait. Jenks, Rogers, assist Taylor. Nurses Summers and Dowlin will also assist."

The men and women he called nodded but kept busy with their patients. Lydia gave her a quick thumbs up. Brook ran to the changing room for a fresh gown.

The doctor sent her easy cases. Simple bullet removals, lacerations that required deep stiches and simple breaks. She sent two men to him, both with missed internal injuries.

When she straightened from her last patient, her back ached and head throbbed.

"Leave this. We'll clean it," Lydia said. "Eat before you head to triage; that's an order."

"Yes, Mum," Brook said in her primmest voice, making Lydia laugh.

Brook blessed the kind soul who'd brought sandwiches, tea, and cookies to the dressing room. She'd just finished her second cup of tea and taken a cookie when a commotion drew her outside. Three trucks of new wounded pulled up and parked before the main doors. Her hands began to shake. She hated this part, the climbing inside and meeting their terrified, painfilled eyes. Not one of these boys wanted to die and all thought themselves immortal until the first bullet hit.

She took two deep breaths and straightened her spine before climbing into the back. Daylight was just breaking, and she checked for plumes of breath in the frosty air, going first to those she knew where alive. She peeked beneath rough dressings and felt pulses and gave reassurance she didn't feel, ordering the orderlies to take this one, and that one could wait, all the while knowing her choices might result in someone's death.

In the second truck, she hurried to the three screaming men and examined them quickly before injecting morphine. Orderlies pushed past her, jostling her hard into the stacked stretchers. Her voice was growing hoarse from offering constant reassurance when she spotted Pryor. Her heart constricted and began to beat so fast she thought she might faint.

"No, oh no."

She dropped to her knees to see him better. He lay on the bottom-most pallet. Men were stacked six high with bare inches between them in the back of the canvas covered truck. Blood had stained the pallets and made the floor slippery, and the air smelled of death and feces.

Her breath left her body in a loud whoosh when she felt his pulse. "You're going to be just fine," she said for her own benefit.

He remained unresponsive. Her hands shook as she checked his vitals and searched his body for wounds. One eye remained fully dilated with no pupal contraction. A head injury. Tears dripped off her chin unheeded as she continued her examine. His abdomen was distended and bruised on the right side. She grabbed the next orderly who passed.

"Get him into x-ray. I want a lower GI and a chest scan. Keep someone on his blood pressure and call me immediately if it spikes. Tell Doctor Roberts I'll be sending him a critical head injury and I suspect trauma to the liver and spleen. He should prepare to perform a trepanation and maybe a hepatectomy although I'm hoping it's the spleen. Begin the blood work and put a STAT on it."

She backed away to make room for the men

to grasp the handles and followed them from the truck. She checked his vitals again and kissed his brow.

"Take care of him, please."

"Yes, ma'am," one said.

"This one's important to the Birdie," another said as he pushed through the men heading to the trucks.

Brook watched them out of sight, then angrily wiped her face on her apron before heading back into the truck. She joined Doctor Roberts as soon as the truck emptied.

"Burns was already here. Your young man's next in line."

She bit her lip and wrung her hands. "Have you seen him?"

"Not yet. I put Lydia on him."

"Please..." She began to cry, not knowing what to say. Doctor Roberts always did his best.

"We'll do our best," he said in a gentle voice. "I hadn't realized you had a young man."

"He isn't." Her breath came hard over the lump in her throat. "He's important to me though."

She wanted to blurt out she loved him, but she didn't even know his name. She wanted to beg the doctor to help her, to make everything okay. Everything she felt must've shown on her face because the doctor glanced at her with sad eyes and said, "Take five minutes and have a glass of tea before reporting to theater three. We'll all do our best."

She nodded numbly and wiped her face again. She hadn't even realized she'd begun crying. Voices and movement around her seemed dim and far away. With all her soul, she wished she'd kissed him. That one moment when she could've opened her eyes and been brave would haunt her for the rest of her life.

She'd heard the longing and loneliness in his voice and had turned away, selfishly using him to hold off her nightmares and offering him no comfort at all, not even the talk and smile she offered the injured who came to her, and for what? Because she was afraid to love and lose? afraid to disappoint parents she didn't even know if she'd ever see again?

So what if strangers thought her loose or of low morals. There was nothing loose or low about what she felt for him. She sat limply on the bench in the changing room, just then realizing where she was. Nurses talked and changed around her, but she remained lost in her what ifs.

Penny poked her head in the door. "Brook, your patient is waiting."

Brook rose and grabbed a new gown from the stack beside the door. "I'm coming," she said as she hurried to the scrub room. "I won't waste my chances again."

Penny followed her in and glanced at her doubtfully as she helped tie the hat and mask in place while Brook scrubbed.

"Are you okay? You look a bit peaked."

"Let's go," Brook said and headed through the curtain with her hands raised.

She treated her patients with mechanical precision, letting their faces and bodies blur, treating each injury as if it were a wound made on a cadaver to practice on, not wanting to see their faces and feel their pain.

"This one's the last," Penny said.

Exhaustion lined her voice, and Brook felt a twinge of guilt. She was using these men to block thoughts of J. Pryor and overworking her good friend. She hadn't even noticed Lydia had entered until she spoke.

"We're off duty for twelve hours, and I for one can't wait to hit my bunk."

"Pryor?" Brook asked hopefully.

"Out of surgery. And doc says the prognosis is good."

Brook sagged. So great was her relief, the room darkened and began to spin. She clutched the metal frame of the operating table to hold herself up.

"Take a few deep breaths," Lydia said and patted her back.

The anesthesiologist glanced up from his machines. "I can keep him out longer if you need a break."

"I just need a minute." She ran from the room to the nearby bathroom where she used the toilet and cried for a minute before rising to wash her face. She re-robed and scrubbed up again grateful no one had followed her.

"Okay, let's see what we've got here," she said briskly when she entered the operating room. She examined the x-ray and traced the path of the bullet with her fingertip. "Tricky, but far enough from the aorta I should be fine. How's his vitals?"

"Steady. We're good to go," the anesthesiologist said.

"Scalpel." She held out her hand.

Lydia handed her the tools as she asked for them. The bullet plunked into the metal tray followed by two small pieces of shrapnel the x-ray hadn't shown.

"I think I got it all," she said as she examined the bullet and the shrapnel beneath a microscope. "Let him up. I'll have the stitching done in minutes.

The anesthesiologist nodded and began the process of waking the patient. Brook stripped off her gown and gloves when she finished and donned a fresh one. The head nurse let her onto the recovery ward without protest, used to seeing her visit after her surgeries.

Pryor lay beneath a white sheet with an equally white bandage around his head. She read his chart and checked his vitals before grabbing a chair and placing it beside his bed to take his hand.

"He hasn't woken yet," the head nurse said in a kind voice.

"I'm going to sit with him a bit."

"That's fine, but you need rest too. We'll have more by nightfall; you mark my words."

Broke nodded tiredly. She longed to lay beside him and breath the scent of his neck. *And wouldn't they think me barmy? I am barmy*, she thought in disgust. She still didn't even know his name. It was crazy to be this upset, this worried for a stranger, but she couldn't make herself leave.

She was dozing when his hand tightened on hers.

"Did I dream you, Birdie?" he asked in a cracked voice.

"Oh, thank God, you remember me." Tears clouded her vision as she gently smoothed his hair.

"I'll never forget you."

She laughed, so relieved the injury or surgery hadn't appeared to harm his mind, she'd kissed him before she realized she was going to. His lips felt soft beneath hers, and his stubble scratched her cheek when she rested her face against his.

"I must be dreaming. Kiss me again."

Laughing and crying, she complied. His hand lifted an inch before fluttering to the bed.

"I shouldn't be tiring you," she whispered with her lips against his.

"Stay with me."

"Until you don't need me anymore." She kissed him again, and overcome with emotion, cried against his cheek.

"There, there now, young lady."

"Leave her be," Doctor Robert's said and drew the head nurse away.

Brook fell asleep with her cheek against his and woke when he stirred and tangled his fingers in her hair.

"Not a dream. I've died and gone to Heaven," he said.

"You're going to be fine."

Embarrassed now at her lack of control, she straightened and moaned. A spasm gripped her back, and she bit back another moan as she stood and stretched, then handed him a glass of water. He took a few sips, his eyes locked on hers, before handing it back. She finished it and set the glass down, feeling awkward and unsure now that he was awake and aware.

"Sit by me. I want to take your hand and kiss you again, unless that was dream," he added sounding horrified.

"Not a dream," she said softly and leaned down to kiss him again.

This time he returned the kiss and deepened it, using the hand that wasn't constrained by the IV to cradle the back of her head. She never wanted the kiss to end. She didn't care who saw or disapproved. He made a soft sound she couldn't decipher, and instantly she was remorseful and pulled away.

"I'm so sorry. You need rest."

"I need another kiss," he disagreed.

"I shouldn't. I want too," she added hurriedly when sadness replaced the sparkle in his eye. "You really do need to rest." She laid a hand on his cheek. The expression on his face caught her breath in her throat, and she wondered if she looked so love-struck to him. Reminded of her disheveled state, her hand rose to her head. It hadn't occurred to her to clean up and change. She still wore a paper hat over her hair, dangling now, and stains marred her dark-blue dress.

His eyes drifted closed.

She wanted to say I love you, but he'd think her addled. She settled for," I'll be back. I have patients to check on."

Unable to resist, she quickly kissed him again when she rose, and turned back at the door. He smiled after her and closed his eyes.

She hoped he'd have good dreams and remember her when he woke. Sometimes patients didn't remember a thing when they first woke from anesthesia, and she wanted him to remember her and that kiss. She wanted him to ask for another and giggled to herself, practically floating down the stairs. She'd ask Lydia to recommend a private spot to take J. Pryor, and she might even ask his name first.

News Reaches Home

"Put the tray by my chair," Edwin said without glancing up from the mail spread out on his desk.

"Yes, sir" Marie said.

"Lay a fire in the library and have a late tea prepared for four. I'm expecting guests before dinner this evening."

"Yes, sir. Might I ask, sir, if Master Jack is well?"

Edwin glanced up and slid the mail into a stack. His lips thinned as he eyed the maid.

"You may not. Keep to your place."

He waved her toward the door.

"Sorry, sir. I meant no disrespect; it's just Jack—"

"Is none of your business. If you wish to keep this position, you'll keep that in mind. In future, keep your eyes from my mail. If simple courtesy is too much for you..."

"No. I'm sorry, sir."

Marie bobbed her head and gathered her long skirt in one hand to scurry for the room.

Edwin rose to close the door she'd left open, irritated by her pestering. He hadn't yet decided what to do about the letter he'd received. His eyes narrowed as he watched Marie run up the stairs.

"Going to tell the old man, are you? We'll see about that." Edwin stomped back to his desk and snatched up the telegram from Jack, making sure his bottom desk drawer was securely locked before striding for the stairs.

As he suspected, Marie was already in his father's room. Both glanced to the door with guilty expressions as he entered.

"Marie tells me she thinks we received a telegram about Jack," Francis said in breathless voice.

Marie straightened his pillow and took his hand.

It was clear they both thought the telegram was bad news. Edwin had to fight to keep the grin off his face.

"I planned to inform you after lunch, but as our maid doesn't know her place...I tell you, Father, I have no use for snooping servants."

"Marie is family. Sit, dear," Francis said to Marie and tugged her down to his bedside.

"Father..."

"Let's not go into this again. Marie is family and that's that. She works for me, not you. She has every right to inform me of correspondence pertaining to Jack. I assure you, she isn't snooping through your mail. Now stop stalling. What was in the damned telegram?"

Edwin wished he could say it was a report of his brother's death. "Jack was injured!" he snarled and dropped the telegram onto his father's lap.

The old man took a long quavering breath. His hands shook as he picked up the telegram. Marie stood, poured him a glass of water, and handed him a small white pill.

"Take it, sir.

Francis swallowed the pill absently as Marie took the letter from him.

"Not injured too badly, sir," she said, sounding relieved.

The two exchanged smiles, and Edwin wanted to slap them.

"See how you've upset him," he said and snatched the letter from her hand. "This is none of your business!"

"Marie," Francis said and sat straighter. His voice had firmed, and color had returned to his face. "See if Mrs. Schmidt has any more of that delightful soup she made. I find myself hungry after all.

Marie's smile widened, and she patted his hand before scurrying from the room.

"Sit!" Francis commanded as soon as she'd left and pointed to the wooden chair beside his bed.

"I'm not a child to be ordered around," Edwin said.

"I won't have the help mistreated. If you can't get along with my choices, find yourself a new place to live."

"You're being ridiculous. No wonder she gives herself airs. Calling her family. Chastising me before the help as if I'm a child—"

"Stop acting like one, and I won't have to!"

Francis sighed hard and squeezed the bridge of his nose. "Marie is family. Sylvia's cousin in case you've forgotten. This is her home and will be as long as she lives. That she chooses to work is a choice, not a necessity. It's you who've forgotten your place, not her. I was against the uniforms and this is why. Marie isn't a maid, she's a dear friend. For crying out loud, she practically raised Jack. Sylvie was busy building Sylvan." Francis stopped speaking as Edwin turned away. Please, son, can't you try to get along with her for my sake?"

Edwin snorted. "For Jack's sake, you mean. Everything is for Jack's sake. You haven't even asked how the merger went."

"Yes, you're right. I'm sorry, but this damned cold has me knocked out. I can't seem to shake it. How did it go?"

"Fine," Edwin lied. "Everything is going as I planned. I'll have the new mill up and running within the month." He strode to the window and stared out over the manicured grounds. A gardener was busily pruning the apple trees that bordered the pasture that had once housed Janice's pony. Reminded of his dead half-sister his eyes narrowed. Jack had inherited her shares of Sylvan and Francis' other businesses too. When Francis died, Jack would own the majority of shares. The unfairness of it threatened to choke him, and it took him a moment to speak past the rage.

"Perhaps we should—"

"I thought I was in total charge now," Edwin interrupted harshly.

"Yes, of course. I'm officially retired. I only meant to offer a suggestion. Phips mentioned Frank's place will be up for sale within the year. If we have the capital, it would practically give us a monopoly."

Edwin let the curtain fall and turned back to the bed, his anger, if not forgotten, at least subsumed by his greed. "That's interesting. Did he happen to say what Frank would be asking?"

"Four million for the main building and two each for the four outlaying ones, but that's including the machinery. While it would be expensive, the savings of taking over a fully functioning mill would more than make up for it. I'm just not sure we're as solvent as we'd need to be to take advantage of it."

"It's too good an opportunity to miss. We could always sell Sylvan—"

"No! Absolutely not. Sylvan is Jack's. It isn't like we need Frank's mills too. Ours do plenty of business."

His father began to cough and reached for the water glass beside his bed. Edwin absently handed it to him, deep in thought.

"Besides," Francis said as he caught his breath. "There should be almost that much in the accounts. Speak to Groger about a loan for the rest."

Edwin turned to the door. "I'll handle everything!" he called over his shoulder as he left the room.

He practically ran down the stairs to his office. The funds his father spoke of were long gone. Some he'd hidden away but most had been spent on buying shares in the shipping line.

Reminded of that fiasco, his stomach churned.

"How was I supposed to know they'd be sunk?" he muttered irritability as he sat behind his desk. That should've been a surefire profit and a big one. He'd expected to quadruple his investment and had planned to use the funds to buy out Jack's half of the business. A business Jack had never had any interest in and didn't deserve.

But, if he could raise the funds himself and buy out Frank, he could set the prices and it wouldn't matter at all if Jack held the majority of shares. Jack had no interest in the business and would likely sell out at a good price.

He grinned and rubbed his hands together. Despite his losses things were looking up. He was glad now he hadn't told his father about the shipping line. Now he'd never have to hear the lectures.

The money he'd taken from the store wouldn't be nearly enough to buy Frank's mills but maybe Agnes's father would be interested.

His father-in-law was sick and a loan from him wouldn't even need to be paid back. He needed to get his wife on board with this.

Jack Falls in Love

When Jack woke, Birdie sat beside him holding his hand and reading to the man in the next bed.

"Hey," he said, and she dropped the book and rose a trembling hand to her flushed cheek.

He tightened his grasp on the hand he held, not wanting her to dart away. She looked scared to him. He was becoming a bit of an expert on recognizing that look. It wasn't an expression he wanted to see on her face. He wanted to see her smile.

"I'd give you a hello kiss if I could sit," he said.

The flush on her face deepened but her eyes sparkled, and she leaned down to kiss him.

"Aww," the man beside him complained. "How about my kiss?"

A red-headed nurse laughed and slapped the clipboard she held to the small table between the beds. "Will I do?" Without waiting for an answer, she kissed the man to loud cheers from his buddies.

Laughing, Birdie pulled away from him. "Hush, you'll get us in trouble."

She'd no sooner said it, then a stern-faced, gray-haired woman marched in the door. The men quieted but chuckles and guffaws followed the redheaded nurse from the room. The older nurse pursed her lips and narrowed her eyes after her, but her eyes sparkled when she glanced at her patients, and Jack didn't think she was really mad or unaware of her nurse's behavior.

He kept Birdie's hand in his. "Don't let her scare you off," he whispered.

She smiled and reached for her book, her breast brushing his arm. The slight contact aroused him, a state the white sheet over him did nothing to hide, and he shifted uncomfortably.

"You look beautiful," he murmured and brought her hand to his lips.

The small effort tired him enough to leave his hand trembling. It occurred to him he might be dying. He hadn't asked about his condition or his squad. Maybe she treated all the terminal this way and he was misreading the warmth in her eyes.

"Am I dying?"

Tears leapt to her eyes as she jumped to her feet. She released him to feel for his pulse, then fumbled for a stethoscope that lay on the small table between him and the next man.

"No. Does your head hurt? Can you see me okay? How many fingers am I holding up?"

He grabbed the three fingers she waved in front of his face and brought them to his lips. His question had scared her. Her hand trembled and tears trickled from her eyes. He tugged her down until she half-sat on the bed beside him.

"I feel good. Real good," he said truthfully, relieved when she gave him a tremulous smile.

He didn't know if it were the meds or her attention, but he couldn't remember ever feeling this content before. He let his eyes drift closed, then recalled his squad. "My men?"

"I don't know. I can ask for you though. Only one man in that truck, Private Schmidt, died. You're going to be fine."

He was relieved but knew as well as she did that meant nothing. His entire squad could've been killed, their bodies left for later pickup, or they could've been in a different truck. *They could also be fine*, he reminded himself forcefully as she continued to speak.

"You have a concussion, and the doctor had to drill a small hole in your head to relieve the pressure, but if you rest quietly for a week or two, you'll be good as new."

"And this?" He released her hand to touch his fingertips to the white bandage peeking from beneath the sheets.

Her hand trailed his, sending a bolt of desire through him that made him groan.

She immediately looked concerned.

"Does it hurt?"

He trapped her hand beneath his as she went to draw back the sheet.

"I'm good. What happened?"

She tried to free her hand.

"Leave it," he whispered roughly. "Your hand makes me feel too good," he continued and flicked a glance at his erection and away.

A blush burned across his cheeks. Her glance followed his and she rose and cleared her throat. The heated look she gave him didn't help his situation.

"Stop. Your killing me," he whispered when she licked her lips.

She giggled, slapping a hand over her mouth and glancing around guiltily. He grinned back.

Her eyes smiled into his a moment before she dropped her hand. "Just a small operation," she said in a brisk voice. "No major damage. Doctor Roberts repaired a tiny tear in your artery. Something hit you hard. It didn't break the skin but caused a small internal bleed. Tests and X-rays show no damage to the organs, and the doc thinks it should heal and you can rejoin your platoon within the month.

"So— good and bad news."

He was immediately sorry he'd said it. Again, tears threatened, wiping the happiness from her face.

"I'll be fine. Ask anyone in my squad and they'll tell you I'm a lucky bastard." A yawn interrupted him, and her expression lightened. She smoothed his hair and checked his pulse and breathing again before straightening.

"Shall I read to you?"

"Sure," he said in a strangled voice.

He regained his composure while she read and took the opportunity to examine her. She wore a white apron bearing a red cross on the left breast over a dark-blue dress with white cuffs and collar. Unlike the other nurse, who wore a small white cap, she wore a flowing veil-like hat, and he hoped that didn't mean she was a nun.

He had no idea what the different style of dresses the nurses wore signified, but they wore three distinct types. Four if you counted the female orderlies who wore dark gray gowns. He ran his thumb over her knuckles and her breath caught. She let the book fall to her lap, her eyes going wide, her lips parting and leaning closer.

No way was she a nun, he thought in satisfaction.

So, he did it again and tugged her closer. She kissed him, and he released her hand to place his on the nape of her neck, wishing her hair were down instead of in the tight bun. The pulse under his fingertips accelerated when his tongue touched hers, and she made a soft, barely heard, moaning sound that went right to his groin. His head began to throb. *My blood pressure must be going crazy,* he thought in the back of his mind.

Hers was. Her pulse fluttered under his

hand. Only the fact that his other hand was attached to the IV kept him from caressing the breast that brushed his arm.

A woman cleared her throat sharply before speaking. "Nurse! If you won't let the patient rest, I must ask you to leave."

"Sorry, ma'am," she said in a soft, embarrassed voice.

Jack grinned as Birdie drew away flushing. He dozed off, and when he woke, she slept in the chair beside him still holding his hand. He caressed her fingers with his thumb and her eyes opened. The smile when she saw made his heart expanded. He wanted to see her smile like that every day.

"How are you feeling?" she asked and leaned forward to rest the back of her other hand across his brow.

He wanted to hear her speak to him every day too.

"Nurse," a man said, jerking Jack's eyes from her.

He glanced around and realized he'd been moved while he slept, and he wondered how long he'd been out. He flicked a glance back to her face and winced as he realized he was telling time by the bruises on her face, but they looked better than they had though she appeared tired. Dark crescents ringed her dull, blue eyes and she appeared thinner than he remembered although he hoped that was his imagination.

"Nurse," the doctor repeated.

"Sorry, sir, I dozed off."

"You need to get some sleep. I understand you're worried, but his condition is stable. The men need you able to work with a steady hand. I'm sure your young man won't mind if you leave him for a few hours to rest and eat."

"Go eat," Jack said and released her hand.

She rose, the lost look she gave him nearly braking his heart.

"I'll be here when you wake." He wanted to say I love you, but she'd think him crazy.

She nodded and smoothed her skirt, pasted on a fake smile, and strode away. The doctor watched her leave, then read Jack's chart, speaking with his eyes on the paper.

"She's a good girl. Frankly, half the men here owe her their lives. We're a doctor short and she's been doing the smaller operations on her own. I can think of five men off the top of my head who will still have their limbs or lives because of her quick work." He glanced up and frowned hard at Jack. "I'm going to take it really badly if you're playing with her affections." He jerked his chin at the nurse two beds down. "So will they— and if you think your life was hell before you reached this hospital, imagine the hell we could make it." The doctor slapped his chart back onto the hook and stomped from the room.

The man in the bed beside his snickered. "Private Jones— and how the hell did you do that?"

"Do what?"

"Get Birdie to fawn all over you? She hasn't spared a minute for any of us since you arrived." Head tilted, he regarded Jack quizzically. "I don't see it. Where's your halo?"

"I have no idea why she loves me." A grin threatened to split his cheeks, and he closed his eyes, relaxing into the pillow. She did love him. Her every action spoke of it.

"You sure are a lucky bastard," Jones said enviously. "These nurses are something else." He was silent for a minute. "Birdie isn't like Nurse Summer though. The doc is right, Birdie is a lady. Not that I don't appreciate Lydia's charms."

"Lydia?"

"The redhead. She'll give you a kiss and sometimes more if she likes you and you ask her real nice. Lydia Summer— the name suits her. She's as hot as a summer day. It's going to take a real man to tame her. I wouldn't mind giving it a try."

Jones continued to speak of Lydia as Jack fell asleep to the memory of Birdie's kiss.

Frank woke him from a sound sleep by dropping his pack beside the bed.

"What time is it," Jack asked muzzily as he tried to push himself up.

"Don't move. Doc says you need to lay still a

few more days." Frank sat in the chair beside him and dropped his helmet at his feet beside Jack's pack. "The squad is fine. John caught a bullet, but it was just a scratch. Our medic patched him right up. He'll be back in a day or two." He laughed ruefully and slapped a stack of wrinkled paper on the bedside table. "He's more worried about his damn letter reaching his girl if he buys it than he is himself. He wrote a new letter on the back of his orders and asked me to give it to you and this one he wants you to put in your pack."

Jack laughed, then winced and rose a hand to his throbbing head.

Frank stood. "Glad to see you're going to make it. You had us all worried." He leaned closer and winked, lowering his voice to a whisper. "Word has it you caught yourself a nurse and a real fine one. The same one from before?"

"Yeah, I'm going to marry her."

Frank burst into laughter and straightened. "I'll grant you, she's a pretty thing, but marriage? Are you nuts? They just give it away—"

Jack could feel his face turning red, and Frank apparently realized he'd made him mad.

He straightened and grinned apologetically, waving his hands in a what have you gesture. "No offense. I'm sure she's a real nice girl." He grabbed his helmet and muttered, "For someone you've known for ten minutes." When he straightened with his helmet in hand, he smiled again. "We go back out tomorrow. Doc says they're keeping you at least two weeks." His glance strayed to Lydia as she passed carrying a lunch tray. "Lucky bastard."

Jack grinned and offered his hand.

No one is luckier than me, he thought as he drifted to sleep.

The Engagement

Brook headed to Pryor after her shift. This time she took a minute to wash up and fix her hair first. She was tempted to let it down and leave her cap behind. Her black eye had almost disappeared, and the scrape was mostly healed. Her blue dress didn't look too bad, she decided as she straightened the cuffs.

Her gaze returned to her hair, and she frowned but put her cap back on, wishing she could wear makeup and curl her hair instead. She wanted to look her best for him and not so... she pursed her lips and doubtfully regarded her reflection. Before she could lose her nerve, she spun away and hurried for the first floor where he'd been moved into the main ward.

Men greeted her with friendly hello's, which she returned, but she didn't stop as she would've in the past to see if they needed a letter written or read but headed straight to Pryor. He was awake and grinned when he saw her. She was glad to see he was sitting more upright now and plucked the chart from the foot of his bed.

"What, no kiss?" he asked, sounding disappointed.

His smile fled when she glanced up and bit her lip. A quick glance showed the matron busy changing a dressing at the other end of the row. When she glanced back to him, he looked sad and nervous, and it occurred to her she wasn't the only one confused by her actions. What she felt to her toes, he probably thought was a silly flirtation on her part. Maybe he thought she kissed all her patients. The blush that followed that thought scalded her skin.

He held out his hand to her. "I missed you. Come sit by me at least."

He grinned that happy devilish grin she loved when she took his hand. *To hell with propriety,* she thought as her gaze traveled his bandages. He could die and then she'd regret not kissing him. His eyes darkened and grew intense when she leaned down to kiss him.

"Mmm," he said and pulled her back for another deeper kiss when she drew away.

His hand slid from her neck to her cheek and he cradled her face, staring into her eyes from inches away.

"Say it," he whispered in a voice thick with emotion.

"I love you," she said so breathlessly she could barely make out her own words.

He pulled her closer until her forehead rested on his.

"Will you marry me?"

Shocked, she drew back, her hands flying to her burning cheeks.

"Don't." She cleared her throat and sat beside him, leaning closer so they could talk privately although she was certain the man in the next bed could hear every word. "Never ask that again unless you mean it. You don't even know my name. I don't expect anything from you. Don't make me promises you won't keep."

"Jack. My name is Jack, and I love you."

She began to cry and leaned closer, hiding her face in the curve of his neck.

"Tell me your name. We're going to be so happy together. When this war is over, we'll raise a family together and every morning for the rest of my life I'll hear your sweet voice. I'm going to take such good care of you." He rubbed her back and cleared his throat. "Please say yes," he whispered.

She straightened, wiped her face on her apron, and grinned at him. Her soul burst with happiness and terror. He was a soldier who would return to the front lines. To give her heart to him was foolish but it was too late, he already owned it.

"My name is B—"

A siren cut her off, and she jumped to her feet. A distant explosion was followed by screams and more alarms. The floor shook as a plane flew overhead. A bomb exploded so closely the glass in the windows blew out.

All around her men began to struggle from their beds and nurses and orderlies raced into the room.

"We're evacuating!" one of the male nurses shouted, his words almost drowned by gunfire and the shriek of planes overhead. Another two bombs went off in rapid succession. She glanced from Jack to the nurse.

"We can't move them!" she said in horror.

"We have to. The line has been overrun." Another explosion punctuated his words. "Get the mobile ones first. Save the worst for last.

She ran back to Jack and pulled him to his feet. Men began rising and heading to the door. Jack leaned hard on her shoulder, staggering her as they limped to the door. Loud voices rose in question and command competed with a shattering roar of another bomb exploding nearby.

Brook glanced at the men tethered to their beds by machinery or injury. Her pulse pounded, adrenaline making her hands shake. She needed to get Jack safe so she could come back and help. Machine guns and mortars added their noise to the din.

Trucks began arriving and armed men jumped from the back to form a perimeter around the hospital. More men followed and pushed past the exiting patients. Injured began boarding with the help of nurses and orderlies.

Doctor Roberts ran outside. "Go with your patients." Another plane flew over, strafing bullets that kicked up gouts of dirt from the road. "Jesus Christ," he bellowed. "Can't they see this is a hospital?" He grabbed Lydia's arm and pushed her toward the truck. "Go!"

"Come with me," Jack said and tried to tug Brook closer when she stepped away.

"Get on! I have to go back. I have patients upstairs!"

"No! Come with me!"

She could barely hear him over the rumble of approaching planes. He glanced over his shoulder.

"Ours," he said and tugged her forward. Another round of explosions had them both turning as plumes of smoke and gouts of debris rained into the air about half a mile away.

Another truck pulled up and skidded to a stop. This one crammed with fresh wounded.

"Don't bring them here!" Doctor Roberts yelled. We're falling back to Charleroi. Take them there. Burns, round up the staff and get them the hell outa here." The doctor turned and ran back into the building.

"Go! I'll see you in Charleroi!" She pulled him to the back of the truck. For a minute, she didn't think he'd get on, but he seemed to realize he was slowing her and she was needed elsewhere. He kissed her quickly.

"I love you!" he shouted after her as she

gathered her skirts and turned.

She'd reached the doorway when the planes passed overhead. All around her people screamed and crouched, throwing their arms over their heads as bullets kicked up dirt and debris from the street. Glass shattered, the tinkle almost musical to her ear.

"Birdie!" Jack screamed, his voice carrying to her clearly through the din.

She turned in time to see him jump from the back of the truck and time slowed. She saw the bullets rip through the canvas truck top, could almost make out the path of each one through the air. Jack's terrified expression deepened as he reached a hand toward her and his other hand clutching his side as debris rained down on him. She didn't hear the bomb but felt the concussion. It rocked her entire body and pushed Jack to his knees.

Something bit into her leg and hot blood splashed across her face. She tried to put down her hands to stop her fall but didn't make it in time. Her head grazed the wooden step, and someone fell on her, and they both tumbled down the stairs as the world darkened.

Brook is Shot

"No!" Jack screamed and pushed himself to his feet.

Brook lay beneath a pile of unmoving bodies. Blue material of her uniform peeked from beneath the pile of dead and injured. The stiches in his side pulled painfully as he yanked at the corpse on top, revealing the painfilled eyes in a blood smeared face of the man beneath.

Jack's head pounded in time with his rapid heartbeats. Warm blood coated his hands, and he prayed it wasn't hers that she was only knocked down and winded and knew he was kidding himself. The smell of death covered the scent of smoke and cordite.

Men shouldered past him and began pulling out the wounded and stacking the bodies to the side to make room for those inside to exit. He couldn't hear a thing, not even ringing in his ears. His gaze stayed locked on the blue of her dress visible beneath the khaki uniform of the dead man who sprawled across her. The world spun, colors and shapes merging, and his head pounded so hard he expected blood to rush from his nose or ears.

He must have passed out, although he didn't remember doing so. But he laid in the mushy snow and stared at the sky now. His hearing had returned. Bells clanged in his head as he tried futilely to push himself up.

Men yelled orders around him, but the gunfire had ceased. He tried to turn his head, but white-hot agony stopped him. He groaned and grabbed at his temples.

"Stay still. You caught the edge of a blast wave and it rattled your skull good," a man said as he shone a light in his eyes.

"Send this one to Hoegaarden. He doesn't need anything except rest."

Jack grabbed his pant leg as the man stood.

"Burns, right? How's Birdie?"

Burns stilled but didn't turn back.

"Hit."

The way he said it filled Jack with dread. "How bad?"

"Burns, quit your yacking; we don't got all day!" someone called irritably.

"Hold your fucking horses. I'm coming!" Burns shouted back and squatted beside Jack. "They're sending the foreign nationals to Charleroi. Our evac hospital is overrun, so they're only taking the critical cases. She's going to lose her damn leg."

"No!" Jack again struggled to sit and vomited in the snow. Pain lanced his head and his vision darkened. "Don't let them send her. Tell them she's my wife. They have to help her!" he gasped out as he choked and heaved.

"Burns!" the other man yelled, sounding aggravated.

He ran over and grabbed Burns's arm. "Sorry, man, I get he's a friend, but he's just puking. He'll be fine and there are others who won't be."

"My wife!" Jack bit out and grasped at Burns's leg.

"Yeah, I'll tell 'um." Burns yanked the dogtags from Jack's neck.

Jack let the darkness claim him.

When he woke again, he lay on a cot above one man and beneath another. Somewhere close, a woman murmured something too quiet for Jack to hear.

"Nurse!" he called and lifted a hand to his head.

The simple word had made his head pound. He wanted to yell again but the pain in his head stole his voice.

"Lydia!" he gasped when he forced his eyes open. Her green eyes examined him with no sign of recognition. "Where's Birdie?" he bit out over the pain.

Her eyes softened. "They sent her to the thirty-ninth in Namur. You must be her Pryor.

Shh, don't try to talk," she said as she smoothed his hair back. "Lay as still as you can and remain calm. Birdie will be fine." Her breath caught on a sob, and she pressed her hands to her mouth. "I can't stay, but I'll return if I find out anything. Get well for her." She hurried off to another man yelling for a nurse.

Jack lay with his eyes closed and listened to the moaning men around him. He was a fool for falling in love with a combat nurse. His wife should be safe at home so he could concentrate on the damned pain in his head, not be worried sick that she was alone and in pain somewhere. Jesus, she must be terrified. He tried to stop his dark thoughts, but there was no scenario he could picture that didn't have her frightened and alone.

For three days, he lay on that cot unable to move himself. Three days of not knowing if she lived or died while his head throbbed so hard he thought it might kill him. Lydia had taken pity on his raging headache and had him moved to a quiet section of the ward with men so far gone they didn't move or make a sound. He almost preferred to be with the screamers. The orderlies coming and removing the dead was freaking him out.

Lydia brought him a cup of lukewarm broth and held the straw so he could drink it.

"Haven't heard a word," she said before he could ask. "I ship out tomorrow. Their moving us back, and I'm assured we'll be off the front lines this time." She sniffed with displeasure. "Twice now we moved out under fire, and while I want to help, I volunteered and all— but this is too much." She softened her voice and patted his hand. "You're safe enough here, and they'll be moving you as soon as the swelling in your head goes down. You need to take it easy and avoid stress."

She laughed when he snorted.

"You love her, don't you?" she asked wistfully.

"With all my heart. Tell her that, will you? Even if she loses the leg, I still want her. I'll want her until the day I die."

"I'll tell her. They're so disorganized though I'm not sure when that will be."

A man hollered for a nurse, his voice muffled by the wall, but she straightened.

"Got to run."

"You're a good woman, Lydia." He kissed her hand and closed his eyes.

Mrs. Pryor?

When Brook woke, the first thing she noticed was the pain in her leg. The next was the bright light overhead and a man sobbing beside her.

All around her men moaned while others issued orders in tense voices. She recognized the sound of hospital triage and her heart began to pound; she'd been injured. She turned her head to see an IV connected to her hand. The slight movement sent a lance of pain through her leg.

Maybe I'm awaiting surgery, she thought and tried to sit so she could peer beneath the sheet that covered her.

"Stay down, Mrs. Pryor. The doctor has ordered complete bedrest for four days and then we'll see if you're up to taking yourself to the bathroom." The orderly who spoke drew a curtain closed around Brook's bed and offered her a bedpan.

A blush burned across her cheeks. "I'm fine. What happened?"

"Piece of shrapnel nicked your femoral artery. Doc stitched it right up, and baring infection, you should be fine in no time." As he spoke, he shone a light in her eyes and checked her vitals. Tasks familiar to her on post-op patients. They rarely had female patients though and always a female nurse helped them. Not a male orderly who by rights shouldn't even be doing the tests he was.

"We're under staffed?" she asked.

He chuckled grimly. "You could say that. Six doctors and twenty-seven nurses were killed. Another sixty-four orderlies and about a hundred or so auxiliary personnel were killed in the initial strike. A good portion of the remaining are injured. I was a field medic they pulled out of the field for this. Not one women is available to help you here. By rights you should've been sent to Charleroi. Lucky for you they didn't though, or you'd have lost the leg for sure and maybe your life."

"Twenty-seven," she said in horror. "And Jack? What happened to Jack?"

"I'll see if I can scrounge you a list of the injured and dead."

"This can't be happening. None of this." Tears clouded her vision as the room spun.

"Try to rest, Mrs. Pryor. I'll do what I can to locate your husband."

The orderly hurried off before Brook could gather her wits enough to say they weren't married. She cried herself to sleep and woke to a friendly face.

"Doctor Roberts," she cried in relief.

"Mrs. Pryor," he said and winked at her. "I'm glad to see you awake. Don't worry about a thing. The VADs are all accounted for and being sent to Charleroi. Your husband is reported in stable condition. I heard from Lydia, and she asks me to send his love."

"My husband?"

"This hospital is for American personnel and critically injured." He winked at her again and gave her a half smile.

"My leg?"

"Give my stiches time to heal and then some therapy. You might have a slight limp. I had to snip a bit of muscle, but it looks good, no sign of infection."

She gestured around the busy room. "I wish I could help."

"You can help best by getting well."

"Has anyone heard anything about my parents?"

"I couldn't say," Doctor Roberts patted her hand and rose. "I wish I could stay, but duty calls."

She nodded and closed her eyes. The doctor was giving her his best shot at saving her leg. She knew as well as he that moving her would drastically increase the chance of infection. She hoped the lie would hold for at least a week.

Who is Birdie

Jack sat up in bed and fed himself, proud over the minor accomplishment. Earlier, he'd been able to walk himself to the bathroom with the help of an orderly. It had tired him and left him shaking, but he'd done it, and best of all, his headache had receded to the occasional dull twinge. Now, if he could only find someone who knew where Birdie was.

"Hey, pal," Jack said to the next orderly who passed him. "Can you get me writing supplies? I need to write my dad."

"Sure."

"I was out of it when they brought me in. Where am I?"

"Hoegaarden, but don't get too comfortable. We're sending you to the thirty-ninth as soon as we can. This place is closing up and moving out."

Before Jack could ask another question, the man scurried off.

The thirty-ninth was where Birdie was, he

thought in satisfaction.

It took him a day to write a simple letter. The effort left him shaking with a pounding headache. When he woke in the morning, his filthy pack sat at the foot of his bed. Mud splatter and damp with new stains, it sported the familiar bullet holes. He laughed weakly and grabbed it, surprised to not only see it but shocked it still contained his hidden wad of cash.

"Hey, could you do me a favor?" Jack waved the folded money at the orderly.

"Maybe," the man said doubtfully.

"Can you send a telegram for me? I sort of left home on bad terms, and I really want to send my wife home. Please? There's more than enough here to send it, and the rest is yours."

"Write out what and where and I'll do what I can. No promises though. The lines are real unreliable."

Jack nodded and wrote quickly. His father was sure to be angry, but he was also sure to be happy Jack wanted to come home, at least he hoped he would be. He'd written but didn't often get the chance to send the letters home. In the three and half years since he'd left, he'd received twenty-one letters of the hundreds he was certain his father had sent. The last ten at the same time eight months ago when he'd been on leave in Paris.

In every letter, his father had begged him to reconsider and come home, offering to pull whatever strings he needed to get Jack out. For the first time, Jack was tempted. Fear for Brook left him cold and trembling. The need to have her be safe was a physical pain, and he felt bad for his father now. If his father felt even a fraction of this worry, his actions in signing up were beyond cruel.

He forced his guilt away and concentrated on what he wanted to say.

The orderly took the note and money. Jack closed his eyes and tried to remain calm. Worry only made his head pound.

"I'll find you," he whispered. *Please be okay.* He repeated that like a mantra until he dozed off. When he woke, a different orderly was helping the man beside him from his narrow cot.

"Any word on when they move us?"

"They already started, but you'll be here another week. The doc wants you still to give the head time to settle down. How's the headache today?"

Jack winced and closed his eyes. He wanted to lie and say fine, move me now, but his head throbbed and killing himself wouldn't help her.

"Hurts," he said shortly.

"I'll be back with ice and a meal for you. Stay as still as you can."

The days passed in a blur of pain-filled sleep. Nightmares haunted him. The vision of Brook's pain filled face as she fell grew until he saw it even while he was awake.

In the distance, guns roared. It took Jack a

second to realize this wasn't his nightmare but actual guns firing close enough to hear. He wasn't surprised when the medical staff ran into the room cursing and ordering the patients to trucks. Jack gritted his teeth and got himself to his feet. The ride to Namur and the thirty-ninth field hospital passed in a haze of pain. The hospital was crowded with both new and old wounded. Brook and the thirty-ninth had already been transferred. He'd missed her by a day. He was there a week when he saw Burns.

He'd never been so happy to see someone.

"She's in Charleroi and doing well. I saw her myself. I don't expect they'll keep her there long though," Burns said as he lightly slapped Jack's shoulder. "She asked for you. I didn't get much of a chance to speak with her." Burns leaned closer and lowered his voice. "Doc Roberts and I lied our asses off, saying we attended your wedding. Father Neilly was killed and half the records destroyed, so it'll be hard to disprove but not impossible. She's okay to be moved now but we'll be in the shit if we're found out."

"I can't thank you enough," Jack said sincerely

"Didn't do it for you. I did it for her. She's a good one."

"Well, I'm grateful."

"The leg will need time to mend and might not ever be a hundred percent."

Jack nodded his understanding and couldn't

make himself stop grinning. His heart sang with joy. She was well and behind the lines. Now, if he could just get her home..."Burns" —a flush climbed Jack's cheeks— "I never got her last name."

Burns chuckled. "Taylor. She's nurse Taylor."

"Birdie Taylor," Jack said and grinned.

Burns threw his head back and laughed. "That ain't her name."

"It isn't?"

"Nope. It's what the guys call the kind nurses. The good ones who take special care of them. A nickname, see, for Florence Nightingale. There's hundreds of nurses called Birdie. I have no idea what her first name is."

Jack's stomach sank. "How the hell will I find her?"

Burns shrugged and shook his head, his face sad. "I don't know. The way they're moving the patients around... and her a foreign national— well, it'll be tough. Lydia might know where she is though or Penny. They're both still in Charleroi stationed with the thirty-ninth. This lot here will be shipped there soon. She might be going by Pryor now though, but if you ask for her without knowing her first name, you'll get us all in the shit."

Our Boy is Coming Home

Francis glanced up and half-rose as Marie entered his study. She was pale and shaken.

Dread weighted his voice when he asked, "What is it?"

Marie held out a yellow envelope in a trembling hand. "Another telegram, sir. From Belgium."

The blood rushed from Francis's face, leaving him lightheaded. He slowly sank back into his seat as Marie placed the envelope on his desk. She lifted her hands to her cheeks as he gingerly picked it up. He wanted to throw it away unread and pretend he'd never seen it. Nausea roiled in his stomach and his pulse pounded.

"Jack, sir? Oh, God, not Jack." Marie began to cry.

Sweat broke out on his forehead, and he had to swallow hard. "Sit," Francis said gruffly and waved her to a seat. His hand trembled badly and vomit burned his throat. He wished Marie hadn't answered the damned door. The maids would be hysterical. He'd have to read this damned letter.

He ripped it open and his breath left him in a loud whoosh. Relief left him lightheaded. Jack had sent it. He began to laugh as he read it.

"He's fine, better than fine, he's getting married!"

"Married, sir?"

Francis pressed the letter to his chest and closed his eyes. When he opened them, Marie stood wringing her hands before his desk. "Shall I call the doctor, sir."

Francis waved at the chair before his desk. "Sit," he said again and grinned at her. "This is great news. He says he'll write soon, but he wants to send her home. Home, Marie! He asks if the job is still waiting for him. My boy is coming home and wants to live here. We'll be a family again."

Marie smiled and rubbed her teary face with her white apron. "And maybe children, sir."

"God willing, Marie, God willing." Francis reread the note, committing the short phrases to memory. 'Getting married. Can I send her home? Is my job waiting? Do you forgive me? Longer letter soon. Love Jack.'

"Send for Phips and Groger."

"Your banker, sir?"

"Yes, and then begin cleaning out my rooms. Jack and his new wife should have the master suite."

Marie inhaled sharply.

"It's time. I should've done it sooner. Pack up Sylvie's things. Leave her jewelry but put the clothing in storage or maybe have it cleaned and put in the green room. Maybe Jack's wife could use it. Goodness, I wonder if she speaks English."

"Is she German, sir?"

"He doesn't say, but I assume Belgium. It doesn't matter. I love her already. She got my boy to come home where he belongs. See about freshening the rooms. Order new bedding and drapes; something modern and welcoming. I want her to feel at home here."

Marie bobbed her head, looking a hair overwhelmed.

"We have time, my dear. It all doesn't need to be done today. One assumes it will take him at least a week to arrange for her to come. They'll probably wish to spend Christmas together." Francis pursed his lips thoughtfully. "Have it done by the new year though."

Francis rose and paced to the double French doors leading to the garden, speaking over his shoulder. "See that the staff is prepared. No one is to speak harshly to her no matter her nationality."

"Yes, sir."

Her dubious tone of voice made him wince.

"I'll speak with Edwin and Agnes," he said without turning from the window.

A light dusting of snow covered the gardens. He wished it were summer. The gardens his Sylvie had planted were still magnificent. He'd let the house go, not caring if the furnishings were outdated or shabby. In truth, he hadn't cared about anything except Jack since his Sylvie's death.

Agnes would need to be told firmly she was to be polite. Maybe it was time to encourage Edwin to move out. Francis rested his forehead against the cold glass. "Marie, send Mrs. Schmidt in with tea for me please and make those calls."

"Yes, sir." The light swish of skirts as she crossed the room reminded him of Sylvie and he had to close his eyes against the tears. The door closed quietly behind Marie, and he sagged. "Our boy is coming home," he said to the empty garden. "I'll make her welcome here, and we'll be a family just like you wanted."

He wasn't surprised when Edwin followed the housekeeper in with the tea.

"Marie tells us Jack wrote."

Francis resumed his seat and nodded for Mrs. Schmidt to pour. "Yes, he did. He's getting married and asks if his wife can come here. I'm sending our assurances she'll be well looked after."

"A foreign nobody? Is he crazy?"

"A woman and obviously one he loves, so we'll treat her with the utmost respect."

"This is all highly irregular. Is she with

child?"

Teacup halfway to his lips, Francis halted and set it back down on the china saucer. "I hadn't considered, but I hope so."

"Good grief, Father. This is just ridiculous. He can't marry a nobody! Especially a foreign enemy nobody."

"Now who's being ridiculous? It isn't like he needs an heiress."

"Father— you really can't separate Sylvan from the rest of the—"

Francis sliced his hand through the air and slapped his desk. "Enough. We aren't arguing this again. Sylvan is Jack's! It has always been Jack's. His mother grew that company from scratch for her only son."

"Pfft. We grew it. She had nothing."

A hot wave of anger flushed Francis' face. "Never speak of her in that tone again. Yes, I gave her the capital, but the idea and work were hers." Francis took a deep breath, trying to calm his ire. "Son," he said in a kinder tone. "Sylvan will be Jack's but the rest will go to you. I've already relinquished control to you."

Edwin glowered, not seeming at all appeased by this. "The button factory makes more than the store and mill combined."

"Don't be ridiculous. The store and mill provide more than enough income to live on." Francis narrowed his eyes and leaned forward, folding his hands on his desk. "Are you in financial difficulties?"

He examined Edwin's florid face as his son angrily sipped his tea.

"Son, I can't help if you don't tell me what the problem is."

"The problem is times are changing and the business you've saddled me with don't have the potential for growth that Sylvan does. I'm the first born, and by rights Sylvan should be mine. Let Jack have the damned store."

Francis pinched the bridge of his nose and took a deep breath. "Why is this so hard for you to grasp? Sylvan was never intended to be yours. If you don't wish to run the store, sell it. Buy whatever business you wish. Hell, for all I care sell the mill too. Sell the fabricating plants and the textile mill and retire. You and Agnes could live like royalty on those proceeds.

Edwin slashed his hand through the air, the gesture making Francis smile despite himself. Francis had learned it from his father and passed it to Edwin. The smile faded as he eyed his childless son. The one time he'd asked if he could hire specialists to see Agnes Edwin had gone ballistic. And he was right, it wasn't any of his business, but he so wanted grandchildren. Agnes wouldn't have been his choice for a wife, large dowry or not, but Edwin seemed content with her.

As if his thoughts conjured her, she entered his study.

"Mrs. Schmidt, I'm expecting a delivery. See

that it's sent directly to my rooms and tell cook to expect three more for dinner tonight," she said over her shoulder as she removed her long gloves and settled into the chair beside her husband. "The help is in a twitter. No one even escorted me inside. I had to ring. What has happened?"

"Jack is getting married and sending his new bride here," Francis said as Edwin opened his mouth.

Edwin snapped his mouth closed, looking angry.

"A German," Agnes said, sounding horrified.

"We don't know, but if she is, I expect politeness. She's more likely to be Belgian," he said cajolingly.

Agnes sniffed.

Francis narrowed his eyes at her. "Jack's wife will be treated cordially."

"Of course," Agnes said brusquely. She rose and gave Edwin and irritated glance.

He waved a negligent hand at her.

The irritation on her face grew, but she said nothing. Without another word, she strode from the room.

"I should tell you, I've ordered the master suite made ready for Jack," Francis said.

Edwin slapped his teacup onto the saucer so hard it cracked.

"What will the servants think? This is intolerable. If you're moving out of the master suite, it should rightfully come to me."

"This is still my home. My home, Edwin, and I get to decide what happens in it. There are thirty rooms. If you don't like yours, choose others or move out."

"You'd like that, wouldn't you?" Edwin snapped as he rose.

Francis rose too and followed Edwin to the door. He laid a hand on his arm. "Now, son, you know that isn't true. But this was Sylvie's house. She'd want Jack's new wife to have her room."

"Sylvia is dead. She's been dead for years. Spoiling her son won't bring her back!"

Francis' hand dropped from his son's shoulder. The words felt like a blow, and he tried to tell himself it was just jealousy. For the millionth time he regretted sending Edwin away to school at such a young age, but Edith had wanted her son to attend the best prep schools, and he'd wanted to make her happy. Guilt softened his voice. He'd been happy enough to send him then and concentrate on business.

"Your mother left you well provided for. Didn't I give you the home we shared and her jewels for your wife?"

Edwin made an annoyed sound and grasped the door handle.

Francis stared after him unhappily as he slammed out the door. Edith had been a kind woman but frivolous and without depth. She'd gone through most of the fortune she'd brought to the marriage with nothing much to show for it.

They'd been happy enough though. Until he'd met Sylvie, he hadn't realized how different true love would be. Sylvie had come to the marriage with nothing except her spirit and love, and she'd worked hard to build a dowry for her children, not wishing to take anything from Edwin. She'd tried to be a friend to Edwin, but he'd rebuffed her. And it must've been awkward having a stepmother barely older than himself.

Francis closed his eyes and took slow breaths, trying to calm his rapid pulse. Thinking of her death hurt, and Jack was all he had left of her. Again, he cursed the man who'd killed his wife and daughter and said another prayer of thanks that Jack hadn't accompanied them that day. Without Jack, his life wouldn't be worth living.

What difference did wealth mean if you had no one you loved to share it with? Brow furrowed, he stared at the closed door. Edwin lived such an empty, shallow life. He had no close friends and his wife was a cold shrew. Thin, with no curves to speak of, her expensive clothing and expertly coiffed hair gave an illusion of attractiveness, but Francis had never thought her pretty, even when she'd been young.

Her pinched lips and haughty expressions had always turned him off. He'd tried to talk Edwin out of marrying her, it wasn't like he needed either money or her family name, but

Edwin had been insistent.

His frown deepened when he gazed up the stairs. Agnes was also addicted to shopping. Maybe he shouldn't have let Edwin take over all the businesses quite yet.

"Too late now," he muttered and shrugged irritably. Edwin was forty-eight and college educated with the best education money could buy. He should be capable of handling his finances and his wife.

He'd just reseated himself and picked up his cold teacup when someone rang the front bell. A minute later Marie escorted Groger into the room.

"Francis, old boy, Marie has told me the charming news." Groger offered his hand in a hearty handshake and took Edwin's vacated chair.

"I'll return with fresh tea, sir," Marie said as she gathered the used cups.

Francis nodded to Marie as he spoke to Groger. "Yes, Jack telegrammed, and we're all thrilled."

"I assume you wish to set up an account for her?"

"Eventually. I don't even know her name yet. What I'd like is if you could see that Jack gets some cash."

"He has access to his account and there's a healthy amount in it."

"He might need cash there to get her home safe. Can we courier some to him? Say ten thousand?"

Groger crossed his long legs and smoothed his thin mustache. "Shouldn't be a problem. I can see to it."

"I'd like to send his mother's ring."

"That... insurance or not— that's risky."

"I really want him to have it."

Groger smoothed his mustache again and nodded slowly. "I'll see to it. It might cost rather more than you think to get it to him in a timely manner."

"Hang the expense. I want him to know how welcome she is and we're waiting for her."

"They'll live here then?"

Francis couldn't contain his grin. "Jack says he wants to get to work in his factory. I'm tempted to pull strings to get him out early."

"Your contracts make it feasible."

"He'd never forgive me. I'll wait until he asks, but if you could start nosing around, putting some feelers out?"

"How many years has he served?"

"It will be four in June."

"Shouldn't be too hard to get him home then. You could retire and let him take over Sylvan. Buttons aren't glamorous, but they are needed for uniforms."

Marie returned with hot tea. "Agnes has ordered us downstairs. She has a headache," she said as she poured.

Francis exhaled heavily. "Hire some

temporary help and work evenings during her dinners and afternoons while she shops, but get this done, please. And, Marie, try to remember you're just as much family as she is. Don't let her push you around."

"Yes, sir." Marie smiled at him and bobbed her head to both men before scurrying from the room.

Groger rose an eyebrow.

"I'm having some work done," Francis said and sipped his tea.

"I remember how grand this house looked with all the Christmas decorations. It'll be nice to see it come alive again.

A soft smile formed on Francis's face. He remembered too. Sylvie had loved holidays and decorating. His smile grew sad when he remembered his daughter's love of the Christmas lights it took three men four days to hang.

"Next Christmas we'll go all out," he promised.

Agnes thought lights vulgar and hadn't hung them once since Sylvie's death. She'd hate having them hung, but he didn't care.

"In fact, I think I'm in the mood to hang some lights this year."

"Can I expect you to attend my Christmas party?"

"I think I will." Francis grinned at Groger who smiled back happily. To Francis's surprise, he looked forward to it when he hadn't looked forward to anything in four years except Jack coming home.

Groger set his tea down and rose. "It's good to see you coming alive again too," he said as he offered his hand.

Edwin Begins to Plan

Perfume buffeted Edwin when he jerked open the door to his wife's bedroom. He waved a hand in front of his face as he strode inside.

Her lips twisted in a slight sneer as she glanced over her shoulder a moment before returning her attention to the mirror. His angry gaze took in the bags dropped carelessly on the king-size bed. Pillows mounded and tumbled across the monogrammed bedding. The edge of a brown fur peeked from the corner of a linen garment bag, and his lips tightened.

"I don't know how I'll get any rest for tonight what with all the racket they're making in your father's rooms. I saw them moving your mother's dressing table—"

"Not my mother." Edwin strode to the window and yanked back the frilly curtains to peer out. "Not father's rooms anymore either." Edwin craned over his shoulder to see her expression.

His wife straightened and turned to him, a smile tilting the corner of her thin lips.

"And before you go making plans, I've been informed those will be Jack's rooms."

"What!" She rose and pulled her pink dressing gown tighter about her narrow shoulders.

"You heard me. Jack gets Sylvan, and I get the scraps."

"All of Sylvan or just the button factory?"

Edwin glared over his shoulder and let the curtain drop. "I'm tempted to have Father's competency tested. What is he thinking leaving my company to a child?"

"Jack isn't a child anymore, Edwin, and you'd never win," Agnes said worriedly.

"I know, but it's so damned unfair. That company was bought with my mother's money. It should come to me."

"I thought your father gave Sylvia the startup capital."

Edwin irritably waved his hand. "My mother came to the marriage with a very large dowry. Father thinks because he gave us their house, that piddling little shack, and her jewels, that Jack should get this one. He's giving Jack everything that was Sylvia's.

"Jack's getting the house too? That's entirely unfair. This is our house!" Agnes said indignantly. "I've spent hours with the gardeners. I won't be a pensioner in someone else's home, Edwin. We must find our own place at once!"

"With what money? The store is bankrupt and the mill..." Edwin rubbed his temples. Tension sent bolts of pain from his temples to his shoulders. The bank wouldn't give him another loan. Groger had been sympathetic but even with the store as collateral he couldn't raise the funds to purchase Frank's mill and without that mill, he'd have nothing.

A perfumed cloud surrounded his wife as she rose to place a hand on his shoulder. "What about the mill? How could that possibly be doing badly?"

"You wouldn't understand."

She snorted and spun away. "I understand quite enough. You fired the managers your father taught and put your choices in. Toadies whose only skill is kissing your ass. Fire them, Edwin, and beg—"

He yanked her to face him. "Never say that again! A Pryor doesn't beg; we command! If you'd just stop spending until we get our feet under us again." He gestured at the shopping bags on her bed. "How many times do I have to tell you we can't afford all this? Not with the store going under. I'm working fifteen-hour days, and I can't keep up with you."

A disgusted expression on her face, she slapped his hand away. "My money, Edwin, and I'll spend it how I see fit."

"Fine. Spend it all on dresses and fripperies.

In fact, take over the running of the textile mills. I wash my hands of it. It's all yours. Hire whomever you like, but don't come crying to me when the dress makers and jewelers send past due notices. I won't pay them."

A flush climbed her cheeks as he spoke, and he smiled in triumph. Finally, their situation was sinking in.

"My father—"

"Is in a nursing home and can do nothing," Edwin said with vicious satisfaction. His anger at being turned away like a beggar surged. Her father had been contemptuous and quite clear he wouldn't loan him a dime.

"But, by all means, go tell him. Cry your eyes out and maybe he'll feel sorry for you and give you a few thousand dollars, but I wouldn't count on it. Hester has him wrapped around her little finger, and if you think to inherit, think again."

"You have to make your father see sense."

"You don't get it, do you? Even after all this time. You saw how he was with his precious Jack. God, it sickens me how he carried on when Sylvia and his brat died. He'll never change his mind. If he could, he'd give everything I worked so hard for to Jack. He's giving him the home we've lived in now for twenty-five years without a second thought or hesitation."

Every word Edwin spoke inflamed his anger more. He began to pace and slap his fist into his palm. "And now some foreign whore will come here, and we're supposed to treat her like family. God, we'll be the laughingstock of the town. Well, I just won't have it! It's beyond ridiculous!"

He snatched a bottle from his wife's vanity and threw it against the wall. Glass shattered and trickled down to the thick blue carpeting. Creamy white liquid splattered on the rose wallpaper and the scent of roses grew overpowering.

Agnes ran to her vanity and slapped at his hands. "Stop it! Breaking my things won't help. You just have to convince him. Tell him she'll want her own home or buy this one from him. I'll speak to him. Surely, he won't kick me out of our home, Edwin. And maybe you could convince him to let you take over Sylvan. So what if Jack owns it if you're in charge of it."

"It should be mine!" Edwin shouted and threw another bottle.

Agnes slapped him. Without thinking he slapped her back and laughed when she shrieked. He hit her again.

"Stop," she cried and held her hands before her face.

He fisted his hands in her hair and yanked her head back to smack her again, being careful not to hit hard enough to bruise. She slapped weakly at him. Her panting breaths excited him. It had been years since she'd excited him in any way.

She screamed when he ripped her dressing gown off, exposing her breasts.

"You're still my wife, Agnes, and a man has needs," he said as she struggled in his grasp. The weak blows made him feel powerful, and he laughed again as he pushed her backward onto the bed. Wide-eyed, she stared up at him as he dropped his pants.

He finished in minutes and slapped her ass hard as he rose. He'd never hit her before, too afraid of her father, but the old man was dying, and once he was dead, Edwin wouldn't need to hold back. A smile bloomed on his face. His bitch of a wife would do what she was told and like it.

"No more shopping. At least until I sell the store. It might be a good idea to speak with your father. Maybe he'll leave you the house. God knows Hester doesn't need it."

He grinned as Agnes turned bright red. She'd always hated that her sister had a bigger house than she. Edwin preferred their house with its spacious grounds and elegant rooms. Hester's home seemed gaudy and tasteless to him with its gilt and mirrors but every time they visited Agnes was consumed with envy.

A bottle broke against the door after he closed it. He paused, considering returning to show her who was boss but continued to his room. Maybe she could talk her old man into a loan, and it wouldn't do to burn that bridge. He'd have to ensure she didn't leave him and go running back home. A divorce would play hell with his finances. He frowned as he considered what to do if Agnes found out he already controlled Sylvan.

Marie had left a plate of cheese and crackers beside a bottle of brandy and laid a fire in the hearth as he liked it. He debated sending his regrets for dinner, but it was important to keep up appearances.

His finances were plummeting, but he wasn't broke yet. If he could sell the store and refinance his loans... and maybe Agnes was right, and he should rehire some of the old fogeys, at least until he got things straightened out. *And who knows, Jack could always die.* War was dangerous. There was hope Sylvan would be his one day, and if it happened soon enough he could take out a loan against Sylvan to purchase the mills. There must be something he could do. Surely, his father wouldn't give it to Jack's widow. The thought angered him so much he threw the brandy against the wall. The two-hundred-dollar bottle broke with a satisfying crash.

He rang for another bottle.

Brook Waits for Jack

Brook sat gingerly and swung her legs to the floor. Puffy and red, the healing gash on her leg throbbed in time with her heart.

"Mrs. Pryor, you should be laying still." The nurse hurried to her side and laid a hand on her brow. "No more fever. That's good. Do you need the bathroom?"

"Yes, please, and has there been any word on my husband?"

"Sorry, no, but I'm sure he's fine. My Alfred serves with the thirty-eighth and he tells me the push is almost over." The nurse continued to talk of rumors on troop placement as she escorted Brook the twenty feet to the bathroom. Each step felt like a knife in the leg. Pain flared into agony and it was all Brook could do not to cry out. Tears of pain clouded her vision.

The nurse made a tsking sound. "Don't get yourself all riled up. No news is sometimes good news. I'm sure we'll hear something as soon as the lines are back up."

The red stamps look like blood, Brook thought unhappily as she neatened the small stack of mail before her.

All bore the same message. Whereabouts unknown. She'd tried everything she could think of and no one knew what had become of her family and now Jack. Tears filled her eyes, and she laid her forehead against the cold tabletop.

"Miss?" a passing nurse asked in a hesitant voice.

"I'm fine," Brook said hurriedly as she straightened and dashed the tears from her face.

"Still no word?"

"No. I need to go home and ask in person."

"Someone is bound to know."

"I'm sorry, I forgot your name," Brook said.

"Helen. And don't worry about it." Helen helped Brook lay back in the bed, tsking over the redness in her leg. "You're rushing it. Give the wound time to heal. If you rupture the stiches, you could bleed out before you even know you've done it."

"I just hate being useless," Brook complained.

"I'll see about getting you a wheelchair and maybe you can help some of the injured read or write letters home?"

"Yes, I can do that." Brook bit her lip against

the pain straightening her leg caused.

"Everyone is missing someone. You'll find them," Helen said in parting.

Brook closed her eyes to better picture Jack's face. Come for me soon," she whispered and held her letters to her chest as slow tears leaked from the corner of her eyes.

Jack Searches for Brook

The two weeks Jack waited to get sent to Charleroi felt like a year. Communications were so disrupted he wasn't able to reach anyone, not his platoon or the hospital. He was in a fever of impatience when he finally arrived. It had been over a month now since she was injured, and his wounds were almost healed. He'd be sent back to the front lines soon. The thought of never seeing her again made his head hurt. Pain traveled in waves from his back to the top of his head. Every bounce and jolt in the jeep made him clench his teeth. He was pale and shaky by the time they unloaded his truck.

"Lydia Summers?" he asked the first nurse he passed.

She scowled and shook off his grasping hand. Jack wished he'd paid more attention to the other nurses. He cursed himself for not asking her damned name. The next nurse he asked eyed him dubiously.

"She'll be on shift tonight, but you don't look like you're up for it. Give it a day or two. She isn't worth a stroke."

A blush heated Jack's cheeks. "No, it isn't like that. Lydia's a friend of my wife, and I'm hoping she's had word. My wife is a nurse too." Calling Brook his wife sent a thrill up his spine and filled his heart with happiness.

The nurse's expression softened, and she glanced at his chart. "Ah, you're Brook's Pryor."

Brook, Jack thought in satisfaction. It suited her, unrestrained, strong, and refreshing.

"Do you know where she is?"

"Sorry, no. Last I heard the walking wounded were shipped to Paris. I have no idea what her status is, being a woman noncombatant and all." The nurse patted his arm. "I did hear she was doing well. Doctor Roberts is here. Shall I ask him to come speak with you?"

"Yes, please, and thanks, Miss."

"It's Mrs.— Mrs. Penny Dowlin and Brook is a good friend of mine."

Jack watched Penny leave the room and settled back on his bed. "I've got you now," he whispered and closed his eyes to envision Brook's smile. Her terrified expression as she fell stubbornly replaced the smile he was trying to see, and he opened his eyes. His dreams wouldn't ease until she was safe at home. Despair made his head ache. *Who knew how long that would be?*

Jack's Pack Saves the Day

February 15, 1945

"Pryor!"

"Here," Jack said and sat, his head barely throbbing at the change of position. Any day now, the doctor would discharge him.

"Special delivery. Who'd you bribe? Never had so much blasted red tape to sort through. Top secret my ass. What's in this thing?" The speaker held out a thick manila envelope wound with packing tape and covered with stamps. "Uh-uh ID first," he said and withdrew the package as Jack reached for it. "Fuckers put me in a delivery convoy and it took we me two days to get here. You bet your sweet ass you're signing for this shit in triplicate." He slapped a clipboard into Jack's hand and jerked a thick thumb at the pen. "Sign!"

Jack debated opening the package first, but the man's hostile tone dissuaded him.

"This better not be girly magazines," the man

muttered as he handed the envelope over.

Jack laughed. "No one would send me..."The weight surprised Jack who'd thought the bulk was from tape. A cold sweat sprang up on his brow when he saw the return address. Mr. Phips, his father's lawyer, had sent it. His hand shook as he reached for his knife to cut the tape.

"What is it?" the man asked in a concerned tone, his eyes on Jack's face.

"I hope not news that my father has died." He rubbed his brow with a trembling hand. "Please don't be change of ownership papers," he murmured as he slit the envelope. His eyes widened at the neat stacks of cash. He laughed in relief when he saw the small black box.

"Good news, then?" the delivery man asked.

Jack glanced at him, amazed the man hadn't peeked when it was obvious he was dying of curiosity.

"Yes. My father approves that I'm— I got married." Jack grinned and withdrew the single sheet of paper and the black box. He tucked the envelope into his pack to hold out the ring for the man's inspection.

"Jesus, is that thing real?"

Jack held the ring up to the light and examined it critically. He'd never really considered the cost of it but now that he did, it astonished him his father had risked it. "It was my mom's."

"She die?"

"Years ago. She'd love Brook. My wife." Jack's grin widened as he read the letter.

The man craned forward, and Jack held it out.

"Can't wait to meet her. Send her home, love Dad? Seriously? He had the ring couriered? He couldn't fucking wait? It must've cost him a fortune..."

Jack shrugged and debated a moment, then stuffed the ring into his pack beside the money.

The delivery man glanced around and whispered, "You better keep that on you. I wouldn't let it out of my sight."

"It'll be fine and thanks for bringing it. Now I just have to find her."

"You lost her?"

She was injured" – Jack touched the healing scar on his forehead with a fingertip— "and we've been sent to different hospitals.

The man nodded sagely. "Command is in an uproar. We're running around like chickens with our heads cut off. Half the time we're acting on lost orders. Paperwork won't catch up to us for months yet, but we got them on the run." He waved in a half salute and sauntered out, calling back over his shoulder. "Congratulations and good luck!"

"Thanks!" Jack called after him, but he was busy counting the cash without removing it from his pack. His nearest neighbors looked on curiously, but none questioned him. Most were too lost in their own misery to care what he was up to, but the delivery guy was right, leaving the ring in plain sight was tempting fate and even his lucky pack couldn't protect him from stupidity.

He took everything out except the envelope and examined his gear with pursed lips. Mildew had stained his spare uniform beyond the laundry's ability to repair it, but he hadn't yet received a new one. The thick canvas of the pack itself hadn't stained, and he'd been able to get the musty odor out of it, but his copy of *The Grapes of Wrath* was ruined, not that he got much time for reading anyway. He eyed the book thoughtfully. A little trimming and it might make a good spot to stash the cash. His eyes widened when he surreptitiously counted it. His father had sent him ten thousand dollars.

With this much money, maybe I can bribe someone, he thought excitedly. He began to repack his bag as he considered who he'd need to pay off to get Brook safely away. The list was depressingly long. *Finding her would be the easy part,* he realized with a sinking feeling. Without a marriage license, she couldn't get transport to America until the civilian lines reopened, and who knew how long that would be? He needed a marriage license. His eye caught on the soaked remains of the letters he carried for his friends. John's was on top. The lettering had faded and washed away leaving an unreadable smudge of blue, but the seal was still visible. He opened it carefully, trying not to rip the paper that had stuck together when it dried.

"What are you doing, pal," the man in the next bed asked when Jack drippled water over the edges, hoping it would help them separate without tearing.

"Seeing if these orders are still readable."

The man flopped back on his pillow, clearly not interested in orders. "Don't bother. Just take them to the nearest HQ and ask for new ones. That was some ring. Your wife will be thrilled. When are they releasing you?"

"I'm not sure." Jack peeled the paper apart and frowned. Using his fingernail, he tried to scrape the still legible black ink from the top. To his delight he managed to smear it into unreadability. He glanced around the crowded ward. Most of the men laid in bed either sleeping or reading although two groups playing cards had formed comprised of men with casts on legs and arms. Penny entered, carrying a pile of fresh linens followed by Lydia. The card playing men invited them to a game.

Jack rose and grabbed Lydia's arm.

"Can we talk privately a minute?" he asked.

Cat calls followed him from the room.

"Have you heard from Brook?" Lydia asked anxiously.

"No. But I had an idea. My father sent me enough money to get her home, but there's no way she can get on transport to America without a marriage license." He held out the smeared papers. "I'll ask for a new one, claim these are ruined, but I'll need witnesses. I know you already lied once for her, but this would be serious. A signed statement."

To Jack's relief Lydia nodded. She bit her bottom lip and glanced over her shoulder into the busy ward. "Brook does need a place. Her family was killed."

"Killed? Jack asked in dismay.

"She's been searching for word, but they were caught in the blitz. It's been two years now and she's heard nothing. Give me a few days. Let me speak with Doctor Roberts."

"You sure that's a good idea? I like the man and all, but will he really risk his career and lie for us?"

Lydia shrugged. Her green eyes sparkled as she grinned. "He already did, but I'll ask before we claim him as a witness on paper. And there's Burns and Penny." She patted Jack's cheek and stopped speaking as two orderlies exited the ward.

Jack waited until they were out of earshot to continue. "Lydia, you've been a good friend and I won't forget it. If you ever need anything, look me up."

Lydia's smile darkened, and she turned away, saying over her shoulder," I can take care of myself. You take care of my friend."

"Next!" the clerk called in a bored voice.

Jack rose and smoothed his uniform shirt. Despite the cold air, sweat beaded his brows and dampened his palms. Brook's safety rested on his getting a copy of a form that had never existed, and her good friends risked their reputations and maybe jail time if the lie was discovered.

"Name," the man asked without glancing up from the form he was filling out.

"Jack Pryor."

The clerk held out his hand.

"I'm not here for orders."

The clerk glanced up and frowned.

"I need special permission to marry."

The clerk exhaled heavily and removed his glasses to rub the bridge of his nose. "Is she claiming to be pregnant.

Anger clenched Jack's fists and heated his cheeks. "No, she *is* not. It isn't like that." His anger evaporated, and guilt made his flush deepen. "We'd just been married in Wiltz. My wife is an English nurse and she was injured in the attack. She can no longer work, and I want to send her home, but our paperwork was also destroyed."

"I see," the clerk said thoughtfully in a kinder tone. He leaned back in his seat and absently rubbed his glasses on a handkerchief he took from his pocket. After a moment's consideration, staring at his files with pursed lips, he replaced his glasses and began to flick through a thick notebook on his desk. "Let's see, you'll need this form signed and dated by the officiating—"

"That's going to be a problem as he was killed in the attack."

The clerk halted in his rummaging. "Your wife—"

"Is in Paris with the thirty-ninth and unable to travel."

The clerk frowned now. "Without proof—"

Jack interrupted again, handing him the stack of now sweaty papers he clutched. "I have signed affidavits from the witnesses. See?" He unfolded the letter Doctor Roberts had signed while blessing the man for perjuring himself.

With his fingers mentally crossed, he handed the clerk John's orders. Water had made the paperwork mostly illegible, but a seal imprinted the paper and a corner of a signature remained.

"My copy of our license was in my pack when I was injured," Jack said and held out his abused pack for the clerk to examine. "All of my wife's things were destroyed in the attack."

The clerk took the papers and smoothed them out on his desk. "I can fill in a request, but you'll have to wait on confirmation."

"Confirmation?"

"The father who officiated will have sent a formal request to his parish registry."

"But the entire church was destroyed. What if he hadn't sent it in yet?"

"He would have sent it within days of the

service."

"That's what I'm saying. The attack happened that day."

Jack's voice had risen to shrill, and he took a deep breath, trying to speak in a calmer tone when he said. "My wife needs a copy of the marriage license. What if I don't make it home? She needs it! She has no home to go to! I can't send her to my family without—"

"What's going on out here?" a gruff voice asked, and Jack flushed as he realized he was yelling again. Both men saluted the general who glared from the doorway.

"Sorry, sir," the clerk said and gave Jack an annoyed glance.

"Excuse me. I'm sorry I lost my temper. My wife, you'll remember her from Wiltz? he asked the general hopefully. "The English nurse, the night of the accident, in the rain. The men stuck in the barbed wire?" He snapped his lips closed, realizing he was babbling. The general wouldn't remember.

"Yes, I remember her. A fine, brave woman."

Jack nodded eagerly. "Yes, she was injured in the attack there a week later. We'd just been married." He held out his papers and blushed when he realized he'd mangled them in his hand.

"Not badly, I hope?"

"A leg wound. The doctor thinks she'll recover the use of it in time, but they're sending her home. But she can't go to our home without a marriage license."

"His copy was ruined," the clerk put in helpfully. "The problem is the priest who officiated is dead and his records destroyed."

"I have signed letters from the witnesses," Jack said and winced as he again offered the mangled papers.

"He'll need to wait to get copies of the license or official notification that they weren't received," the clerk said.

"I can't wait. She needs somewhere safe right now."

The general held up his hand. A slight smile built on his face, and he cleared his throat. "As I recall, you didn't know the nurse when I met her?"

"No, sir," Jack mumbled. He held out the papers. "Doctor Roberts signed as a witness and Burns and Summers..."

The general took the papers from Jack and examined them a moment before handing them back.

The smile on the general's face built. "While I can't blame you're, ah, enthusiasm, she seems a lovely girl, perhaps the wait would do you good?"

"No, sir," Jack said emphatically. "Brook will be safer in America. Her parents are missing; her home destroyed. Her leg... she won't be able to walk on her own for a bit."

The general's smile faded, and he nodded and pursed his lips. "Yes. Too many have been injured by this damned war." His glance flicked from the clerk and his stack of forms to Jack, and his smile returned. "The solution is simple. Issue him a new marriage license. I'll write and attach a letter. Find someone to officiate again. If you found one priest willing to marry you in a few days, I'm sure you can find another."

He glanced down at the papers Jack clutched and lowered his voice. "Lucky for your wife you'd married and she was sent to our American hospital." He cocked an eyebrow and his smile grew. "But we've got these bastards on the ropes now." He waved a hand at his clerk and motioned Jack to follow him. "Get me the papers to sign," he said over his shoulder and gestured Jack to a seat. He pulled a fresh sheet of paper from his desk and wrote briskly a moment, stamped it, signed it and blew on the ink.

"There you are, and good luck to you, son."

"Thank you, sir. We're quite obliged."

"Not at all. It's funny, I don't' recall signing that order." His eyes twinkled when Jack's flush deepened. "That's my stamp, but that paper is generally used for orders, but I do admire a man who's willing to put it all on the line." He smiled widely and waved Jack to the door. "Dismissed."

Jack saluted and practically ran from the room.

Edwin's First Murder

"Marie!" Edwin called crossly as the maid entered the main door.

Marie waited at the front gate every day for the postman, and Edwin was getting sick of it. They hadn't heard a thing in over two months. He was sick of the entire house treating Jack's impending arrival like the second coming.

He opened his locked desk drawer and eyed the letters inside in satisfaction. For four years now, he'd intercepted his father's mail whenever he could, removing the letters Jack sent and his father's replies. At first, he'd taken them out of spite. Now he was glad he had. His father was sick from nerves and had handed the management of every one of their businesses over to him and had stopped inquiring as to their welfare.

Edwin patted the front pocket where he kept the papers he'd had drawn up transferring Sylvan to him permanently. Is all he needed was his father's signature. He needed him distracted but ill would do and a letter with bad news might be just the thing to push him into a deep depression where he didn't care what he signed.

"Marie!" he called again, but she barely glanced at him as she headed for the stairs.

By Marie's excited expression, Edwin assumed she held a letter from Belgium and he wanted to read it first. Good news might energize Francis, and he couldn't afford interference.

"Stop!" he snarled and ran after her.

She halted on the stairs, gripping the bannister with one hand and the long skirt Agnes insisted the staff wear in the other.

"Excuse me, sir, but I have an important missive for your father. He's instructed me to bring him the overseas mail at once."

"I'll bring it to him." Edwin panted slightly as he strode up the stairs.

"Sorry, sir, but I have my instructions." Marie continued to climb, ignoring his outstretched hand.

Edwin grabbed her arm and spun her to face him. "I said *I* would bring him the letter. I'm in charge here, not you. *You* will do as you're told, or you'll be out on your ass!"

To Edwin's shock, she glared and yanked her arm from his grasp. "I'll do as I'm told by the mister, not you! The mister wants immediate word of Jack. You can't fire me. I don't work for you. I work for the mister and Jack. I was his nursemaid, and when he returns, I'll be his housekeeper. Jack is like a son to me. I know you've been stealing the mister's mail and it's cruel. His heart is breaking for word of his son."

Fury caused Edwin's hands to clench. That this little gutter snipe dared to speak him in such a tone in his own home enraged him. He slapped her face. She gasped and rose a hand to her cheek. He snatched at the letter.

"No!" she half-yelled and yanked it away as she tried to push passed him.

Edwin pushed her back. Her wide brown eyes fastened on him as she fell and reached for him, scrabbling, trying to grasp anything to stop her fall.

He stepped back, making no attempt to help her. When her head cracked into the wall, he winced and closed his eyes. Dull thuds and small whining gasps followed as she tumbled down the marble stairs. Edwin didn't open his eyes until he heard the wet splat.

He glanced over the rail. The edge of Marie's navy-blue skirt and a small streak of blood were all he could see. He ran to his room and closed the door behind himself. Panic began to replace his anger.

"No one saw," he assured his pale reflection.

He poured himself a double shot of brandy and threw it back. Color flushed his cheeks and his pulse stopped racing.

"No one saw a thing," he repeated in a calmer

tone. *What if she's not dead,* he thought in sudden worry. She'd say he pushed her, and he'd lose everything even if he didn't go to jail. "I didn't mean to hurt her," he said indigently to his reflection and poured himself another double. *Surely, they couldn't blame him for a simple accident.* He leaned on his hands, trying to catch his suddenly short breath.

A muffled scream jerked him upright. "You don't know anything," he muttered as he ran to the door and into the hall.

"What is it!" he called.

"Oh, dear God, Marie, Marie!" Mrs. Schmidt yelled in a tear-soaked voice.

Edwin stopped halfway down the stair. "Call for an ambulance."

Mrs. Schmidt leaned over Marie who lay with her arms out-flung. Greying-brown hair had come loose from its knot. Long strands snarled around her shoulders and across her face, not quite covering the wide, staring eyes. Her legs remained on the stairs while her head and chest lay in a growing pool of blood on the marble foyer.

"What is it, Edwin," Agnes asked from the top of the stair.

Edwin hadn't heard her arrive. The brandy numbed him. He felt as if he'd just woken from a dream. "Marie has fallen. Go back upstairs."

"Oh, the poor dear is dead. She's dead!" Mrs. Schmidt wailed.

"Dead!" Agnes gasped.

Her hand flew to her throat, and she took a trembling step backward.

"Go lay down, dear. I'll see to this." Edwin ascended the stairs and turned his wife, giving her a small nudge.

"She can't be dead. Why, she's the same age as me. No, it isn't possible."

Edwin escorted his mumbling wife to her bedroom and called the family doctor. He was still on the telephone with him when he heard sirens approaching. Cold dread made his hands shake. Mrs. Schmidt had called the police.

He knew he should go back downstairs but he couldn't bring himself to face them. A few minutes later, an officer joined him in his wife's bedroom. Edwin sat on the side of his wife's bed patting her hand, trying to look innocent and not scared to death.

"Should I ask the medics to come up?" the officer asked kindly.

Edwin had to clear his throat to speak past the lump lodged there. "No, thank you. I've phoned our physician. Is she really dead?"

"I'm afraid so, sir. Looks like she was running up the stairs and fell. Your housekeeper, Mrs. Schmidt, found a letter and informed us she was likely hurrying to bring it to your father."

"Oh, dear God, we have to tell him. He'll be heartbroken," Agnes said and pushed herself upright. Edwin put an arm around her.

"We'll wait for the doctor. God knows what

this news will do to him. Marie was like family," Edwin said and had to bite back his giddy laugh.

The officer nodded and strode to the door. "The body will be brought to Central. I don't expect they'll want to autopsy. I'm very sorry for your loss." He bobbed his head and left, closing the door behind himself.

Edwin sagged, relief making him lightheaded.

Agnes hugged him a moment before pushing away and heading to the door. Edwin coughed to cover his laugh; she thought he was sad.

"Marie?" his father said in a quavering voice.

"I'm afraid so, sir." Mrs. Schmidt handed him a blood-smeared, wrinkled letter. "It appears she fell while bringing you this."

Tears sprang to Francis's eyes.

"I'll be right back with some nice, hot tea. Doctor, can I bring you anything?"

"No. Tea will be fine. If you could show me to a bathroom so I could wash up?"

Mrs. Schmidt bobbed her head and gestured the doctor to proceed her from the room.

"Shall I read you the letter?" Agnes asked.

Edwin fumed, cursing himself for not grabbing the damned letter. But maybe this was better. Everyone seemed convinced she'd fallen because of her hurry to bring the letter upstairs. While he pondered, Francis nodded.

Agnes read:

'Dad, I can't thank you enough for your support. You're going to love Brook. She's an English nurse. We only just met, but I'm certain she's the one for me. She's sweet and kind and so brave it worries me. She was injured in an attack in Wiltz, and I've lost touch with her, but as soon as I find her again, I'm sending her home where she'll be safe.

I know you probably think I'm nuts but wait until you meet her. You'll see immediately why I love her. Her soul is more beautiful than she is and that's saying a lot. I still can't believe she loves me.

Take care of her until I get home, Dad. The hospitals are so swamped here it's been a nightmare trying to find her, but I've got a good lead now. For the longest time, I didn't even know her name. Have I got some stories to tell you. To get her medical care I lied and said we were already married but the papers were forged, and my witness were lying their asses off. It's a long story that I can't wait to tell you in person. Thank God, Brook has such good friends. If Lydia Summers contacts you, I beg you to help her in any way she asks. Brook and I owe her so much.

I'm so sorry I didn't listen to you. I didn't understand. The thought of Brook here shrivels my soul. Don't worry about me though. I have good friends too, and they can tell you what a lucky bastard I am. We take good care of each other. As soon as I find Brook, I'll telegram so you know when to expect her. We'll be home before you know it, and I'll gratefully take my place in the family business.

Much love,
Jack'

"Read it again," Francis said weakly.

Agnes sniffed hard but complied. The doctor enter as Agnes finished reading, and he hurried to Francis's bedside where he took out a stethoscope and listened to his heart. Light glinted from the dome of his bald head as he leaned over Francis to check his pulse and eyes.

"Whirlwind romances seldom amount to anything. I bet she's forgotten him already and found herself another soldier," Agnes said.

"Ha." Edwin snatched the letter from his wife. "Not if she realizes he'll inherit a fortune."

"Please," Doctor Ames said and made a calming motion. "Mr. Pryor needs peace."

"I'm not dead yet," Francis said crossly and tried to push himself more upright in the bed.

Doctor Ames frowned and made shooing motions at Agnes. "Still, a shock of this sort should be treated with care. We don't want to have to bury you too."

Edwin grimaced and busied himself covering his father in a faded quilt Sylvia had made him twenty years ago. Any moment he expected someone to yell out, *'He did it!'* but no one seemed to be contemplating Marie's death had been other than an accident.

Francis sniffed and rubbed his face hard. "My poor girl. Marie was a sweet thing, always so happy, and she took such good care of me."

"It's a real tragedy," Agnes agreed and patted his hand. "At least Jack's wife is English though. Such a relief.

"This damned war!" Francis snapped.

"Don't get yourself all worked up. You need to rest. I'll see to everything," Edwin said as the doctor opened his mouth. *Likely to chastise them again,* Edwin thought bitterly, annoyed he couldn't throw this man out on his ass.

Francis plucked at the quilt with shaking hands. "I want her buried in the family's plot. We were all she had."

He panted a minute, trying to catch his breath. The doctor leaned over him with a stethoscope again, and Francis irritably nudged him away.

"See to it, son. It's the least we could do."

"Don't take on so," Agnes said as she stood to pour a glass of water. "It's hardly our fault Marie slipped and fell while running up the stairs. I'll speak to the help and remind them of proper behavior. No one should be running inside the house."

Francis glared at Agnes and batted away the water she offered. "She was trying to bring me the letter." He snatched the paper from Edwin and waved the wrinkled missive, then smoothed it out on his blanket-covered lap. "Poor dear was trying to ease me and it cost her life."

Doctor Ames shook his head and said, "As Mrs. Pryor says, it isn't anyone's fault but a tragic accident. You rest and no getting out of bed until I say you may. Your blood pressure is still much higher than I'd like. If you want to live to see your son return home, you'll listen to me."

Francis exhaled heavily and leaned his head back on the pillows. "You'll see to her, Edwin?"

"I'll take care of everything, Father."

Edwin escorted Doctor Ames to the door. Mrs. Schmidt appeared as he held the door for the doctor. Red rimmed eyes and pale cheeks revealed her distress, but she spoke in her normal brisk tones.

"I've spoken to Father Mattis and arranged the ceremony already. Shall I arrange for a wake and dinner?"

"Yes, please. Father would like her buried in the family plot. Arrange for some temporary help and give the staff the rest of the week off."

"Very good, sir. And the mister?"

"Will be just fine. The doctor wants him to rest, so if you'd call his secretary and inform him I'll be handling his meetings that would be helpful."

"At once, sir."

"Such a tragedy," Edwin said sadly, shaking his head and tsking. "Such a waste for a mere note." Laughter built, making his voice thick.

He patted Mrs. Schmidt on the back, earning a surprised glance and hurried away afraid he'd burst into laughter right there.

No one suspected a thing. He wished it were Agnes he'd pushed down the stairs. The laughter faded to simmering anger. It'd be suspicious as hell if his wife fell down the same stairs. He'd wasted a golden opportunity on a minor annoyance.

He halted at the top and walked the wrought iron railing that encircled a landing overlooking the main entranceway. Fanciful curlicues decorated the black metal, matching the chandelier that dangled over the foyer. Gilt legged chairs, cushioned in blue silk, lay against the paneled wall, bracketing the wide window that overlooked the interior courtyard. This landing curved and narrowed, leading to the guest wing before widening again and overlooking the ballroom. He rarely noticed it as he always turned left at the stairs into the family's wing.

It had never occurred to him before how easy it would be to push someone over this low railing and rid oneself of their annoyances. The floors were marble, and the landing was a good twenty-feet high. It was almost certain to be a fatal fall. The death of Marie, while not planned, had given him access to all his father's records, and maybe permanent access to Sylvan if his father succumbed to his high blood pressure, so maybe it hadn't been a complete waste.

He frowned and spun away. Jack and his damned wife stood between him and his inheritance. Another slip and fall would be suspicious, but surely he could think of something. People died in accidents all the time.

Jack Finds Brook

March 3, 1945

Jack's heart pounded hard and his palms sweat. He'd found her. It had taken two months but here she was and more beautiful than he remembered.

Her hair hung in loose waves over her shoulder and the dressing gown she wore floated to the floor, exposing a v of milky skin with just a hint of the curve of her breast and the glint of his dog-tag.

She sat on a chair beside a bed where a man lay holding a hand to his bandaged eyes while she read. Her soft lilt filled Jack's heart with joy.

"Brook," he said, and her head jerked up.

The book tumbled to the floor as she stood and took an unsteady step forward.

"Jack?"

Love and longing laced her voice, bringing tears to his eyes.

"What took you so long," she said through

her tears as she took another trembling step toward him. He caught her in his arms and hadn't realized he'd moved from the doorway. They were both laughing and crying as they embraced. Her kiss tasted salty from her tears and her hair smelled of strawberries. He clenched his fingers in it, as he'd dreamed of doing, and pulled her back for another kiss.

"Hu-hum," a woman cleared her throat loudly, and Brook broke away from him giggling.

"Oh, Jack, I'm so glad you're well." She kissed the hands she clutched and tugged him to the door.

He realized she limped and pulled her even closer, his arm so tight around her waist their hips brushed as they paced slowly forward.

"And you. God, I was so worried." He drew her to the side of the door and kissed her again. Brook Taylor, will you marry me?"

She laughed and kissed his lips, then his cheek and chin and nose. Tears sparkled in her beautiful eyes.

"Yes! With all my heart, yes!"

Relief made him sag against the wall. She rested against him, a fragrant, delicious armful.

"It might be a bit tricky to marry though," she went on a moment later.

His shoulders tensed.

"They think we are married. You saved my life, Jack."

A wave of relief made him lightheaded. Still holding her tightly against him with one arm, he slipped his pack from his shoulder and wedged it between them so he could rummage one handed.

"I got that covered." He produced a crinkled paper with a flourish. "Your friends helped me. We claimed the marriage license was destroyed in the blast and this"— he waved the paper triumphantly at her— "is permission to remarry. Is all we need to do is get it signed with witnesses." He stroked her hair and kissed her neck. "I wish you could have a huge church wedding with all your friends and family there but please don't make me wait."

Two men exited the doorway and stopped talking as they passed them. Brook ducked her head and pressed harder against him. He realized she was embarrassed, and knew he should release her, but couldn't make himself.

"Find us an official, Jack."

Her laughing blue eyes sparkled, and he hoped he looked as happy to her.

"I wrote to my father. I know how much nursing means to you. I really do, but I need you safe. After we marry, I want you to go my dad in America." He tightened his grasp when she tensed.

"Please, Brook? For me? I know it's unfair, but I can't stand the thought of you here. You'll like him, and you'll be safe there."

"My parents," she said faintly.

"We'll go together after the war. Please, Brook, I'm begging you."

"I don't want to leave you."

"And I don't want you to leave, but it isn't safe here or in England. In America, you'll be safe, and everyone says we've got this almost licked. I'll be home soon. My stint is up in June." He closed his eyes, not wanting to see the pain in hers, and pressed his cheek against hers. "Please," he whispered.

"I'll do what you ask but can't we stay together for now? How long is your leave?"

"One week and you can thank Doctor Roberts for that. Hell, you can thank him for finding you."

"How did you find me?"

"I'll tell you later." He rummaged in his bag again and removed a thick manila envelope. "My dad sent me this too. Crazy of him when he knows they lose more letters than not, but I appreciate it. My mother's ring." He dumped the ring into his palm, and her breath caught.

"You really mean it," she said breathlessly.

He frowned. "Didn't you?"

"Yes, but Lydia warned me men will say—"

"I've meant every word I've ever said to you." He slipped the ring onto her finger and closed her hand around it. "Never take it off."

"Your mum passed, then?"

"She died when I was sixteen. She was my dad's second wife, and he never recovered. It killed him when I joined, and now I feel like a heel, but they would've drafted me anyway. He wanted me to finish college, and I wanted to see the world and live this grand adventure." He snorted, stirring her hair.

The smell of strawberries wafted over him and he breathed deeply. "I'll tell you everything, and you can tell me about you and your family, but I need to go find a preacher and rent us a room."

The sharp staccato of high heels pulled him from her kiss. She left him dazed, so in love his breath came hard and it was physically painful to leave her in the hallway.

He glanced back at the door, and she lifted her still clenched hand in farewell. Bright eyes alight with love and lust followed him from the building. He practically ran down the street, his pack thumping against his shoulder.

An ear-to-ear grin lined his face, and he realized he must look like a loon as pushed through the crowd, but he didn't care. He hesitated at the bus stop, debating going to buy her ticket to America or finding a preacher first. He opted for the ticket home. He had no idea how hard it would be to find someone to marry them, and he wanted to make sure he had enough money left to get her to safety. He blessed his father and recounted the money he'd sent.

His leaving had been a bigger blow than he'd meant it to be.

"I'll make it up to you, old man," he whispered to the dirty bus window. "You're going to love her."

His grin deepened. His father would be thrilled to have another woman in the house and hopefully children. Agnes, his brother's wife was quiet and cheerless. She and Edwin had no children, and Jack doubted they ever would. They'd been married for almost twenty years now. The thought made him sad for his brother.

The bus pulling to a stop before the port authority jerked him from his thoughts, and he grinned as he pushed through the men thronging the entrance. She was almost his.

Port authority bustled with activity. Soldiers sat on the floor and leaned on the walls while they waited their turns. Few civilians seemed to be about.

It might be harder than I'd anticipated to get Brook a ticket to America, he thought uneasily as he eyed the harried clerks.

"Heading home, Mack?" the man behind him asked.

"Not yet. Soon. I have enough points to make the short list and my time is up in June. You?"

"Lucky. I got another year and a half. Maybe we got these assholes whipped into shape by then though."

Jack examined the crowd as the men around him spoke of troop movements. His attention sharpened as a man before him mentioned his wife.

"Damn lines are so long I'll have to report back before I can get her a ticket home. I'm going to be eating mud soup for a year if I don't get this done. Her mam is convinced I'm a bounder."

"They aren't taking civilians?" Jack asked.

"The muckety mucks get the few berths they have open." He jerked his chin to a booth in the far corner where a clerk spoke to a well-dressed man. Only a few men waited in that line and all wore civilian clothes. The soldier patted his pocket and lowered his voice. "I brought me a hefty bribe this time. I want my wife outa here."

"Me too. I'm hoping because she's an English nurse I can get her on soon. She was injured and can't work now."

"This damned war," the soldier behind him said.

Jack glanced at his watch and frowned. This was taking longer than he'd planned.

"You got at least another two hours," the soldier behind him said. "Maybe longer."

"Damn. I really need to find us a room too. I can't take her to the barracks."

"She doesn't have a room?"

Jack had no idea where Brook stayed but assumed she lived with the other nurses. "She's stays with the other nurses. Any hotels or boarding houses around? I just have a week of leave."

"Finding a room might be harder than you think. This city is crowded as shit and every Tom, Dick and Harry is renting out their extra rooms for huge sums." The man grinned and winked at him. "Me and me buddies took rooms in a brothel when we first got here. Give 'um enough cash and they always make room, and they don't have any asinine rules on when you come and go and whether you can smoke or drink."

The two men nearest him began trading brothel stories. Jack tuned it out and examined the civilians. The few civilians in the room were well dressed and seemed to be getting fast service. He left the line and headed to the short line.

"Sorry, sir, war effort business only," the clerk said as Jack stepped up to the counter. He jutted his chin to the waiting soldiers. "If you'll just be patient someone—"

"Check your list for Sylvan Industries outa PA." Jack crossed his fingers as he handed the man his ID's, hoping his father had put his name on the lists as a part owner.

The clerk eyed him doubtfully but opened his book.

"Well, I'll be damned. Jack Pryor owner and general manager of Sylvan Industries. What the hell are you doing on the front lines?"

"My brother is taking care of my company until my wife gets back to take over. She's was volunteering as a nurse but was injured, and I need to get her home."

"Let me see what's available." The clerk opened another book and ran his finger down the page. "Got one leaving for New York in twelve days or London in six where she could catch—"

"No. I don't want her on the ocean either."

"She'll be sharing a cabin with at least two others. Tell her to bring a few days' worth of nonperishables and to pack light. It's better to ship your belongings separately."

"That isn't a problem. She doesn't have much. As I mentioned, she's injured though and might need help boarding."

"Crew will see to her. Tell her to leave early and expect long waits to board." The clerk leaned closer and lowered his voice. "If it were my wife, I'd buy her some books or something and tell her to stay in the cabin as much as she can. The returning soldiers can get a little rowdy and while the crew tries to keep tabs on the ladies..."

"Thanks, I will."

"She should be able to get a train to Pennsylvania. I hear the railways are business as usual back home."

"If not, my family will go get her. I appreciate the advice." Jack paid for the ticket and tucked it into his pack.

Outside, a cold rain had begun to fall. The air smelled of fish, smoke, and freshly baked bread. His stomach rumbled but he ignored it and jogged to the nearest church. Wet to the knees, he wiped his feet on the muddy mat before he entered.

Somewhere in the building, a children's choir practiced in French. Jack let the door swing shut behind him and poked his head into the small office.

"English?" he asked when the woman inside greeted him in French.

"Yes. Can I help you?" she said in heavily accented English.

"I hope so. I need someone to remarry me. My original marriage license was destroyed and the priest who officiated killed in the attack that injured my wife. I have all the paperwork and signed letters from the witnesses. What I need is a clergy to perform the ceremony and to refile. My wife is returning home in a week, and I don't want her to go without proof in case something happens to me."

Guilt reddened Jack's cheeks, and he hoped she thought it anxiety.

"I see," the woman said and pursed her lips thoughtfully. She rose and peeked from the door before shutting it. "Father Donovan is a bit of a stickler. He'd do it, but it could take him months to satisfy himself all requirements are met. Try Father Giovanna at Saint Thomas. Here, let me give you directions and add a note of introduction."

Twenty minutes later, he was telling his story to Father Giovanna.

"She's a nurse, you say?" the father asked in heavily accented English.

"Yes, an English nurse, but she's been wounded and can no longer work. She'll return home in a week, and I'd like her to have a copy of the marriage license in case something happens to me."

Jack handed him the paperwork as he spoke. "See? My commander signed stating the original records were destroyed. Dr. Roberts, Private Anthony Burns and a friend of my wife's, a fellow nurse, Miss Lydia Summers signed as witnesses. If you could just spare a few minutes, I can refile here."

Father Giovanna tapped the papers thoughtfully, then smiled. "I don't see why not. I shall sign them today. Bring your wife, say fiveish, and I'll preform a quick ceremony and you can file tomorrow." His smile widened. "I have a friend in the clerk's office who can get you copies."

"Thank you so much!" Jack enthusiastically shook Father Giovanni's hand. "You have no idea what this means to me. It will really ease my mind knowing she'll be taken care of if I don't make it home."

"God willing, you and she will have a long life together."

"I hope so, Father."

Jack shook his hand again and ran from the building. He still had to find a room.

Brook gazed doubtfully at her reflection.

"You look beautiful," Margery said.

"You do," Lucy agreed.

"Brook smiled at her fellow nurses and handed back the lipstick Doris offered her.

"Jack won't recognize me if I wear to much makeup," she said jokingly.

The women here had been very kind to her. Volunteers like herself, they'd welcomed her and let her stay in their crammed apartment even though she wasn't yet able to work. Her leg still pained her, cramping horribly if she stood for too long.

Every day it gets a bit better, she told herself as she absently massaged it.

"The leg hurt?" Doris asked.

"A bit," she admitted.

"No dancing on your wedding day," Margery said sadly in her musical French accent.

"Oh, they'll be dancing," Doris said and winked.

The women erupted into peals of laughter. A blush scalded Brook's cheeks, and she smoothed her dress and tugged the cuffs. The dress was clean but well-worn, the hem let down for Brook's height, but the stained white cuffs left her wrists bare.

She only owned two dresses and one nightgown. All had been generously donated by the other women. Her kit hadn't caught up with her and neither had her pay.

"I should've joined the QAIMNS," she

muttered irritably.

"Pfft." Doris separated another thick strand of Brook's hair and wounded it around the metal rod she took from the stove. "Don't be silly. If you had, you'd need permission to marry, and you could forget about taking a night off. I like my freedom too much, thank you very much, to give anyone that much authority over me."

A familiar argument erupted, and Brook let it wash over her as Doris curled her hair. It had grown and hung in a heavy mass halfway down her back. A smile flitted across her face. She'd no need to trim it now. Long hair would be fine as a civilian's wife. She'd have time to wash and dry it and clean water to do so. The thought of taking a long hot bath made her sigh deeply. She hoped Jack would find them an apartment with a big bathtub when they returned home.

Home— the word brought tears to her eyes.

"Are you okay?" Doris whispered. "You don't have to do this."

"Fine. How did he become my life so quickly?"

Doris smiled and smoothed the hair she was pinning up on one side. She tucked a white cactus flower behind Brook's ear before saying, "Men have a way of doing that. Sometimes lust can make us do things...I mean, there's no hurry. If he really loves you, he'll wait."

"I want him with all my soul," Brook said.

Doris smiled and kissed her cheek. She

lowered her voice to say, "Then take him. But marriage...Who would know or care. Paris is bursting at the seams. The Germans are marching, and we could all die tomorrow. Believe me, no one will think worse of you."

"No. I really want him. I love him. I want him forever."

Doris snorted lightly. "You don't even know him. For all you know he's a thief or a liar." She sighed, then laughed. "I see my words of warning are wasted. I like you, Brook, and I hope for your sake Jack is the man you think he is."

Brook grinned at her, then held out her hand to admire her ring. The diamond sparkled in the light. "I'm certain he's exactly who I think he is."

Dusk had fallen while Brook stared anxiously from the window. Jack had been gone for hours. Two men ran beneath her window shouting at a third, and they all disappeared around a corner. The sight reminded Brook this was a big city full of dangerous men all on edge. Tempers were high and violence common. Fights that ended in death and bloodshed erupted daily. Men and women thought to be sympathizers were keeping a low profile when they could and being harassed and sometimes harmed when they couldn't. The further the Germans were pushed back the more aggressive the mobs became.

Brook never left the safety of the hospital,

grateful she had a safe place to live where food and shelter were provided. Long lines snaked around the building during the day for rations and medicine.

Doris sticking her head in the room and calling her jerked Brook from her reverie.

"He's here and sent this up for you." She grinned and held out a paper wrapped package. "He asked me to tell you he's found a preacher who will renew your vows and begs you won't take too long as the appointment is for five tonight."

Brook opened the package and held up a blue dress.

"He's so sweet," Margery said.

Brook had to agree. She removed her dress with hands that shook. *We're really doing this.* The dress was a bit loose but much prettier than her hand-me-down. Doris patted her hair a final time and the girls crowded around grinning as she slowly descended the stairs.

Jack waited at the bottom, and she wanted to run to him and feel his lips on hers, but her leg protested each step, forcing her to a decorous walk.

"Brook," he said in a breathless voice when he took her hand.

"No second thoughts?" she asked.

"Never," he said as he leaned down to kiss her lips.

Giggles made her pull back. She'd kissed him

much longer than she'd intended but the touch of his lips made all thoughts flee her mind.

He laughed huskily and traced her bottom lip with his thumb. "Can we go?"

She held up her small sack. "Yes. This is all I have."

"I'll be all you ever need," he whispered as his fingertips skimmed her cheek. He took the bag from her and threw it over his shoulder where it bounced against his pack.

His slightest touch excited her, made her stomach clench with anticipation and her skin feel alive as if her nerve endings lay exposed on the surface.

A cab waited outside the hospital. The cabby grinned and held the door for them. The brief ride to the church passed in a haze. Jack's presence, his body heat against her side enthralled her utterly.

"Did you find us a room," she asked hopefully.

"I did."

To her surprise a flush reddened his cheeks. "I'm not sure though. It isn't really an appropriate place, but all the hotels and boarding houses are full."

"Appropriate?" The embarrassed hesitant way he'd said it alarmed her.

"It's sort of a, um, working girls house."

Brook slapped a hand over her mouth to stifle her giggles. "A whore house?"

"We don't have to stay there. I can look again

tomorrow," Jack hastily assured her.

Brook leaned in and kissed him. "We aren't waiting."

He moaned and pulled her closer, kissing her so hard he left her mouth feeling slightly bruised. She drew him back when he pulled away. His hand slid up her leg onto her thigh beneath her dress. The cabby loudly clearing his throat made her flush and spring away.

"Saint Thomas's," the cabby said as proudly as if he'd built the cathedral himself. "Best of luck to ya!" he called after them as Jack helped Brook from the car.

The father greeted them at the door and spoke with Jack. Brook couldn't concentrate. Her hand strayed to her lips where his kiss lingered. She wanted to kiss him again.

"Miss?" Father Giovanna repeated it twice before Brook realized he was speaking to her.

He smiled and handed her a bouquet of ferns and flowers.

Brook wondered where he'd found flowers at this time of year as she held it to her nose.

"All brides should have flowers," the father said.

"I'm not really a bride," Brook murmured.

"As your husband explained, you'd been married two days before the attack that injured you and killed the officiating father."

"And we've been separated since," Jack added. He tightened his grip on her hand. "I won't risk us being separated again. Brook needs a copy of the marriage certificate. I'll feel much better when you're home— safe with my family. You are my bride. I'll love you until the day I die."

His fingertips traced her face, remembering the injuries she'd sustained the first time he'd seen her. The touch was so full of love, her eyes fluttered shut. Love shown from his eyes when she opened hers, love she felt in her soul from the brief caress.

"Yes, it's best to be prepared in these uncertain times." Father Giovanna gestured to the front of the church.

Jack held her hand firmly without a trace of tremor or nervousness. The ceremony passed in a blur for Brook. Her only clear memory was the look in Jack's eyes and the timber of his voice as he repeated his vows. Sometime during the ceremony two nuns and a woman in a plain brown dress had entered. They all signed the marriage license as witnesses and wished she and Jack well in thick French accents.

"I'll buy us wedding bands at the first opportunity," Jack said when he broke from their first kiss as man and wife. "How did I get so lucky?" he continued in a thick voice and kissed her again.

She laughed, his thoughts matched hers so exactly. She'd gone from being alone in the world to having a loving husband. He made her feel safe and secure as if nothing bad could ever happen to her with him by her side.

"I'm going to take such good care of you. You deserve every good thing," he said.

Tears of happiness trickled down her cheeks, and she rested her face on his shoulder. "I'll be the best wife, Jack." She grinned. She didn't even know what he did for a living in civilian life, and it didn't matter. She could support them while she finished her degree. She didn't care if they lived in a one-room room shack as long as they were together.

"The ladies have prepared a small supper," Father Giovanna said, interrupting Brook's musings.

Jack's frustrated sigh made her giggle.

"Thank you," Brook said and straightened. She took her husband's hand and followed the women who now talked rapidly amongst themselves in French. "We can't stay long," she continued, and Jack tightened his grip on her hand. "Our lodgings have a curfew."

Sexual tension vibrated so thick between she and Jack, she found it hard to make pleasant conversation. His every glance and gesture flushed her skin and tightened her muscles until she thought she might burst if she didn't kiss him soon. Judging by his heated glances and lingering touches he felt the same way. The thirty minutes they spent in the rectory felt like a year. It was the longest thirty minutes of her life.

As soon as the cab pulled from the curb Jack was kissing her, his hands hard in her hair his body pressed tightly to hers.

"You sure about that address," the cabby asked in mangled English.

"Yes. Unless you know of a nicer place renting rooms," Jack asked hopefully.

The cabby grimaced in the rearview mirror and shook his head. Jack resumed kissing her, and she couldn't keep her hands from wandering. She had his shirt unbuttoned by the time they reached their 'hotel' and didn't even remember doing it.

Jack overpaid the driver, not even glancing at the bills he dropped into the front seat. Neither heard the cabby's effusive thanks.

Jack and Brook's Wedding Night

Brook giggled when he swung her into his arms, and she dropped the flowers she held to use both hands to hold his face while she kissed him. Her touch made his pulse leap.

He kicked the door open with his foot and let their bags tumble to the floor. Thanks to his foresight, the room was warm and smelled of fresh baked bread with just a hint of cheap perfume. Clean linens covered the bed and warm water sat in a porcelain ewer on the table before the window.

"Our temporary home, Mrs. Jack Pryor."

"Wherever you are *is* my home, Jack," she said and kissed him again. She continued to kiss him as he let her slide to her feet.

The dress he'd bought was a bit too big, but he'd picked it because it matched her eyes and had a zipper. She moaned softly and dropped her hands to his belt when he slid the zipper down. His fingers fumbled on his buttons, tangling with hers, as they removed his shirt.

He had to break from the kiss to pull off his t-shirt. She kicked off her shoes, holding her dress up with one hand. The laces on his boots seemed fiendishly tight, and he was tempted to cut them, but they finally gave, and he was able to kick off his boots while she giggled.

"A honeymoon in Paris. You're every women's dream," she said breathlessly as she again reached for his belt, still holding her dress up with one hand. The glimpses of her skin made his hands shake in anticipation.

"Mmm." He kissed her lips lightly, then her neck, making her shiver and press closer.

She released her dress and ran both hands through his hair and over his back, the press of their bodies keeping her dress in place.

Her obvious excitement excited him. Every sigh and shiver flushed his skin until he'd thought he'd combust from lust.

He tugged down her dress with one hand, using the other to cradle the back of her head beneath the warmth of her hair.

Her dress pooled on the floor by his feet. She was naked underneath and more beautiful than he'd imagined possible. He let both hands drift over the curves of her body while her fingertips lightly skimmed him. His skin shivered under her hands, and he was so hard his cock throbbed against her leg. He wasn't going to last long at all.

His palms whisked across her soft skin with a

sound like angels sighing, and he wanted to kiss everywhere he touched. With both hands, he cupped her buttocks and pressed her against his arousal.

"Jack," she whispered, barely above a sigh of sound, but he heard it in his soul.

This was true desire, not a whore's paid interest, and he hadn't realized how potent the difference would be. She wanted him, his hands, his lips, it was clear in every sound and gesture she made.

She moaned louder when his thumb brushed her nipple.

"Ahh!" she gasped out and took a staggering step back when he dropped his head to kiss it.

He remembered her leg then and walked her backward to the bed. On his hands above her, she stared up at him as he spread her legs with his knee.

"I love you," she whispered as he slid inside her.

He slid easily without needing the lubrication he'd brought. Her hips bucked up to meet him, and she groaned loudly as he seated himself deep. He'd felt the slight resistance of her maidenhead and stilled to give her time to adjust.

He'd never asked about her previous liaisons, and hadn't cared, but knowing she was his alone filled him with pride. A guilty wince slowed his thrusts as he hoped she never asked about his.

Balanced on one hand above her, he ran his other over her full breast and lightly pinched the pink nipple between his thumb and forefinger until it stood out hard, then took it in his mouth.

The sound she made, caused his hips to jerk. Both of her legs were around his waist and she was rocking with him. Without meaning too, he was pounding hard and came moments later in hard jerking thrusts that left him breathless.

"Sorry," he whispered and kissed her neck, embarrassed over his lack of control.

"Don't," she said and tightened her legs around him when he shifted his weight afraid he was crushing her. "Stay inside me."

A wave of desire scorched him. Her words heated him and clenched his stomach muscles. He wanted to make love to her for hours.

She made a soft disappointed sound when he slipped from her body to lay beside her. The sound changed to an excited hum when he slid a finger inside her.

"Oh, God," she moaned when he sucked her nipple into his mouth, licking it in time with his finger. "Jack, she said in a voice that was almost a wail as her body began to surge with his hand. "Jack," she said again louder with a tinge of desperation.

He kept his finger moving in short jerks, blessing the woman who'd taken him to bed and tried to make him a man as Brook's body tightened, and she screamed his name, hips jerking hard against his hand. He stilled, feeling her inner muscles contracting around his fingers.

She'd gotten him hard again and writhed beneath him, crying out when he entered her.

He paused surprised by the shrillness of her cry. Maybe he was going too fast and she needed more time. "You okay?"

"God, don't stop!"

Laughing, he complied. She pulled him closer for a kiss and before he knew it they were rolling on the bed, thrusting and groaning.

She was wild for him, calling his name, raking her nails down his back, and pushing hard against him. He pounded so hard he could hear their wet flesh slapping together.

He came again, harder than the first time, each jerk of his hips a glorious release. Her soft sighs were a symphony his body danced too. Weak and spent he collapsed, rolling them over until she lay across his chest, and realized she cried when her tears wet his skin.

"God, did I hurt you?" he asked in concern when she continued to cry, clutching him hard with her face buried in his neck.

"I'm sorry. I got carried away." He continued to murmur words of love and reassurance, growing more concerned by the second. She was pressed so tightly against him he could feel her trembling.

"Sorry," she finally whispered as her crying eased and she pushed away.

He leaned over the edge of the bed and yanked his jacket over to grab the handkerchief in the pocket.

She took it with a shy smile, wiped her face, and blew her nose while he examined her.

He'd left small bruises on her breast, bites he didn't remember making. When he brushed his thumb over them, she shuddered and grabbed his hand. The handkerchief fluttered to the floor forgotten as she pushed him back on the bed and straddled his knees.

"It doesn't hurt." She cupped her breasts with her hands and gazed down on them. "It felt good. Do it again."

"Soon," he said ruefully, glad he hadn't hurt her and amazed by her passion. He didn't know it could be like this, his body and emotions so entwined he lost track of them.

She released her breasts to run her hands over him, stopping to trace his scars with her fingertips, then easing backward to fondle him, touching his balls so lightly and hesitantly it tickled.

"Am I hurting you?" she asked as his body jerked.

"It tickles, but I like it."

A smile tilted her lips and she rose to wet the cloth beside the warm water. He leaned on his elbows to watch her wash herself. Dusk had come and darkened the room but there was enough light for him to admire the curves of her body. He'd thought her beautiful in clothing but naked she was a goddess, perfect in every way. Even the red scar on her leg didn't detract from her perfection. He could stare at her for hours.

She came to him and wiped him too, then settled beside him, one hand trailing over him, lingering on his biceps before sliding lower.

Warm breath caressed his chest, and he was surprised how good it felt when she sucked his nipple into her mouth. He hadn't realized how inexperienced he was but whores were nothing like her. Every touch felt new; every sound she made unique.

She leaned over him now, her hair brushing his skin as she kissed across his chest. One hand stroked his body, his shoulder, arm, and hip as if she couldn't get enough of him. He kept both hands on her back, not wanting to disturb her exploration. His hands slid to her shoulders and tangled in her hair as she eased lower, still kissing him.

"You don't have to," he said through gritted teeth when she hesitated, her warm breath teasing his cock.

"I want to; I'm just not sure how."

"You want too?" He winced at the surprise in his voice, hoping he hadn't discouraged her.

"I want to kiss you everywhere." Her fingers teased his length, and he didn't know if she were doing it purposefully to arouse him or if she was exploring.

"Yes, kiss me," he said eagerly and pressed

her shoulders, urging her closer to his throbbing cock.

His body jerked when her lips brushed him.

"That's so good," he moaned, making her giggle.

It emboldened her because she ran her tongue over him next.

"Oh God," he moaned, and she did it again.

She made love to him with her tongue and lips until he thought he would burst.

"My turn!" he gasped and flipped her onto her back.

Her giggle changed to a groan as he took her nipple into his mouth. He knelt between her knees and rubbed her nipples while watching her face. She had her head tipped back and her eyes closed, thrusting her breasts into his caress, more responsive and uninhibited than any fantasy he'd ever had.

He'd never imagined a woman could be like her. He'd been prepared for shyness, not enthusiasm. In his experience, women urged a man on but wanted it over quickly. But she seemed to enjoy caressing him as much as he did her.

Her eyes opened as he hands went lower and she craned her neck to watch him part her.

"You're beautiful," he whispered as he traced her delicate folds with his fingers. She widened her stance, letting him look, not at all shy with him. He wondered if it was because she was a nurse and used to seeing naked bodies, but whatever the reason, he liked how uninhibited she was.

He watched his fingers slid in and out of her as she writhed. *I could watch her for hours*, he thought again but his cock throbbed now. He leaned forward to lick her, wanting to taste her excitement.

She moaned so loudly he did it again. She tested salty and wild like a stormy day at sea. He continued to lick her, holding her spread with both hands until she sobbed his name. She sobbed it again louder when he slid inside her and sat with her legs around him, rocking slowly as she kissed him. He'd never felt anything like it and tears filled his eyes.

"You're not going to cry again are you," he asked as he brushed a trickling tear from her cheek with his thumb.

"I might." Her shaky laugh made his heart swell with tenderness.

"I might too," he whispered and jerked his hips harder. He lost himself in her, caught up in emotion as they strained against each other becoming one.

"I love being married," he said when she collapsed against his chest breathing hard.

She laughed and snuggled closer. They fell asleep with their arms and legs entwinned, his sweat, semen, and love holding the together.

Brook Delivers a Baby

Cold air made Brook shiver as she eased from the bed, being careful to keep Jack covered so he wouldn't wake. She slipped her dressing gown on and hurried down the hall to the bathroom without bothering to put on her shoes. The house was quiet around her. Dawn was mere hours away and the working ladies had found their beds for the night.

She giggled and slapped a hand to her mouth to muffle the sound. Drunk on love and lust, she hadn't cared where he'd brought her and surprised herself by liking the women here. She still felt drunk. His touch heated her entire body, and made emotion overcome her until she had to cry out. And here no one noticed or cared. The room was clean and well insulated. The music from downstairs barely traveled through the walls, and it was rare to hear another woman cry out in passion.

If they didn't have to share a bathroom it

would be perfect. Jack usually escorted her to the bathroom and waited outside, afraid she'd run into a client and be mistaken for a working girl. Reminded, she hurried her shower. He'd be angry if he woke and she was gone.

When she slipped into their room, he still slept sprawled across the bed. The room had cooled in her absence. The wet hair against her neck made her shiver. She peeked into the picnic basket and frowned. Only a hunk of cheese and a loaf of bread remained. They'd have to go out for food today, and she didn't want to. Every moment they had was precious, and she resented the ones she had to share with others. These quiet hours, when it felt like they were the only two people in the world, were her favorites. She longed for peace, a safe place they could come to every day and share their thoughts and be safe together with no worries or fear. To see him sleep and know he was safe and warm was a gift.

She let her robe slip to the floor and snuggled up to him beneath the covers. Still sleeping, he turned on his side and pulled her closer. She felt when he woke by the tensing of his body.

"I told you to wake me if you needed to use the bathroom." His hand glided over her head, and she heard the frown in his voice. "And you showered. Brook, promise you won't do it again. There's no lock on the door. Anyone could walk in, and in a place like this..." He sighed hard and rolled to his back, bringing her with him. "I should've found us a better place, but I was rushed and the hotels full. We can go out and look today."

"This place is fine." She kissed his neck, then his chest, letting her hands wander through his hair and across his thigh. The feel of his skin beneath her hand heated her from the inside out. His low chuckle clenched the muscles of her stomach and tightened her nipples. "I don't want to miss a minute with you." Tears filled her eyes at the reminder of their impending separation. She squeezed them shut and kissed him hard, not wanting to upset him.

The kiss heated, and she welcomed him eagerly when he rose on his hands above her and nudged her knees farther apart with his.

"Sore," he asked when she hissed as he slid inside her.

"A bit. Don't stop."

He laughed but slowed, barely moving as he kissed her. Four days of making love hadn't sated her for him. Every time they made love she wanted him more. She craved his touch, his kiss, his whispered words of love. The slight soreness she felt didn't stop her from arching into his caress and grinding against him. Lust made her forget her discomfort. His slow thrusts were driving her crazy. She wanted him to surge hard and leave love bites across her skin.

She sucked above his left breast, making him moan and push harder. When she drew back, she'd left a red bruise behind beside a nearly faded one. She licked the mark and flicked her tongue over his nipple.

He laughed and pinned her arms above her head and kissed her nipples until she moaned before licking the skin beneath her breast and sucking that. He left a trail of small red marks to her other breast that left her panting beneath him.

He kept her arms pinned as he made love to her slowly, his eyes intent on hers.

"No, look at me," he said when she closed her eyes.

He released her arms to lay a hand on her cheek. Sweat built up on his brow and chest. He was holding himself back hard so she could reach orgasm. His excitement excited her. Staring into his eyes as she came was strangely intimate. It left her feeling vulnerable and exposed in a way making love didn't.

Watching his eyes, seeing the love in them when she reached her release was the most intimate thing she'd ever done. It affected him too, he threw his head back and shouted her name.

She pulled him to her chest and hugged him tightly while he breathed hard and her hips jerked in small orgasmic aftershocks.

"You need sleep. We have the rest of our lives to make love," he said when he'd caught his breath.

She said nothing. They both knew war made their future uncertain.

"Don't leave this room alone again. It would kill me if anything happened to you."

"I love you so much," she whispered.

He settled her against his chest and ran his fingers through her wet hair. "I know you're worried, and I'm so sorry for it. I wish I didn't have to go back, but I do. I'll be careful. Only death will keep me from you."

She began to cry, angry with herself for upsetting him and ruining their moment but not able to help it. The thought of life without him felt like a knife in her soul.

"Promise me you won't die. I need you, Jack."

He continued to smooth her hair. "I hate this war, but I'm more grateful then I can say that it led me to you. When I imagine how empty my life would be without you... I've never loved anyone like I love you. I could never love anyone like I love you, but if I don't make it back, I want you to remember me but to find love again and be happy."

"Shh," he said when her crying escalated. "I'm not giving up. I just want to picture you being happy and surrounded by grandchildren."

"Our children, Jack."

"God willing." He kissed her softly. "I'll remember these days for the rest of my life. When I close my eyes, I can see your smile and hear the sounds you make when I kiss your breast."

His warm palm closed over her breast, and she tried to memorize the sensation. If this week was all they'd ever have, she didn't want to forget a minute of it.

"We aren't going to be sad over this separation but grateful we have each other and look forward to meeting again."

She knew he meant the words as comfort but there was nothing he could say that would ease her. The thought of never seeing him again made her tears fall faster. He made love to her slowly and sweetly as if he were memorizing her body and tears filled his eyes too as he shouted her name.

"We belong together, Brook," he whispered and cuddled her close, his heart pounding beneath her ear, the sound more reassuring than his words.

She kissed him until he groaned and made love to her again.

A sharp knock on the door woke Brook. She sat groggily as Jack rose.

"What time is it?" she asked.

"Early," Jack said as he opened the door.

Brook debated going back to sleep. Sunlight streamed through the curtains, but the streets were still quiet. They'd just fallen back asleep, and she'd hoped to snuggle for a few hours before they had to leave to buy more food.

The panicked tone of the woman at the door disabused her of that dream. Brook rose to wash her face in the ewer before the window as the girl pleaded with Jack.

"Please, I'm sorry to disturb you, but Alice said your, um, wife is a nurse and Lisbet really needs help. Please, *Mademoiselle*, will you come?" she asked louder in a mix of English and French.

"I'm coming," Brook said as she scrambled for her discarded dress.

"What's the problem?" Jack asked at the same time.

"Lisbet's baby won't come, and she's in horrible pain. *S'il vous plaît, Mademoeiselle!*" The woman clasped her hands and took a deep breath obviously worried Brook couldn't understand her mangled English but unable to remain calm for more than few words at a time. "The midwife won't attend her, *et il est trop tard pour l'amener à l'hôpital!*"

Brook gathered her hair as she strode to the door. "Fetch hot water and boil a stack of clean rags for ten minutes. I'll need the sharpest smallest blade you have and a needle and fine silk thread. Boil everything and then use a clean cloth to pick them up. Show me to my patient."

Jack kissed her cheek as she stepped into the hallway.

"Jack, see about finding us food while I deal with this," Brook said.

"Shall I go for help?"

"Yes, see if you can find an ambulance. I can deliver a child and even perform a c-section, but I lack the equipment to preserve the life of a baby." She turned to the woman who wrung her hands in the doorway. "Do you have access to ether or chloroform?"

"Yes, both. This way, Miss, and thank you."

The floor felt cold beneath Brook's bare feet, and she wished she'd taken a moment to put on her shoes but the woman's fear urged her to hurry.

"Call me Brook."

"I'm Charise and Lisbet is my best friend. I told her she should go to hospital but..." Charise trailed off and rubbed her face with trembling hands.

"I can help her," Brook assured her.

The two women ran up the stairs at the fastest pace Brook could manage.

"It's just down there, Charise said unnecessarily. The sound of low moans and encouraging voices traveled to them down the narrow corridor.

"I'll see about the supplies," Charise said and ran back down the stairs.

Brook hurried to the door, knocked once, and entered uninvited.

A naked woman lay on a narrow bed cradling her swollen stomach and moaning. Bloody fluid had stained the blanket beneath her. Another woman leaned over her smoothing her hair and holding a wet compress to her forehead, urging her to push in French.

"No, don't strain," Brook said. "I need to do a quick examine. Do we have soap and water?"

Another woman who mumbled prayers beside the door gestured to an ewer on a rickety dresser.

Brook washed up and soaped her hand good, eyeing the shabby furnishings and wondering if all the upper rooms were so poor. A cold draft fluttered a candle set beside the ewer. Brook could see her breath as plumes the air was so chilly.

"We'll have to move her after the birth. This room is too cold. If a bedroom can't be prepared, my husband and I will move up here, and she can have our room. This might be a hair uncomfortable, but you're almost finished," Brook said as she gently eased Lisbet to her back and reached between her legs.

Lisbet screamed shrilly when Brook's fingers entered her. She screamed again as Brook pushed back the small foot. Lisbet's stomach rippled with a contraction as Brook withdrew her hand, and she groaned loudly as she bared down.

"Good, the baby is coming right now," Brook said.

All eyes were on the feet that protruded. Brook eased the child out and flipped it over to rub its back.

"You have a son," she said as the baby

gurgled then cried.

The watching women exclaimed in delight and relief.

Brook sat back in relief, glad it had been such a simple matter handled so quickly and handed the baby to the sobbing mother.

While the women cooed over the child, Brook delivered the afterbirth.

"Merci, Mademosielle," Lisbet said.

"You're welcome. He's a beauty, isn't he?" Brook said admiringly as she took the baby back to examine.

"I thought we would both die," Lisbet said in halting English and began to cry again.

"There, there," the woman by her head said and smoothed her hair from her sweaty face.

"They'll be okay now?" she asked Brook.

"Everything appears normal," Brook said as she clipped the cord.

The baby waved his legs and cried, making all the women laugh.

Charise entered, carrying a large steaming pot.

"Just in time," Brook said and the women chattered happily in French as they dipped rags into the hot water to clean mother and child.

In no time at all mother and son rested comfortably in Brook's old room.

"Thank you for this too," Lisbet said shyly and gestured around the room.

"It's no problem. My husband keeps me

plenty warm." She winked, making Lisbet laugh then groan and clutch her stomach.

"You'll be sore until the bleeding stops. No sex for two months. Give your uterus time to heal. And when you resume sexual relations, use birth control."

"Some of the men don't like it."

"Then you'll be in this state again in a year. Buy a diaphragm, or, if you really can't afford that, at least use sponges. But a diaphragm is much cheaper than a child."

Lisbet nodded and bowed her head over her infant.

"What shall you call him?" Brook asked.

"I'd name him for you, but Brook isn't a masculine name. What's your father's name?"

"Eugene. Doctor Eugene Taylor."

Reminded of her loss, tears filled Brook's eyes.

"That's a fine name. I'll encourage little Eugene to study medicine," Lisbet promised.

The women were still cooing over the baby when Jack returned with fresh supplies. Brook had sent the ambulance away, glad it wasn't needed. Both mother and child and were doing fine.

"I'll get it," Brook said ruefully as she left the cozy warmth of their bed and her husband's embrace to answer the door.

Jack chuckled and pulled the thin sheet higher. "It's kind of them."

"I know, and I appreciate they mean well, but I hate the interruptions," Brook whispered, then pasted a fake smile on her face and opened the door.

Charise handed her a pot of stew that still steamed slightly. "Are you sure you're okay up here?" she asked doubtfully.

"Perfectly fine and grateful for the room," Brook assured her as she took the pot.

"Well, okay, but if you change your mind, I can switch rooms for the remainder of your stay. We don't usually allow guests up here..."

"Jack and I are fine," Brook repeated and tried to close the door.

Charise laid a hand on the door to stop it from closing. "If you need a place when he returns to his unit— not to work," she added hurriedly. "The girls all agree you can keep this room rent free until you find a boat back to England."

"That's kind of you," Brook said as Jack said, "Brook won't be returning to England. We really are married, and she'll be going home to my family."

"I'll be staying at the hospital with the other nurses once he leaves," Brook added.

"Well, if you ever need a place, our door is always open." Charise bobbed her head, then scurried away. Brook leaned against the closed door and laughed.

"They don't believe we're married." Brook hardly believed it herself.

Jack felt like a dream to her. This week with him was so different from her previous life it held a dreamlike quality that persisted even when they did the most mundane things, like eat stew. His company, his caring, learning how he thought and hearing of his friends and family while warm and comfortable and safe all filled her with a wild longing for a home of their own. Somewhere to return every day and share life's worries and triumphs.

"We are," Jack said as he rose to take the pot from her.

She stared after him, her eyes feasting on his naked body. Every day she thought him more beautiful. The fading scars made her wince. He'd been hurt many times, and he had months to go.

"I'll be fine," Jack said as if reading her mind. A flush covered Brook's cheeks. He hadn't read it but seen her staring.

"I like seeing you naked too," he said in a deeper voice and turned from the stew to pull her close. Stew forgotten, they fell to the bed. The stew was cold when Brook finally served it.

Jack Returns to His Duty

"We'll be together soon, sweetheart. I love you with all my soul."

"Sorry, I—" Brook took a deep hitching breath and rubbed her red cheeks. "I just know how dangerous your job is. I've seen all the horrible ways a soldier can die."

She was crying so hard now he could barely make out her words. He kissed her temple and rocked her in his arms, murmuring endearments that didn't ease her.

"You have to go,' he said and gently pushed her away. "Promise me, you'll get on the boat, Brook."

She nodded without looking up. Both her hands grasped his uniform lapels. She'd stopped crying, but misery radiated from her.

"Write me as soon as you get there and again when you meet my dad. He's going to love you so much." Jack kissed the soft hair on her temple.

"My brother can be a bit stuffy, but I mostly ignore him. He was always too busy for me. I think he kind of resented the attention I got from our father. Not that he was ever mean or anything. He was more like a second father— always giving advice— than a brother."

She made a sound of profound distress that made his eyes tear up. Jack pulled her closer and rubbed her back in small circles. He cleared his throat and tried to speak normally, hoping that acting as if this impending separation wouldn't be so bad would reassure her. He felt the hugest hypocrite as he said cheerfully, "Let's see, he'll be forty-eight this year. His wife is a shrew, but again, we can just ignore her. They're hardly ever home. If you hate living with them, we can get our own place. I have a job waiting and the pay is good."

"We can start a family," Brook said in a choked voice.

"A big one," Jack agreed.

The thought of seeing her heavy with his child made his eyes tear and he hastily wiped his face on his sleeve as he dropped his hand to her stomach and kissed the top of her bowed head. "I can't wait. We're going to be so happy together, Brook. Just a few months and I'll be out, and then we'll see about finding your family together."

"June," she said prayerfully.

"June," he agreed. "It might take a few weeks

for the discharge to go through and for me to get home, but I'll come to you as soon as I can."

"I'll be waiting."

"Stay with the VADs and don't go out at night."

She nodded and began to cry again.

"I love you," he whispered over the lump in his throat. Her tears hurt. He hated to leave her alone in this dangerous city. He wished now he'd asked his father to pull some strings. As soon as he could he'd write and ask him.

"Three months, Brook."

She kissed him hard and made a deep, unhappy sound when he pulled away. He had to pull her hands from his uniform. Pale and tear streaked, she stared after him as he boarded his train. Tears filled his eyes when he glanced back. He took a seat on the opposite side so he wouldn't be able to see her and disgrace himself by bursting into tears.

"Well," Frank asked when he entered the tent the platoon shared.

Jack dropped his pack and kicked it beneath his cot. "I found her and sent her home to my father."

"You guys are crazy. Who falls in love in a day?"

"She's amazing." Jack flopped on the cot and threw an arm over his eyes. "We got married."

He lowered his arm and glanced around the empty tent. "Where is everyone?"

"Enjoying their leave, except for Henry. Frank squatted beside Jack and lowered his voice. "He thinks he's in love too— with a German."

"A German," Jack said doubtfully.

"Well a Belgian who was living in Germany. You missed it, but while you were gone, he got his ass shot up good. We thought he'd bought it. He was MIA for a month. Hell, he would've bought it if that woman hadn't found him."

"Where is he now?"

"Hospital and then home soon as they can transport him. Took one in the lung. Doc says he'll make it but no more marching for him."

"So, good and bad news..."

Frank snorted.

"All bad for him. He's desperate to get his woman home, but she's a fucking German. I like her an all, but I can't see him pulling that off from a hospital bed. Me and the boys are taking care of her, but we go on patrol in five days."

"Great." Jack flopped back on his cot and threw an arm over his eyes.

Frank snorted again and rose. He kicked the leg of Jack's cot. "I haven't seen my wife in a year and a half. You gotta wait a few months. Suck it up."

Jack sat and reached for his pack. "Let's go see Henry," he said. "I have some money left that my dad sent. Maybe we can bribe someone."

"Now that's the Jack we all know and love." Frank cuffed the back of his head and laughed when Jack swore.

Edwin Takes Charge

Edwin stretched his feet out beneath his father's desk and leaned back in the leather chair, a satisfied smile plumping his thin cheeks. Sylvan's profits were enough to bring his store back up to snuff. Agnes had rehired the textile managers, at an increased wage, but already they'd begun to turn things around in the mills.

He rose to rummage in the filing cabinet and emerged with his father's bank statement. He didn't have access to these accounts yet, but soon. He'd spoken with Frank and was arranging a private sale of the mills. He could easily hold him off a few months until he got his hands on Sylvan or his father's money.

Since receiving that first letter over a month ago, they'd heard nothing from Jack. Edwin took great pleasure in reporting company L's movements though. The fighting in Belgium was ongoing and fierce. The causalities high. Francis had taken to his bed. Nerves had his blood pressure so high he suffered from fainting spells.

The smile on Edwin's face deepened. His father had large savings and even larger stocks and bonds. His hand dropped to his belt, and he fingered it thoughtfully, the smile changing to a leer. He found he enjoyed beating Agnes, and for this much money, she'd let him and not complain. He dropped his hand when a timed knock sounded at the door.

"Come!" he called and returned to his desk.

"Sir, a telegram has arrived."

Tory, the new maid, offered him the yellow envelope with a hopeful expression.

"Very good. Thank you."

She bobbed her head and scurried away after placing the letter on the corner of his desk. His hands trembled when he opened it, praying this would be a notice his brother had been killed in action. His life would be so much easier if Jack had the decency to die.

"Damn him," he muttered and threw the paper to the desk. *Jack had married and was sending his whore home.* He snatched the decorative sculpture formed of metal buttons made at Sylvan and hurled it across the room, then swept the papers from his desk.

"Out," he barked when Mrs. Schmidt poked her head in the door.

The door shut with gratifying swiftness, easing some of his anger. Since Marie's death he'd taken over the household staff. Well, to be more accurate, he'd encouraged his wife to take over, and like her, he appreciated the more formal behavior from them.

His father's illness insured they listened to him, bringing him the mail first despite Francis's requests. Everyone believed it for the best that Edwin deal with bad news first. Restored to good humor by the reminder he was firmly in charge, he began gathering the scattered papers.

It wasn't like he didn't have a plan. Humming happily now, he dropped the dented statuette into the garbage can and chuckled as he threw out Sylvia's desk set and began emptying her drawers. Drawers he'd been forbidden to touch his entire life but who could stop him?

Brook Meets Edwin

"Ma'am?"

The porter's soft question pulled Brook from the light doze she'd fallen into. Travel had never tired her this much in the past, but then again, she'd never been sick for so long before either. She'd gotten seasick the moment the ship had left port and been ill the entire crossing. She'd had to rest for two days in New York before feeling up to train travel.

A deep groan escaped her as she tried to stand. Stiff and sore from the long train ride, it took her three tries to rise. The porter fetched her cane and bag from the rack above her head and offered her an arm.

"Thank you," Brook said gratefully.

"Shall I fetch you a cab?"

"No, thank you. Family should be meeting me."

The porter tipped his hat and scurried away. Brook grasped the metal railing tightly, biting her lip as she attempted to force her leg to bend the mere inches it needed to reach the first stair.

A kind stranger helped her down the three stairs, waving off her thanks with a brusque, "You're welcome. My wife had the polio too."

Brook didn't disabuse him. She leaned on her cane, hoping the walk to the car wouldn't be too long and gazed around the crowded platform as she took slow painful steps. Men and women hurried about their business, seeming to Brook much the same as their English counterparts.

The building had a new feel. Solid and practical, it was made of brick with no added embellishments to make it attractive. What she could see of the countryside looked similar to home as well. Low rolling hills were covered with elms, oaks and maples. Smoke plumed in the distance and traffic wove through the streets. It appeared a busy and prosperous place.

She began cautiously edging across the platform towards the exit sign.

Edwin glanced at his watch as he strode into the station. Fifteen minutes past four, exactly as he'd planned. Late enough she'd become anxious but not so late she'd attempt to reach the house herself. He spied Jack's wife immediately.

She stood to the side of the main door leaning heavily on a wooden cane. Her blue, knee-length coat had fallen open and she fumbled one handed with the tie. Long brown hair tumbled over her shoulder in loose curls. Slim, with pert breasts and shapely legs her ill-fitting dress didn't detract from her good looks.

His brother had married a beauty. Jealousy clenched his teeth, deepening when she offered him a tentative smile. Clear blue eyes shaded by thick lashes set above patrician cheekbones. Skin as fine as porcelain and full lips that begged to be kissed made his voice gruffer than he'd intended.

"Brook?"

Her smile widened.

"You must be Edwin. You look a lot like my Jack."

Her voice sounded like music, and his jealousy turned to hatred. *Why did Jack get everything? It wasn't fair.* He hesitated. Maybe he could entice Brook to marry him when Jack was dead.

"Jack has told me you were like a second father to him."

Her words washed his daydreams away before they had time to fully form. She'd never willingly be his. He was too old for her. He wasn't Jack.

He withdrew an envelope from his pocket and offered it to her.

"More than you deserve but worth it to be rid of you."

Her mouth dropped open and she took a

half-step back, stumbling and catching herself with a hand on the wall.

"What?"

She made no attempt to take the envelope.

"You aren't the only hussy to try to pass herself off as Jack's girl while he's been gone. I admit, you're the first one to get him to go along with it though."

"What?" she repeated in a barely heard whisper.

"I'm aware of the ruse you pulled to use his insurance and get yourself out of your contracts. Come to the house, claim to be his wife publicly, and I'll see that not only you but Summers, and whoever else you involved in your charade is also charged. Falsifying documents will get you all long jail terms."

He smiled as she paled and swayed.

"Your sort isn't welcome here." He wagged the envelope at her. "This is a ticket to London."

"I don't want your money. Jack and I are really married."

"Say it just once more and I'll be forced to take action."

They stared at each other a moment. He was pleased to note tears in her eyes and red in her cheeks.

"Can I assume you won't trouble us further?"

His smile grew when she nodded and bit her lip.

He let the envelope flutter to the ground as he spun on his heel.

Brook stared after Edwin, shock rooting her to the spot. The anger in his voice seemed extreme. She debated calling after him to show him the marriage license she carried in her bag but decided it wouldn't help. He'd already decided she was a liar and fraud.

"Miss," a man said and handed her the envelope.

She took it and absently thanked him. Nausea roiled in her stomach and her legs felt weak.

"Miss? You look a bit peaked. Can I call you a cab or..." the man trailed off.

"I'm—" A lump in Brook's throat threatened to choke her, and she didn't know what to say.

The man took her arm and led her to a nearby bench. "Sit a moment. I'll fetch you a water."

Brook burst into tears as the man hurried off. A total stranger was being kinder than her new family. Jack had been wrong about her reception. Passerbys slowed and stared. Brook took deep breaths and scrubbed her face on her coat sleeve.

The man returned and offered her a paper cup of water.

"Thank you," Brook said and sipped, hoping it would quell her nausea.

"English?" The man smiled as if delighted.

"Yes."

"Can I call you a cab or escort you to a train?"

"A cab please."

She let him help her stand and listened to his chatter about train conditions as they took slow steps to the cab stands. She waited until the door closed before asking the driver to take her to a cheap hotel.

Jack might have been wrong about his family, but she was certain he loved her. She'd write and tell him what his brother had said, and he'd straighten everything out. Meanwhile, she'd need a job and a cheap place to live. *Maybe I can trade in the ticket.* She'd promised Jack she'd wait for him, and she meant to keep her word.

Rain drops pattering against the window woke her. She'd slept longer than she'd intended, and she wished she could stay in bed, but she only had the money Jack had given her and three hundred dollars left from her pay until she could open an account here and get her money transferred.

"First, you need a new dress," she said as she gazed critically at her reflection. "Something to job hunt in."

She put on her dirty dress and went shopping, returning three hours later with two new dresses, a new nightgown, a heavy sweater, and a box of stationary.

She ate a quick dinner in a dingy restaurant across the street from the hotel and spent the evening writing letters. In the morning, she headed to the post office.

"My my, dear, you're far from home," the woman behind the counter said when she took the envelops.

"Yes. I was overseas. I'm a nurse but a friend suggested I come here when I was discharged until my folks can be located."

"Ahh, poor dear. Lost them in the blitz?"

Tears filled Brook's eyes when she nodded. "My parents... I hope they're just relocated, but I haven't had word."

"Well, the mail is getting through regularly now, and the telephones are almost back to normal too." She glanced through the stack of letters. "Have you considered asking the Red Cross for help? I know they keep lists of the American Soldiers, maybe they keep English lists too?"

"No, I hadn't, but that's a great idea. I shall inquire at once. I'm hoping my aunt might have heard something." Brook slid the envelope out and examined it. "We'd fallen out of touch, but she's my only other family and should be safe in North Wales."

"I wish you luck, deary. I'm sure your friends will be in touch. You've quite a lot of them."

Brook smiled at the stack of letters. She'd written to her fellow VADs and a few of the nurses she'd met in Paris as well as Jack, Doctor Roberts, and Burns. "I do. I served with some fabulous people."

"God willing, they'll all return home soon."

Brook nodded and paid for her stamps. Her leg wasn't nearly as stiff today. She was able to manage the stairs herself. She took a cab to the nearest hospital and put in an application, then bought a paper and sandwich in the hospital cafeteria to read the want ads and boarding house advertisements.

Edwin Finds Brook

Edwin glanced up from his newspaper in annoyance as the secretary resumed her seat. She gave him an apologetic smile and nervously shuffled her papers.

How dare the director keep me waiting like this? Edwin deepened his glare. His family practically owned this hospital. The man had nowhere near the capital Edwin needed, but he'd thought acquiring a few smaller, private loans might work out. But not if he had to put up with such disrespect. He rose and stuffed the newspaper into his briefcase. He was two steps from the door when it opened.

"Your credentials are impeccable, but I'm afraid we have no openings at the moment. Perhaps you could try at Memorial, Miss Taylor."

Edwin jerked back in shock. Brook stood before him shaking the director's hand. His pulse began to pound, first in worry, then anger.

How dare she stay? And how had she wrangled a meeting with the director?

"Thank you, Mr. Hardcourt, I'll do that. You've been most helpful," Brook said.

"I'm sorry I can't do more. Thank you so much for stopping in and speaking with me personally. News from the front can be hard to come by, and it eases my soul to hear your reassurances. Volunteers like you made a real difference."

"The thirty-ninth was safe outside Amiens when I left. And last I saw, your son was doing well. Doctor Roberts is well respected. He's a fine surgeon with experience. I'd recommend him to anyone."

Edwin stepped back. Neither had noticed him. Hardcourt's secretary looked up as he passed her desk, but he was out the door before she could speak. He hurried to the men's room and leaned on the sink while he caught his breath.

His anger calmed, and thoughtfulness replaced it. Brook had made no mention of the Pryor name and Hardcourt had referred to her as Miss. Apparently, she'd taken his threats seriously enough to use her maiden name. He should've considered she would know doctors and have contacts.

"Is she in touch with Jack," he wondered aloud.

No, if she was, she'd have shown up at the house and demanded to speak with Francis. The staff would fall all over themselves to escort her to the old man. His hands began to tremble. If Brook made her presence known, it would become much harder to borrow Sylvan's assets. His father was sure to show her the company and maybe go through the books.

"She can't show up," he said to his reflection.

He washed his face and hands, the cold water soothing his hot cheeks.

"It won't even be hard to find you. I know exactly where you're going to be." Edwin wadded up the cheap paper towels and tossed them to the floor.

Hardcourt's secretary lurked in the hallway, looking relieved when he exited the bathroom.

"I'm so sorry for the wait, Mr. Pryor, but—"

Edwin waved his hand, cutting her off. "I'll have to reschedule. I have no time today." He ignored her babbling apologies and marched from the building. In his car, he took a minute to slow his excited breathing before heading to Memorial Hospital.

Brook Finds Her Parents

"Good news then, Brook?"

Brook's smile widened, and she set down the letter she held. "Yes. I'm so relieved." She slid over to make way for Peggy to sit beside her on the narrow bench.

Peggy exhaled heavily and sat, immediately kicking off her shoes and rubbing her foot.

"Heard from your parents, have you?" Peggy nodded to the letter before Brook.

"Yes, thank God. They're alive and well in Surrey. My father writes that he's working in a temporary hospital and is looking for a permanent position in London."

"Will you go home then?"

"No, but I can't stay here either. My good friend has found me a position on staff at Mercy General in New York."

Brook picked up the letter Doctor Roberts had sent and showed it to Peggy. "I can work there while I wait for Jack to come home."

"Well, don't wait too long. An Atlantic crossing with a baby will be a nightmare."

Brook laid her hand against her still flat stomach. "He'll come for me."

Peggy snorted and fussed with the glittery trim on her short skirt, smoothing the material to hide a fading bruise on her thigh. "Maybe so, but you'd do better to wait with your folks than here."

Brook frowned but made no mention of the bruise. She'd treated Peggy after a too enthusiastic client had beat her so badly he'd broken the skin on her back and knew Peggy didn't want to hear her cautions. "I like it here," Brook said. "This reminds me of our honeymoon. I'll be sad to leave you girls."

Peggy snorted with laughter and jammed her foot back into the too small high heel. "You're a good one, Brook, and I'll miss you when you go and not just for the free medical care."

"You're a good one too, Peg, but you're going to cripple yourself if you insist on wearing those shoes."

Peggy laughed as she lurched to her feet. "Got to make hay while the sun is shining. I'm socking all my dough away. I figure I can work for one, maybe two more years, before I head west and put all this behind me. These hand-me-downs are good enough. None of the men give a damn what I'm wearing as long as I look the part. I'll find me a good man and be a good wife.

I got it all planned."

"Well, I wish you luck."

"Pfft, I don't need luck. The men will be home soon and looking for wives to take care of them. I'll pretend to be an out of work secretary. I'll dress real conservative with just a hint of sex appeal. It'll be like shooting fish in a barrel."

Peggy's smile fled, and she looked worried. "You should go home. The jobs for women really will dry up when the men return, and they're bound to be a bit wild. Living here or anywhere like this won't be healthy for you."

Brook patted her hand. "Jack will take care of us."

Peggy nodded but didn't look convinced. "You love him, but are you sure he loves you? His brother said this has happened before. Maybe Jack does this all the time..."

Brook shivered and pulled her sweater tighter. "No. I'm certain he loves me."

"They can be pretty convincing. Half the girls here are here because some cad led them on and their families kicked them out."

"Not my Jack."

"For your sake, I hope you're right, Brook, but please consider going home."

Peggy kissed her cheek and wobbled into the hallway. Loud music billowed through the door she opened. She glanced back and gave her a small wave. For one second, Peggy's expression revealed deep fear, but she wiped the look away with a seductive smile and strode into the main room. Brook shivered again and hastily rose to finish making her sandwich.

The kitchen door opened again, and two women entered laughing. Both said a quick hello but didn't stop to talk, grabbing the already prepared trays of small sandwiches and heading back into the main room.

Brook slipped up the back stairs and into her room, grateful not to meet any clientele in the hallways.

Letters From Home

"Adams, Michaelson, Pryor, Trenton."

Jack jumped up and pushed through the men crowding Walt to get his mail. He recognized the handwriting and clutched the letter to his chest.

This one too, Pryor," Walt said and thrust a bigger envelope at him. Jack frowned when he saw the return address. Unease morphed to dread. He could only think of one reason Phips would be contacting him. With trembling fingers, he ripped the letter open. His breath left him in a loud whoosh.

"Trouble at home?" Frank asked.

"No. Dad's okay..." He flipped the envelope over to check the postmark. "Well, he was three weeks ago when this was sent. He's worried he hasn't heard from me. That's odd though. I sent two telegrams, and I know Brook would've sent one too." Jack's glance flicked to Brook's letter a moment before he reread the letter Phips had sent.

'Dear Mr. Pryor,

Your father has asked me to mail this on his behalf as none of his correspondence seems to reach you, or yours him. Frankly, I'm at a loss as to why. I receive regular missives, albeit not in a timely manner, from my grandson who is stationed in Paris at the moment. You might take this matter up with your commander. If your platoon isn't receiving its mail, there are steps I can take.

I hope this letter finds you well and in good health. Your father has sickened in want of news. Please attempt to contact him immediately. I'm afraid the strain of waiting to hear from you is acerbating his high blood pressure, but he's a tough old codger and the most stubborn man I've ever dealt with. I'm certain he'll hold out to see his grandchildren born.

I wish you all the best and a speedy return.
Sincerely,
Eustace Phips Esq.'

Jack snatched up Brook's letter. She'd sent him a long note telling of her time on board and the crossing and her time alone in Paris. His gaze lingered on the tearstained passages.

'I miss you so much. How can one week have such an effect on me that sleeping alone, without your body tucked tight to mine, leaves me wakeful and unrested? I dream of us, Jack, and wonder if I imagined how good it was. I worry I'll forget the sound of your voice and the scent of your skin. Please come home to me safe.'

Jack reread it five times, then held the letter to his nose, hoping it would smell like strawberries and soap but it smelled of cheap ink and wet paper.

"Letter from your girl?" John asked.

"My wife. God, I miss her. She reached New York safely though and that's a huge weight off my mind."

"Good! Now maybe you'll get your head outa the clouds and pay attention," Frank said sourly.

Jack flushed and ducked his head, holding the letter up to block his face.

"Both of you need to stop mooning over your women or you're going to get yourselves killed."

"Yes, sir," John said and rolled his eyes at Frank when he turned away.

Jack bit back his grin and tucked Brook's letter into his pack. Phips letter in hand, he headed to the communications tent.

The lieutenant in charge set his letter on the desk and removed his glasses to clean them. "Sure, we misplace a few but no one else in your platoon seems to have an issue. Try contacting this"— he picked up the letter to read the signature –" Mr. Phips at his home. Maybe your father is getting a bit senile?"

Jack pursed his lips and doubtfully eyed the lieutenant. "I doubt it, but maybe Mrs. Schmidt, his housekeeper, is misplacing them or something. That's a good idea though, sir. I'll write to my dad in care of Mr. Phips. Any chance of an overseas call? I'd really like to reassure the old man."

"Sorry, no, not from here. You'll be sent back to Paris though to catch a boat home and maybe from there."

"My discharge came though?" Jack asked in excitement.

"I expect we'll all be going home soon. We got these bastards almost licked."

Jack strode from the close confines of the noisy tent into the spring air. Hope filled his soul. The fighting in and around Bastogne had slowed and his patrols felt more like peaceful walks in the woods.

He almost wished now that he'd encouraged Brook to stay. They could've snuck into the newly green fields and spent hours making love in the sunshine. The field hospital here wasn't that busy.

A man grabbing his arm pulled him from his daydreams.

Frank slapped his rifle into his hands. "Our tents are this way. Man, spring fever really got a hold of you." He slung his machine gun higher on his back and gestured around him.

Jack followed his pointing hand.

"Sure, this looks peaceful as shit, but any minute now a horde of Germans could swoop down on us. Don't go off without your weapons. Don't fucking wander the countryside like a goddamn tourist, and don't go anywhere alone. It'd be a fucking tragedy if you get your fool head blown off by a discontent 'cause they see an opportunity. Not all these people love us, Jack."

"Yeah. Sorry, you're right."

"Get ahold of your dad?"

"No. The lieutenant says everyone else is receiving their mail."

Frank shrugged lightly and patted the bulging front pocket of his uniform. "I get mine regular as clockwork."

"Maybe our mailman is throwing out the damned mail or something. We get tons of it. It takes my father secretary hours to sort through it all."

"Maybe he's throwing them away?"

"I doubt it. Peter has been with my father for years." Jack was silent a moment before blurting. "If he is stopping my mail, there's going to be hell to pay. My father is sick with worry. This could fucking kill him. He isn't a young man. He's seventy-four. How the hell will I live with myself if my coming here kills the old man?"

Frank slapped his shoulder but had nothing to say. Depressed, Jack followed him back to their tent.

"Stop picking the posies," Walt snarled and slapped the flowers from John's hand.

He half-turned to eye his troops, then framed his mouth in his hands to bellow, "The next asshole who stops to pick a fucking flower will be on KP for a week. We aren't on a nature walk, boys. I'm going to be angry as shit if you get my ass blown off because you're too busy admiring the bluebells to spot the enemy. Spread out and quiet down. Adams, you take the lead and stay sharp."

Jack kept his rifle in hand and his gaze on the dense trees bordering the road. He thought this patrol was an excuse to save the trucks and have them hike to their new posting. It kept them busy and out of everyone's hair while the muckety mucks repositioned the forward encampments, but he'd rather do this than dig latrines.

They were almost at camp when rifle fire broke the afternoon stillness. His platoon took cover as bigger guns joined in.

"Fuck," Frank muttered.

Jack had to agree. It sounded like all hell was breaking loose less than a quarter mile from them and right on their camp. The men eased forward until they reached the main road. Hunkered in the brush on his stomach Jack peered after the trucks carrying American GIs into the firefight. Canvas tops rolled up revealed men singing and laughing. More than one bottle was being passed around. He exchanged puzzled glances with Frank.

Frank grinned and leaped to his feet. Jack turned back to Walt who spoke on the radio, but he couldn't hear him over the cheering men and gun fire.

"The war's fucking over!" Walt shouted as he stood and let the radio fall to the ground. "The Germans have surrendered!"

All around him, Jack's platoon jumped up and began yelling. Is all he could think about was he could go home. Brook would be waiting in safety and comfort without the fear he'd be killed in action. He added his cheers to the mix and practically danced into town.

His good mood grew when he saw the note to go pick up his mail.

A stack of mail waited for him. All around him men read their letters and ripped the envelopes into confetti. Every soldier seemed to be carrying a bootleg bottle of hooch. Bottles were passed hand-to-hand, complete strangers offering him drinks, grinning and slapping his back.

Jack waved the offered bottles away. He felt chilled and slightly sick. Mr. Phips had written him back. He'd received his letter, but his father hadn't. No one had heard a word from Brook. His wife was missing.

Edwin Plans A Murder

Newspaper pages scattered across the gleaming hardwood floor of Edwin's office as he jumped to his feet. The abrupt movement began a spasm in his back. Two days of sitting hunched in his car to find and follow Brook had left him with a sore, aching back and furious anger that she hadn't left the country.

In the distance, horns honked and people cheered. The din pressed itself into his usually quiet office. Gladys, his secretary, peeked into the room. Edwin knew without being told the war had ended

"Sir, the workers are taking the rest of the day off. I didn't think it wise to try to stop them. This is such fabulous news."

"Quite alright. Take the rest of the day yourself and tell the rest of the management staff. Send for my car, please, before you go."

"Yes, sir. Thank you, sir." Smiling brightly, she closed the door.

Edwin let his pleasant expression fade to a snarl as he strode to his windows to peer out. The street before his building was crowded. Men and women stood in clumps, clutching papers and laughing. Tears and smiles wreathed the faces of his factory workers as they streamed from the building. The whistle blew, one short sharp blast. Another echoed it, and within moments, all the factories sounded their horns.

On the street, men waved their hands in the air, the sirens and horns deafening.

Edwin thought he might vomit. Bile burned his throat, and he had to swallow hard to keep it down. He'd counted on his brother being killed in action but that seemed unlikely now. He'd be home soon. He didn't have the months he'd thought to cover his tracks in Sylvan, not that he could cover many. Anyone examining the books would immediately notice the missing sums.

Jack would have to disappear— and his damned wife. He couldn't put it off any longer.

Edwin grabbed his jacket and headed to the door.

"I must get home to speak with my father," he said to every man who hailed him. All desisted immediately and let him pass. This sign of the obvious respect they held for his father angered him anew.

Two secretaries got on the elevator with him, both talking excitedly about the wars end. Neither woman acknowledged him, too excited to even see him in the corner.

"My Johnny will come home," the younger one said.

"And a good thing too. I'm sure the factory will be shortening its shifts. My Frank says work will be hard to get now that we don't need to supply the front. I, for one, will be happy to return to my home. We're thinking of moving back to the farm and living with his parents. As much as I like living in the city, I'll be glad for the fresh air."

"We'll lose our jobs?" the other secretary asked anxiously.

Edwin didn't know if she addressed him or her friend. But he couldn't have answered anyway. Fresh rage suffused him, and his pulse pounded so hard he thought he might faint. With the war ending, the need for buttons would drastically decline. The lucrative contracts Sylvan had wouldn't be renewed. His income would drop dramatically. *If I'd only had one more year!*

He pushed through the crowded lobby and got into his car. It took him fifteen minutes to drive through the crowds surrounding the factories. Once out of the factory district, the congestion eased. He pulled over on a side-street to consider his options.

Sweat beaded his brow and the sick feeling intensified. He'd have to kill his brother and his wife. It was the only way to ensure Sylvan became his. And he'd have to get Agnes under control. If she cut back on her spending, the proceeds from Sylvan would be more than enough to live off of, and in time his other businesses would turn around.

"People die in accidents all the time," he said and straightened. "There's nothing to connect Brook with me." He started the car as he pondered how to do it. Excitement replaced his sick feeling. He knew where she lived. He could go in disguise as a client. *How hard could it be to sneak into her room?* The police would believe one of the Johns had raped and killed her. They'd never think her brother-in-law did it. They'd never have any reason to connect her to the Pryor's at all. He'd go tonight.

The hard part would be Jack. He'd have to kill him right away before he had time to find his wife. Jack was stubborn like their father and would never stop looking for his wife's killer. He'd know she wasn't a working girl and once he saw Sylvan's books, he might suspect.

"I'll think of something," Edwin muttered as he pulled up to the second-hand store to purchase used clothing.

Brook in New York

"They've surrendered!" a man shouted.

Brook glanced to the doorway a moment before returning her attention to the tray of instruments.

"Go see what that's about," the doctor snapped as loud voices erupted in the corridor outside the operating room.

The assisting nurse ran to the door. Loud talk of the Germans surrendering billowed into the room when she opened the door.

"Please, let the war be over," Brook muttered as she handed the doctor the scalpel he asked for.

She suctioned the incision without being asked, and then blotted the doctor's forehead. The operating room door swung open and the assistant nurse stepped inside the doorway. She held a mask over her mouth and tears streamed from her eyes. "They've surrendered. The war is over."

Without meaning to Brook released a sharp cry. She felt like bursting into tears too but the man on the table needed them.

"Blood pressure one-twenty over eighty," the anesthesiologist said. "Mine is going crazy though."

The doctor snorted with laughter. Brook grinned and handed him the retractor. Her eyes burned and felt hot.

"Hold this for me, will you?" the doctor asked.

Brook accepted the small clamp and leaned closer. She pushed thoughts of Jack away and turned her full attention to the patient on the table. For another hour, she assisted before the doctor straightened with a satisfied grunt.

Again, without being asked, Brook began to close, leaving a line of tiny, neat stiches across the patient's chest.

"Good work," the doctor said as he monitored the patient's vitals. "Nurse Taylor, will you see him to recovery and monitor until he wakes?" The doctor examined the drainage hole he'd made in the patient's skull. "Head injuries can be tricky, and I want someone on his pressure until I'm satisfied the swelling has permanently receded."

"Yes, sir," Brook said and hid her wince as she straightened. Pain throbbed from her feet, traveling to her lower back. *At least I'm no longer nauseous*, Brook thought thankfully as she stretched.

"Leg acting up?" the anesthesiologist asked.

"A bit."

"Go get something to eat and a cup of tea. I can stay with him until you return."

Brook nodded gratefully and scurried from the room. She stopped to drop her soiled gown into the bin and donned a fresh apron over her white dress. The cafeteria was busier than normal and thrummed with excited talk. Doctors and nurses spoke loudly over each other. A kind man gave her his seat, and she listen happily to the talk of reuniting with loved ones while she ate her sandwich.

The tea did little to ease her exhaustion. She was always tired now. The babe, small as it was, drained her energy. The thought of Jack's baby filled her with tenderness. He'd be so excited. Reminded of his continuing silence, tears filled her eyes. She hadn't heard back and hoped it was just his mail missing him. She made a mental note to write her friends and ask them for word as she pushed herself to her aching feet.

"Brook, we're going out tonight to celebrate," her new roommate Fran said when she entered the recovery room.

"I'm exhausted," Brook admitted.

"You shouldn't be working this hard." Fran took Brook's hand and felt her pulse a moment before returning to her patient. "Maybe you should wait for him at home with your parents."

"I can't face another sea voyage. I've never

been so sick in my life."

Fran winced sympathetically and pulled a chair up beside the bed. "Sit. You can monitor him just as well from there. Don't worry about the doc. He's a good 'un and won't mind if you sit." She bustled around busily for a moment before saying, "You're doing a great job, and we like you, but it's just going to get harder. Maybe you need to speak to his family. Surely, they'll help you out until he gets back?"

Brook pressed both hands to the small of her back and rotated, trying to ease the soreness. "Edwin made it perfectly clear he wanted no part of me. I could try to speak his father, I guess, but I hate to waste the money and take the time off. It'll take at least two days to go all the way to Pennsylvania and back. My parents will help me. I can pay my share of the rent if you chaps don't mind me staying when I'm as big as house."

Fran's tinkling laughter interrupted her. "You're welcome to stay as long as you like. Believe me, you're a nice change from my last neighbor. Not only did Bet snore loud enough we could all hear her through the walls, but she was out all hours and her perfume made me sneeze. And, God, her cooking! I pity the man she marries. I'll take a nice quiet roommate who can cook any day."

"I can't thank Doctor Roberts and Lydia enough for arranging this for me," Brook said. "I hate to disappoint them by quitting so soon."

"Lydia was my best friend, and I thought her nuts to volunteer. I still think it was nuts but one of the bravest things I ever heard of. I'm sort of sorry I stayed. I think we all are. Helping you makes us feel better, and it isn't like you don't pull your weight."

"My ever-increasing weight." Brook ran a hand over her barely rounded stomach.

"I envy you," Fran said.

Brook rested both hands on her stomach and closed her eyes to say a quick prayer. "I'm so happy about this it worries me," she said when she opened them.

"He'll be fine and home before you know it."

"God, I hope so."

"I'll speak to Marge and get your rotations cut down, and if they fire you, so what. You can afford to stay five more months, and he's sure to be back by then. We'll work something out to get you into a ground-floor room. Antoinette will have to be made to see reason."

Brook smiled her thanks. Three floors of stairs would likely be beyond her ability when she was further along. Her bad leg made them difficult enough now. "You're a good friend, Fran."

Jack Goes Home

Walt slapped Jack's orders into his hand. "You're out, boy. Someone somewhere pulled some strings. You're to report to Paris for transport home, and then to New York to be discharged.

Jack grasped his discharge papers in both hands.

"Congratulations," John said sadly.

Stunned, Jack stood stupidly as his friends congratulated him.

"Adams, Michaelson, Trenton, Vicks you're out too. Not on the fast track like Pryor, but you're headed stateside." Walt continued to call out reassignments, having to yell to be heard over the excited talk of his men. Finally, he put two fingers in his mouth and whistled shrilly. The men quieted to hear him. "Those of us who still have time to serve will be merging with company D and redeployed. If you have over two years left, but have served over one and a half, you might be able to qualify for home leave. See me after. Transportation is a bit overwhelmed though, so those of you who looked forward to a regular leave might have to wait."

The men groaned and complained.

"Stop your bellyaching. You'll be waiting safe in camp. If you do get permission to travel, I advise being a few hours early and prepared to wait a day or more to catch trains and boats. No one is going to care if you go hungry or sleepless, so carry your own supplies."

Walt reached into a sack hanging off his shoulder. "Our mail has caught up with us. Adams—"

Jack waited anxiously, hoping to hear his name called. He'd gotten another letter from Mr. Phips and two from Lydia but none from Brook. Lydia's' letters reassured him Brook was well, but he was confused on why she wanted a job and wasn't with his family. He wished now he'd given her all the money. Maybe his family had intimidated her, and she hadn't had the guts to meet them once she saw the house. It hadn't even occurred to him to tell her his father was rich.

His breath caught when he recognized her handwriting on the top letter Walt handed him.

'Darling,
I hope you get this. I'm writing weekly instead of daily to save money. I haven't received any letters from you and the silence is growing unbearable. I leave tomorrow for New York.

Lydia and Doctor Roberts have secured me a job. I'll wait for you as long as I can. My family is safe and in Surrey. If I don't hear from you in five months, look for me there. I plan to return to them after the child is born. God, I hope you're getting these letters. You're going to be a father and I don't even know if you know it.

I was tempted to go to my family now, but the thought of another ocean crossing keeps me here. Please come home safe to me.'

Jack had to close his eyes and breathe deeply. She was well and expecting their child. He checked the postmark and frowned. She'd written in April before the war ended. He read the entire letter and still had no idea why she hadn't gone to his family. She spoke of her new friends and daily happenings with one vague sentence referencing prior letters and asking what she should do about Edwin. She'd included her new address though. As soon as he reached Paris, he would telegram her.

A grin bloomed on his face. He'd beat any letter he sent home.

"Good news," Frank asked.

"I'm going to be a father."

"Congratulations." Frank slapped his shoulder and shouted the good news.

Jack's platoon surrounded him, slapping his back and yelling insults and congratulations. Jack's head spun. He felt drunk on a mix of happiness and anticipation. She'd be three and a half months along now.

"We're going to have a baby," he repeated.

He wished he could tell his father right then. Reminded, he opened the letter from Mr. Phips.

His happiness faded as he read it. *Why would Edwin keep his letters from their father?* He didn't like the conclusion Mr. Phips had reached. If his brother was in financial trouble and stealing from Sylvan, what else might he be capable of? *Was Brook afraid of him?* Anger bubbled. *Had his brother sent her away?*

He reread the reports and the last paragraph twice.

Mr. Phips had written:

'I can think of no other reason Edwin tries to block my visits to your father except he's trying to keep him in the dark. Francis didn't even know the war had ended. The news cheered him considerably although he remains very worried at the continued absence of your wife. I've hired an investigator and tracked her to New York where she lives with fourteen other nurses and works in Mercy General. She's going by the name Brook Taylor, which confuses me. This entire situation confuses me. I've taken it on myself to pull some strings to get you home quickly. I can't further investigate Edwin without involving your father, and I fear doing so will put his health at risk. You need to come home and straighten this mess out.'

Jack opened the letter from his father contained within Mr. Phips letter. His father expressed concern over his wife's absence and worry over the lack of communications. Jack's anger built. His brother was intentionally keeping them in the dark. His father had only received that first telegram and had written to Jack daily. There was no way over a hundred letters had accidently gone astray. Edwin had a lot to answer for.

Again, he examined the attached reports. Mr. Phips didn't say it, but it was clear he thought Edwin was stealing from Sylvan to shore up his companies. A fission of fear ran down his spine. It was also clear Mr. Phips thought Edwin was purposely keeping his father on edge. *Was he trying to give the old man a heart attack?*

Something had caused Brook to run. She'd have kept her word and telegraphed his father when she arrived. His father would've greeted her with open arms, he was sure of that, but his father hadn't heard she'd arrived, and yet Mr. Phips reported she had. She'd stayed for almost a month before going to New York. Edwin must've turned her away.

Jack's anger threatened to choke him.

Edwin's Plans for Murder are Thwarted

Cigarette smoke mingled with the scent of perfume and the heavier scent of cheap booze. The main floor of the 'women's hotel' was packed with men. Women in tight dresses, which revealed more than they concealed, hung off their arms.

Edwin pushed through the crowd to the makeshift bar set up beside the stairs. A brawny man stood with his arms crossed on the third stair. As Edwin watched, the man stepped aside to let a laughing woman and her date up the stairs. He hadn't spotted Brook but hadn't expect to see her downstairs.

He picked out a small brunette and, without small talk, asked her price. She led him upstairs and down the narrow hallway. Closed doors lined both sides of the long, well-lit hall.

"How many people live here," he asked.

"It varies." She smiled over her shoulder at him and unlocked her door.

Edwin frowned. He hadn't considered a locked door or a bouncer. He'd never been to a brothel before and assumed it would be dark and mostly deserted but this place was well-lit, and men and women walked the halls.

He paused by her door and glanced over his shoulder at a man kissing a woman as he did up his pants.

Brook wasn't in that room, but doors lined both sides of the hallway.

"Is there a bathroom up here," he asked.

"Last door on the right at each end of the hall," she said as she slid her hands over his ass and tried to pull him into her room.

"Give me a minute."

She sighed and stepped back.

Edwin headed to the far bathroom, taking his time, adding a small stumble to his step as an excuse to lean on doors and listen. He'd eliminated two more rooms by the time he'd reached the bathroom. Thin walls ruled out the room right next door. A man grunted loudly in time with a woman's small shriek and the smack of a belt on flesh.

The sounds excited him, and he wondered if his date would let him whip her. He pressed his ear to the wall and dropped his hand to his cock.

"Tell me how bad you are," the man said.

The woman giggled, the sound traveling

easily through the thin walls. "So bad. I spread my legs for—"

Edwin jerked back as someone wriggled the door handle.

"Just a minute!" he called and flushed the toilet.

He'd have to be fast and quiet when he found Brook. If she managed to scream for help someone would hear her through these walls.

A woman passed him, and he paused to stare after her. Naked breasts jigged with each step she took. She winked at him and added an extra wiggle to her step.

"Room five," she said in a breathy voice and blew a kiss as she closed the door.

Edwin hesitated, tempted to ask his date to let him whip her and get number five to participate. "Don't be stupid," he muttered. "Get in and out quick and no one will remember you."

There are others houses, he told himself as he entered his date's room. He'd find one where he could do whatever he liked. He wished he'd thought to come sooner. He hadn't been this hard in years.

"Almost got lost finding you," he said and began undoing his pants. "Girl in room five offered me a date, and it got me wondering, how do you know who's in which room? I didn't notice any numbers."

"Right side is odd numbers, left is even. I can invite her in if you like. It'll cost extra though."

"Not tonight." Edwin slipped his hands into

her gown to rub her nipples. "Get naked and suck me."

His excitement grew as she stripped, sliding her hands slowly down her leg to remove her stockings. One slow button at a time she removed her dress. Her instant compliance got him even harder. The thought of her mouth on his cock made him moan. Agnes never even kissed him. She'd throw a fit if he asked her to suck him. He giggled and lay back on the bed. Soon her old man would be dead, and he'd make her suck him; suck him and fuck him and he'd beat her until she begged for mercy.

"Mmm, that's so good," he said when her lips encased him, excited more by his thoughts than her tongue.

She drew back and ran her hand along his length. "It's extra to come in my mouth."

"Worth it. Can I buy another hour or two? You go get us a bottle, and we have a private party?"

"If your still up for it after, sure," she said and began licking him again. She made him come in minutes. He flopped back on her bed as if exhausted.

"You can get me up for it. Gimme a few minutes." He fished in his shirt pocket and withdrew a wad of bills.

Her eyes lit.

"Let's see if you can earn it all," he said as he peeled off two twenties and handed them to her.

He gave her another and closed his eyes. "Scotch and maybe some bread and cheese."

She giggled and left him on her bed.

As soon as she was gone, he jumped up and yanked up his pants. The knife he'd tucked in his ill-fitting boots was still there. He didn't think he'd need it. Brook was much smaller than he. She'd open the door and be surprised to see him, but she'd let him in if he said he was sorry. Once inside her room it would be child's play to subdue and strangle her. Too many people roamed the halls and the walls were too thin to do what he really wanted to do, *but there were other houses* he reminded himself. He slapped his hand over his mouth to stifle his giggles. He felt like he'd just come alive.

"So many damned rules. I should've made my own long ago."

He peered out the door. If he were staying here, but not working, he'd want a room by the stairs to limit the time spent passing clients in the hallway, and a room by the bathroom would leave only one shared wall. He ran down the hall and pressed his ear to the door of the room beside the bath. Giggles and muffled moans from the stairs warned him someone was coming. He'd heard nothing in the room but that could mean this girl didn't have a date yet or they were being quiet.

He shrugged and tried the door. He could always claim he thought it was the bathroom. An empty room greeted him. He closed the door behind himself and opened the bureau already knowing there would be nothing inside it. This room didn't smell of perfume and sex as his date's did, and the door had been unlocked. He waited a minute to give the couple time to enter their room before heading back into the hallway.

Sounds of flesh-on-flesh issuing from two rooms confirmed working girls lived inside. He opened the door on the room beside his date's and backed out with a mumbled apology. The man didn't stop his hard thrusts. The sight excited him, and Edwin was tempted to stay and watch. More and more he liked the idea of hiring a few women and maybe a man. He could beat them and watch them fuck, make them do whatever he wanted. His cock hardened at the thought, and he grinned. He hadn't been this aroused in years. Agnes never encouraged him, treating him with cool contempt after they made love and laying like a corpse during the act. He couldn't believe he hadn't considered this sooner. All those years wasted working and for what? Anger made his hands tremble on the next door handle, which was locked. No one answered his light knock.

"This room, silly!" his date called.

He turned and smiled.

"You need door numbers or something," he said as he headed back to her room.

"We aren't supposed to leave our dates unattended. I brought us scotch and snacks."

She held up the basket she carried with an air of triumph. "Want me to get a friend?"

"How many women work here?"

"Twenty-two." She winked and brushed passed him, rubbing her breasts against him. "Think you can handle all of us?"

"You're all, ah, working girls? I thought this was a women's hotel too."

"At the moment, we're all whores. You can say it, you know. It won't hurt my feelings. We had a few boarders, but they've all left." She set down the decanter she carried and began slicing the cheese with a small knife. "I'm going to miss this place."

"It's closing?"

"Soon. Now that the war is over the men won't need us. This was a good spot right next to the railroad like it is, but without the troops..."

Edwin sipped the scotch she handed him and contemplated her. Either she was lying and Brook still lived here, or Brook had left. Since she had no reason to lie, and had readily admitted they were all whores, he assumed Brook had indeed left.

To his surprise, he was disappointed. He hadn't realized how much he was looking forward to their encounter. *It shouldn't be too hard to find her*, he told himself. She was a surgical nurse and should be easy to track down. A smile crossed his face. This trip wasn't a complete waste. He'd learned a lot and could have some fun tonight. And when he found

Brook, maybe she'd be somewhere a bit more private and he could have some fun with her too before ridding himself of his problems.

"See if you can get your friend to join us. The one by the bathroom." Edwin fingered his belt.

His date paled and nodded nervously.

"I don't do the rough stuff, but Peggy and Agnes do."

"Get Agnes. I like that name."

He laughed as she fled the room.

Three days later, Edwin scowled at his handwritten notes. It was proving harder than he'd thought to locate his brother's wife. None of the hospitals he'd visited admitted to having her on staff. He flipped through the yellow-pages to private investigators. His finger traveled the page and stopped on one in a seedier section of town. A man answered on the second ring.

"I see from your ad you promise discretion. I have a somewhat delicate matter to handle."

"I assure you, I'm very discreet. If your wife is cheating, no one will hear it from me."

"Not my wife. I need to find my brother's, err, fiancé. I sent her away when she showed up. I thought her a gold digger and a bit loose and am regretting my actions. He'll return soon and be angry if I've, um, misplaced her."

"I see. Do you have her real name?"

"Brook Taylor. She's English and a surgical

nurse. I can describe her, and I know her last known address, but she's moved on from there."

"My rates are twelve dollars a day plus expenses. I require a hundred-dollar retainer but will refund the balance if I find her quickly. Chances are she found a new man to take care of her. What's the last known address."

The man laughed when Edwin gave it to him. "Your instincts are correct. That's a well-known whore house and one of the risqué ones. You still want me to find her?"

"Yes. If you can get me proof she lived there, that would be great. He doesn't want to see what kind of woman she is. I'll deliver a check today."

Edwin grinned into the phone. This was playing out even better than he'd hoped. He was coming off at as the sainted brother and her the scheming slut. Hopefully, she'd returned to England and forgotten all about his brother. But even if she did surface, he'd be able to discredit her. He leaned back in his seat and pursed his lips. He needed to get his hands on that letter his brother had sent and tie up that loose end but there was no rush if she'd made herself scarce. He could take care of Jack, bury his father, and go to England on vacation. Hell, maybe he could do away with Agnes there too. Humming happily to himself, he hung up the phone.

His secretary knocked once and stuck her head in the door. "Mr. Pryor, Mr. Phips is here. Shall I escort him in?"

Edwin straightened his tie and nodded

nervously. He needed to do something about Phips and his nosing around. She left, returning a moment later with Mr. Phips, his father's solicitor, in tow. Edwin rose to shake his hand, smiling when he felt the weakness of the handshake and noted the circles ringing the old man's eyes. Maybe he would die soon, and Edwin would be spared the effort. His secretary placed a stack of mail on his desk, and Edwin's good cheer evaporated at sight of the overseas stamp.

In the Nick of Time

So much for Gay Paree, Jack thought in disgust as he held a hand to his face to block the stench rising from the stagnant water that had collected in slimy green pools in the clogged gutters along the street. Men and women darted between the slow-moving cars and faster bicycles, cursing the cab drivers, singing drunkenly, laughing, yelling and in general behaving like giddy school children released on holiday.

Jack couldn't wait to get home. He craved the peace and solitude of his father's house. He took another step forward in the crush of men waiting to board the ship and closed his eyes to better envision his mother's flower garden. A smile crossed his face, and he could almost see Brook, the sunlight on her face, pruning the roses, smiling her beautiful smile when she saw him.

Someone jostled him hard, and he opened his eyes to see the line had moved forward another ten inches. He took a step forward and hitched his pack higher.

"Mister, I gots good sausages and fried breads!" a boy called out.

Another yelled in a thick French accent, "I gots the paper and books! Good books!"

"Cigarettes, chocolates, shoes!" another shouted.

"Damned beggars," the man behind Jack muttered. "Stealing our smokes and selling them back to us."

The boys eeled through the crowd, hawking their wares to the men waiting to go home. Most of the men waited quietly. Some even played cards while standing or squatting on their heels. Despite the crowds and the stench, the mood was good. Everyone wanted to go home.

Nine days, Jack told himself and took another step forward.

"Come on, mister, soldier sir. Bring a souvenir to the misses. I gots jewelry and do-dads. Real Paris art." The boy waved a model of the Eiffel tower with one hand, clutching a worn sack to his chest as if he expected a pack of thieves to descend on him.

"Probably stole it all from his mother," the man behind Jack said sourly. Then louder. "Let's see the jewelry."

As if by magic, four more boys appeared and began waving an assortment of jewelry most of it broken, all of it clearly stolen. The first boy was roughly pushed away, and a scuffle broke out.

Jack grabbed the instigator and shook him hard. "Beat it, kid, before I give you what you got coming."

The first boy nodded his thanks and waved his model hopefully.

"How much?" Jack sighed, sorry he'd gotten the kid's hopes up.

"Fifteen dollars," the boy said

Jack laughed. "Try that again, sport."

"Two for fifteen." Look"— he thrust a model into Jack's face— "real well made. Your misses will love it. And two can be bookends or sumptim."

Jack laughed again and grabbed the model to avoid being beaned with it. The weight surprised him, and he hefted it thoughtfully. It was solid metal, not painted wood. The boy kept pace with him as Jack stepped forward, moving with the line. It started to pick up speed, and the boy blurted his entire spiel again. Jack wondered if the kid even knew English or had learned his spiel by rote.

"Fine, fifteen," he said, more to get rid of the kid waving another model in his face. *If the bag was full of these it must weigh a ton* Jack thought as he pulled his money from his front pocket and peeled off a twenty.

The boy hand Jack the other model, took the twenty, and darted away as Jack had known he would.

"Sucker," the man behind him said. "Look. I got my wife a nice ring for five bucks." He thrust a ring, which had once had three small pearls on it but now contained two, into Jack's face.

"Nice," Jack said as he fumbled with his pack, trying to shove the two models in. He was tempted to drop them, but they did remind him of Paris, and Brook might think the reminder romantic. He couldn't stop his wide smile. He was going home to his wife and this shit was almost behind him.

"Listen up, scrubs, any of you assholes give me any shit and you and ten of your friends picked at random will be on KP for three months while we sort paperwork, kapish?"

The Staff Sergeant stood at the bottom of the stairs with his hands on his hips and a glower on his face. He eyed the muttering men and pointed to the back bulkhead. "We have two heads. Keep 'um clean. Breakfast will be served at o-six-hundred. You can fill your canteen then, but it has to last all day. You'll be issued two meal bars with your eggs. This ain't the Ritz, so you'll just have to suck it up for the nine days it takes us to cross. When we get home, you'll be mustered out in an orderly fashion. Some of you lucky sods will be free the moment this ship reaches port. I got your paperwork right here." He shook a handful of files at them.

"Sleep, play cards, talk quietly. No singing dancing or screwing." He glared around the crowded hold and nodded decisively. "Trade bunks if you want. We've found it best to bunk the pukers together. That's what the buckets are for. Use 'em."

He emphasized his words by kicking an empty stack of buckets across the room. The buckets rolled down the narrow isle and clanged against the metal bunks stacked four high. Barely two feet sat between the rows and each bunk offered just enough room you could sit slightly hunched.

"I catch any of you fuckers lighting fires to cook your own slops and there'll be hell to pay. Am I clear?"

"Yes, sir," the men chorused.

The staff sergeant nodded again. "I ain't an asshole. Smoke if you want but go up top or the air down here will get too thick. Deck C is the only deck you can use. Follow the yellow line. The yellow one, not blue, green, or fucking red. Yellow!" he glared for another moment, then grinned. "In the case of an emergency— kiss your asses goodbye."

Laughing at his joke, he turned and stomped up the narrow stairs.

Jack tucked his pack beneath his head and closed his eyes. The sounds of men talking and retching lulled him to sleep. Breakfast the next morning was stale biscuits, cold coffee and reconstituted eggs. The grumbles were at a minimum though as most wanted to be sure they'd hear if their name was called.

Jack couldn't figure out the staff sergeants system if he even had one. He appeared to call names randomly, not by rank or name and Jack guessed it was to keep the men quiet in the hopes they'd hear theirs. And it worked. Whoever thought of it was a fucking genus as far as Jack was concerned. The staff sergeant called names until the cooks headed back up the stairs carrying their now empty trays.

"More tomorrow, lads," the staff sergeant said as he gathered his papers.

"Aww, come—"

"You giving me shit? What's your name, boy?"

The staff sergeant strode through the narrow aisle, instantly silencing all complaints.

He halted and glanced around. "That's better. Carry on." He swung around and marched out to a collective sigh of relief.

As soon as he was safely out of ear shot the men began to complain, yelling at the man who'd spoken up and the absent staff sergeant. Jack lay back in his bunk and took out the paperback he'd brought along. The food was crap, but he'd had worse. Laying in the smelly hold sucked but tromping through mud and snow while being shot at was worse. He'd take this shitty bunk any day. And Brook waited. As soon as they reached New York he'd call her. He touched the pocket where Lydia's letter lay and smiled. Maybe he wouldn't call. Maybe he'd just surprise her. The book fell unheeded to his chest as he daydreamed of Brook.

"Pryor!" the staff sergeant called.

"Lucky bastard," the man beside him said as Jack scrambled to his feet.

He'd almost given up hope. The ship was scheduled to arrive in New York in the morning. He waited with the twenty other grinning men for the staff sergeant to hand over his discharge papers. Now he wouldn't need to telegraph her and ask her to come to the base. He could go to her.

"Okay, you lucky sods," The staff sergeant opened the thick file he carried and sorted the papers. "Sign the papers and you're free men. The pay should be current up to four weeks ago. If you don't receive your last check, there's a form in the file you can fill out and send in, or you can decline this early release and continue with your squadron and cash out with the paymaster on base."

A low-level muttering began among the men, but no one declined the release. Jack would've paid ten times that to get out. He didn't care if he never saw a penny of his missing pay.

"None of you should still have weapons but if you do, sign the release and hand them over."

No one admitted to having a weapon. Jack had happily turned his in. He never wanted to hold a gun again. His grin broadened. The enemy had been left behind and an entire ocean separated them. Some of the men clearly had kept enemy weapons as souvenirs and darted guilty glances to their packs. The staff sergeant snorted lightly and flipped a page.

"You'll find a travel voucher in your file. With it, you're entitled to a ride anywhere in the continental United States on military transport at the military's discretion."

The muttering grew louder, and the staff sergeant rose his hand. "Wait times aren't long at all. If you're going by train, it will take a few days. Bring your own supplies—"

Jack tuned him out and flipped through the packet the staff sergeant had handed him. He signed everything and separated the copies, tucking his copies into his pack.

"Okay, boys, you're free men when this ship docks tomorrow night."

"Tomorrow?" the man beside Jack asked before he could. "I thought we docked tonight and offloaded in the morning.

"We're running a bit behind. A small engine problem, but they expect it to be repaired momentarily."

Loud muttering broke out.

"Who knows, maybe they'll fix it and we'll dock on time." The staff sergeant flicked them a salute and swaggered away laughing.

Jack was glad now Brook wouldn't be

expecting him. She'd worry if they were a day late. Frustration might kill him but at least she wouldn't worry.

Edwin Hunts Brook

Edwin gestured the waitress over. "Coffee, fresh cream, if you please." He waved a hand in dismissal and glared at his watch. Seven thirty-five. The detective was late. Edwin began work promptly at eight every morning. Being late would be noticed although he doubted his secretary would have the nerve to question him. The thought cheered him. He'd give the man ten more minutes, he decided.

He'd almost finished his coffee before the man finally appeared.

"Mr. Pr—Peters." The detective offered his hand, which Edwin ignored.

"You're late."

"With good reason, sir. I've found her. She's still using her maiden name and working at Mercy hospital in New York. I think you can assume she's given up her plans and moved on. I've spoken with—"

"No one was to know of my interest!" Edwin

snatched the papers from the detective's hands.

"And no one does. I assure you, sir, I was most discreet."

Edwin withdrew the envelope containing the cash and held it out. "And no record of our dealings exist?" He didn't release the money until the detective nodded.

"This is all the information?"

"It is. She lives in a house with thirteen other women."

Edwin held up a hand, cutting him off. "It doesn't matter." A tremor of excitement made his voice husky. He wanted this man gone so he could savor his plans. He'd found he enjoyed wielding a whip. He'd returned almost every day to the first whorehouse where Peggy and Agnes greeted him with smiles and let him beat them or watch while another fucked them. The more strained their smiles grew when they saw him arrive, the harder he got. They'd do anything for money.

Imagining Brook kneeling before him, begging him to stop but not having too, with just her beautiful hair covering her pert breast made him hard. He shifted in the seat and cleared his throat. "Our business is concluded."

Before the detective could say another word. Edwin rose and hurried out, leaving the detective with the bill for the coffee.

In his car, he sat and took a few deep breaths before opening the folder. The detective had included a picture, a candid shot of Brook smiling at another nurse as they paused outside Mercy hospital. Jealousy again scorched him that his brother had this beautiful woman, and he was suddenly consumed by the need to mar her beauty.

Anger made his hands shake as he held the picture up to the light. "I'll break your perfect nose. No, I'll cut you. You'll beg me to stop. You should've become my mistress. Who the hell are you to turn down that honor? I would've treated you so nicely... What do you see in him anyway? He's nothing. Nothing! The son of servant's daughter." He threw the papers, scattering them over the seat and floor and started his car. He could be in New York in three or four hours. He'd driven there before, well been chauffeured there, but he knew the route. Agnes didn't expect him home until ten tonight. He would call and say he was staying at the club and would be home for dinner tomorrow. She wouldn't think a thing of it. He'd been spending more and more nights there both to get away from her shrew's tongue, and to spend nights with Peggy.

He'd have an entire night with Brook to do whatever he wished. He wouldn't even need to bring her somewhere else. Even if someone heard her moan, they'd assume she was entertaining a client. No one ever interrupted him, even when he made the girls scream.

Of course, he paid for the special services, but he could gag her. As much as he enjoyed hearing them scream, tears and moans worked for him too.

No one on Earth would think him capable of what he had planned for Brook. There was nothing to link them. He forced himself to drive the speed limit, but he longed to rush. Plans flashed through his mind, and he was almost giddy with excitement. The police probably wouldn't even investigate the death of a whore. They'd see she lived in a whore house and assume she was a prostitute. Everyone knew that was a risky profession.

His excitement built as he realized he had the perfect way to kill his brother too. Is all he had to do was intercept him before he reached home or even if he reached home. He could tell him he knew who'd killed Brook and lure him somewhere private. If he could do it before Jack got home and anyone knew they'd spoken, the police would have no reason to connect him to his brother's death. Even if they realized Brook was his wife, they'd think Jack was killed by the man who'd killed her— a jealous lover. He'd ensure it. He laughed so hard he had to pull over to catch his breath and wipe his eyes. He'd have everything. He even had an idea of how to rid himself of his shrew of a wife.

Humming happily, he started the car and continued on his way. His excitement grew the closer he got. It took him thirty minutes of searching, and he had to stop once to ask directions, but he finally found the address the detective had given him.

Brook lived within walking distance of the hospital in a large brownstone that had seen better days.

When he arrived, it occurred to him he'd no idea which room was hers. He parked a block away and cut through a neighbor's drive to reach her backyard. There he hesitated. To ask would be to give himself away. He eyed a fire escape that climbed the back of the three-story building. He could climb it and break into a room, but he'd have to subdue the woman whose room it was. *Or kill her too,* he thought, both excited and nervous over his own daring.

While he dithered at the corner of the yard, two women arrived. Both wore blue dresses and white caps and Edwin's heart sank. This wasn't a house of prostitution but a home the nurses shared. He should've listened to the full report.

He stepped back into the neighbor's yard as the two women walked down the gravel drive and entered the house using a side door. Edwin cursed under his breath. He didn't even know how many lived here, and these women would notice odd noises. He cursed savagely as he realized his fantasy was just that. He couldn't think of a way to get her alone. If he could speak to her without anyone seeing him, he could talk her into his car. There must be a thousand deserted spots between here and home where he could have a little fun with her before dumping her corpse.

He ran back to his car to read the report. Maybe the detective had noted which room was Brook's.

Edwin slapped the report closed and threw it to the passenger seat. Fourteen women shared that house, and she had a room on the third floor in the back. The detective had noted she worked the morning shift and usually returned home around six. One of her windows overlooked the fire escape. Edwin glanced at his watch. It would be light for hours yet. He could return at dark.

He eyed his clothing and frowned. He still wore a suit and dress shoes. *Would she go with me?* he mused as he absently straightened a silver cuff link. Try as he might he couldn't think of anything to say to explain his appearance in her room and why they needed to leave by the window instead of the door. She was bound to introduce him to anyone they passed in the halls, and when she didn't return, everyone would know he'd done something to her.

"Damn it," he snarled and pounded his hands on the steering wheel.

"You okay, mister?" a young boy asked, startling Edwin.

Edwin straightened and smoothed his hair. He offered the boy an insincere smile and started his car. The boy said nothing just stared from the back of his bicycle. Edwin wanted to shoo him away but who knew where his mother was or if she'd notice. *It was better to drive away,* Edwin told himself and pulled into the light traffic. He needed to buy some dark clothing and light shoes he could sneak around in— and a gun.

"There's always Agnes," he said and snickered. "I'll take you somewhere amazing." He laughed again. "So, what if this one has to be quick. Better to kill her fast and be done with it. It isn't like I have experience at this sort of thing. I'll take my time and plan for Agnes."

In a much more cheerful frame of mind, Edwin drove down the street looking for a clothing store. Brook would be dead before morning.

Jack Reaches New York

Jack slung his almost empty pack to his shoulder and stepped onto the dock. He'd finished the food he'd brought with him, except for one can of beans, and given away his two books. All he had left were the two statuettes, one set of dirty clothes, and a clean set of underwear and socks. He hadn't even bothered to pack up his bedroll. He'd just left it on the bunk. He'd been tempted to leave the entire pack but couldn't bring himself to abandon it.

Men and women crowded the docks. Small children laughed and cried as the adults greeted each other with glad cries or complaints. The grin on Jack's face grew, hearing the familiar language and seeing sunset gilding a familiar skyline eased a tenseness in his shoulders he'd carried for four long years.

He pushed his way through the teaming throng and paused as he reached an intersection. The road split into three, one leading to a quieter boulevard lined with store-fronts and offices. The right hand-road curved along the waterfront while the left was crammed with people heading to the bus terminal and train station. He headed left. He was tempted to stop and buy some clothes and see if he could rent a room to clean up, but she'd have a bathroom, and he couldn't wait another night to see her.

Disembarking had used every ounce of patience he had left. The ship had arrived a little after noon and it had taken hours to release them. Hours spent in a stiflingly hot hold with increasingly angry men. The engine had gone again as they limped into port, and they'd shut them all down, killing the lights and fans in the hold to do so. He was just glad they'd been able to reach the port at all and hadn't needed to spend another night at sea.

Jack hitched his pack higher on his shoulder, drew in a big lungful of city air, and exhaled nosily. All around him men complained, but he couldn't stop grinning. He pushed through the crowd, not bothering with the lines for busses. She was just miles away. He could walk until he found a cab. Hell, he could run there. As soon as the crush broke up enough, he shifted to a slow jog. They'd never spend another night apart.

Life Without You

"Brook!" Fran called from the foot of the stairs.

The repressed excitement in her voice hurried Brook's steps to the door. They'd just come in, and Brook had been looking forward to a long bath but maybe the hospital had called and needed them on shift.

She grabbed her robe from the foot of the bed and grimaced at her dirty clothes. She hated to put on dirty clothes.

Her robe would have to do. Fran wouldn't call her downstairs for anything less than an emergency. The smells from the kitchen always made her sick. She thought Antoinette went out of her way to cook eggs whenever she knew Brook would be home soon. There was no other explanation for it.

"Brook?" Fran called again, sounding closer.

Brook stuck her head out the door.

Fran grinned at her. "You have a visitor."

"I do?"

"Yep. A man."

Brook furrowed her brows in thought but couldn't think of anyone who might visit her. "Doctor Robert's?" she asked in sudden excitement and took a step forward before remembering she wore only a robe. "Tell him I'll be right down. I need to dress."

But Fran was shaking her head. "It's not Doctor Roberts. He says he's your husband." Fran laughed when Brook squealed.

"Jack? Jack's here?"

Fran grabbed her arm as she tried to pass her on the stairs. "Don't hurry so. You'll fall to your death with your bad leg."

"Are you sure it's Jack?"

"He says so, and who else would it be? And a good thing too. These stairs are too much for you. I wish I'd taken Antoinette's room, so I could switch with you. I can't wait until she's gone. The nerve of that girl."

Brook absently patted the hand on her arm. Fran was more incensed at Antoinette than she was.

"It was her room first, and she hates the stairs too," Brook said soothingly. "And besides, who cares? Jack is here!" She laughed with giddy excitement. "Are you sure it's him?" It didn't feel real that he could just show up on her doorstep. "Why didn't he call?"

"You can ask him in a minute. He's in the front drawing room. And you're lucky I came home when I did because Antoinette was turning him away, the spiteful cow."

Brook halted on the second-to-last stair. "Why would she do that?"

"Because she can't get a man of her own. If she'd stop eating for ten minutes, the men might get a chance to approach her but..." Fran shook her head and made an apologetic face. "Sorry, she's just so petty. And don't think we don't know she cooks her eggs on purpose when she knows you're home. I opened all the windows in the kitchen. And don't you go worrying over the house rules. It doesn't apply to husbands, as I told her. She huffed off."

Brook paused before the drawing room door and straightened her hair, suddenly nervous to see him. Maybe he wouldn't be happy about the child or had changed his mind now that the war was over. The thought made her heart hurt.

"Go on," Fran said and made a shooing gesture.

Brook took a deep breath and stepped into the room.

Jack stepped forward with his arms outstretched.

"Jack!" she yelled and threw herself into his arms, doubts forgotten.

He hugged her hard, and they were both crying and laughing. Her knees felt weak and the room spun. Only Jack's face remained clear.

"You're here. You're really here," she mumbled between kisses.

"I missed you so much," he said. "I was so worried when I didn't hear from you, and then, when my father wrote— God, Brook, why didn't you go to him?"

Brook kissed him again and pressed her cheek against his damp one. "I knew you'd come for me. Why didn't you call though and say you were coming home? Do you have to go back?"

"No, I'm out and never leaving your side again. I'm officially discharged. I probably should've stopped and bought some clothes and cleaned up before coming—" his breath left him in a sharp oof as she sagged in his arms.

"Are you okay?"

She began to cry hard, deep raking sobs that shook her body.

"Here," Fran said and held out a glass of water. "It's the shock. Set her down on the sofa here and let her catch her breath. Take a few deep breaths, Brook."

Fran grabbed her hand and rested her fingertips against the pulse in her wrist.

"Is she okay?" Jack asked anxiously.

"I'm fine," Brook tried to say through her sobs as Fran nodded.

Jack sat and pulled her down beside him. He rubbed her back as she cried on his shoulder

"I'm sorry, I'd thought to surprise you but maybe that wasn't such a good idea. I should've called."

"You're really here. I can't believe it." Brook's

tears slowed, but she couldn't make herself release him. Her face burned from her flush. A quick glance at the door had shown four more of her roommates had gathered and watched silently from the doorway. Jack's light laugh fluttered her hair, and she was suddenly consumed by lust.

"Tears are normal in her condition," Fran said and rose. "Let's give them some privacy."

"She can't be alone in the room with him with a closed door," Antoinette said.

"Don't be ridiculous. He's her husband. Why don't you go finish all those eggs you made?"

"How—"

The closing door muffled their words into indistinct sound.

"Are you sure you're okay."

"Perfect now that you're home. I can't believe you *are* home. Did you get my letters about the child?"

Jack dropped his hand to her stomach and his voice deepened. "I did. We're going to be so happy. But why are you here?"

Brook used her sleeve to wipe her eyes, wishing she'd grabbed her bag or had a hankie. Jack set his pack by his feet and reached in as she said, "Your brother sent me away." She accepted the handkerchief he handed her and laughed at his shocked expression. She blew her nose before saying, "He thinks I was lying about being your wife, and I didn't want to anger him more. I knew you'd work it out with him, and it just seemed easier for everyone if I waited for you here."

"Everyone?"

"I was worried he could get Lydia and the others in trouble."

Jack nodded, and his expression lightened. "I understand, but I'm sorry... I'd wanted you safe at home and meant you to be taken care of." He trailed off as she began to cry and grabbed him again. He stroked her hair, resting his cheek against hers and didn't speak again until her crying had stopped.

She used the hankie again and stood. He glanced doubtfully at the door but let her lead him from the room. Women's laughter and talk reached them faintly from the hallway.

"They'll be in the kitchen," Brook whispered and held a finger to her lips.

"Should we be going upstairs?"

She held a hand to block her giggles and shrugged. "They don't allow men upstairs, but we *are* married..."

"I could get us a room somewhere," he offered.

She glanced over her shoulder at him as she said, "I don't want to wait." The heated look in his eyes started a fire low in her belly.

He huffed a light laugh and crowded her on the stair, and she tried to hurry her step. The heat from his body behind her spurred her on and she moaned softly when he placed his hands on her waist. She turned to kiss him before she even realized she was going to.

"You idiots are going to fall down the stairs," Fran said. She shook her head and headed down the stairs toward them.

Brook broke from his kiss and giggled.

Jack cleared his throat, and Brook laughed at his embarrassed expression. She turned to grin at Fran and continue climbing the stairs one slow step at a time, her leg twinging with each step.

"Fran Thompson," Fran said as she offered her hand to Jack. "I'm your wife's nearest neighbor, but I'll be bunking with Beth tonight. Everyone on this floor is going to the movies, too bad you'll miss it." She winked at Brook. "I'll bring up a meal when we come back, and it won't be eggs." She winked again and waved over her shoulder as she ran down the stairs.

"Eggs?" Jack asked.

"Can't stand them now," Brook said and shuddered dramatically, making Jack laugh.

"Beth has the room beneath mine," Brook continued as she hurried her step down the corridor.

She seems nice," Jack said.

"She is." Brook stepped into the bathroom and dropped the sash for her robe. "Mmm, she said and pressed her naked breasts against her husband.

His warm hands trailed her back and pressed her hard against his erection. His hands grew urgent when she deepened the kiss, and she was surprised when he broke away and shook his head.

"Not here on the cold tile, and should we at all in your condition?"

"Yes, it'll be months before we need to stop, and here's fine. The tub is big enough for two."

He frowned, then laughed when she huffed indignantly and rolled her eyes. He helped her with his buttons.

My Brother?

A soft whispery sound drew Jack from the depths of sleep. He woke instantly, knowing an enemy was nearby. Brook slept with her head tucked against his chest, clutching his arm in both hands. Her soft breathing and relaxed state didn't reassure him. He lay in the dark room straining to hear what had wakened him.

He jerked upright, dislodging Brook, as the soft slither came again. Someone was opening the window that overlooked the fire escape. He scrambled from bed naked, wishing he had a weapon. A cool breeze wafted into the room.

On the bed, Brook murmured in her sleep and rolled into the spot he'd just vacated. Moonlight streaming through the window behind the bed illuminated her pale skin. Mussed hair tangled around her shoulders and trailed against her pregnancy swollen breasts. The curve of her hip and one graceful leg lay above the covers, and he wished he could just stare at her. Her beauty tightened his loins. Her defenselessness clenched his hands into fists and a snarl settled onto his face. A dark figure blocked the moonlight from the window beside the fire escape.

He debated waking her but that was sure to notify the man sliding his leg through the window, and he wanted to catch this asshole.

A gloved hand rested on the windowsill now. Jack's eyes had adjusted to the dim lighting given off by distant streetlights enough to make out the darker figure in the dark room. He crouched beside the wall and prepared to spring. The intruder was halfway into the room. The low light caught on a knife in the man's hands, and Jack tensed, his gaze going to Brook.

This wasn't a man bent on robbery but murder. Fourteen nurses lived in this brownstone apartment. The intruder was likely bent on rape and murder to silence his victim.

Jack yanked the knife holding arm and twisted. The intruder grunted and tried to kick out. The knife clattered to the floor as Jack and the intruder struggled. The intruder tried to shove Jack away to escape back out the window as Jack yanked him inside.

"Fucker," Jack muttered as he heaved and forced the man through the tight opening.

Glass shattered, and his opponent swore. Jack punched him hard in the stomach and followed him down to the floor to kneel on his chest. Deep gasps came from the man. He gave up trying to escape and lay still.

"Everything okay in there? one of Brook's roommates called through the closed door.

Brook still hadn't woken.

"Caught an intruder. Call the police." Jack couldn't remember the woman's name.

His wife still slept. Fury gripped him. This man could've done anything he'd liked to her. She was defenseless. If he'd arrived one day later, she'd be dead. The horror of that thought made his stomach clench.

He hit the man again and kneed him hard in the groin. While the man moaned and tried to double over, Jack fumbled with the black ski mask the intruder wore.

"Edwin," he said in shock and stumbled to his feet, dropping the mask he clenched.

His brother glared up at him, rubbing his jaw with one hand and clutching himself with the other.

"What the hell are you..."

"When did you get home?" His brother said at the same time.

Jack peered over his shoulder at his sleeping wife. Shock made his head swim. His brother had come to kill his wife. The crunch of glass brought his attention back to Edwin. He'd risen, his head lowered as if he scanned the floor.

"Looking for the knife?" Jack asked in disgust.

"I can explain."

"Save it. Explain to the police."

"She's a whore, Jack. I was trying to save you."

Jack grabbed him by the ratty black sweater he wore and shook him hard. Pain lanced his foot from a shard of glass, and he released him to pry it out.

His brother shoved him, taking him by surprise, making him stumble backward to catch his balance. Jack swore as he stepped on another shard of glass. A roll of thick black tape dropped from his brother's hand and rolled across the floor. Attention on the glass covered floor, a flicker of movement warned him right as his brother lifted a gun from his waistband.

Jack's eyes widened.

This can't be happening, he thought as his brother snarled and fired at him.

The bullet whined past his left shoulder and ripped through the thin wall. A woman screamed, and Brook sat. Another shot missed him by a mere inch. Jack was thanking his lucky stars his brother couldn't shoot for shit as he grabbed the dresser and yanked it in front of himself.

"Jack!" Brook called.

"Get down!" Jack yelled, terrified Edwin would fire on her next. He grabbed a bottle of he didn't know what from the dresser and threw it unaimed at the window, then risked a quick glance.

Edwin was staring, not at him, but Brook. His lips lifted in a snarl, and he fired again.

"No!" Jack yelled, knowing he was too late. Brook sat in bed clutching his pack to her chest to hide her nakedness. The bullet struck her, knocking her back onto the bed.

Jack screamed and ran to Brook as she sat and wiped her chest.

Beans, not blood, Jack thought in relief and turned for the window Edwin was attempting to crawl back out. He reached for his brother's leg and missed as Edwin stood on the fire escape and fired two more shots in quick succession.

Brook screamed.

Hot and cold waves traveled Jack. His brother had just tried to kill him and his wife.

"Jack!" Brook called again, sounding terrified.

"Get dressed. Careful there's glass on the floor."

Footsteps thudded on the fire escape. Lights had come on in the house behind this one.

Brook's room overlooked the small back lot. On the top floor of a three-story brownstone Jack had a good view of his brother's furious grimace as he turned and fired at the window.

Jack had ducked back as soon as his brother lifted his arm. The bullet thudded into the wall above the door and Brook screamed again. The scream was echoed by women outside his door.

"Am I dreaming?" Jack asked.

He rubbed his eyes hard and glanced around

the still dark bedroom. Moonlight gilded the furnishings and Brook's pale skin. She sat in bed staring at him with the sheet clutched to her breasts and his pack in one hand.

"This can't be happening," he muttered as he peeked from the window again in time to see his brother disappear into the neighbor's yard.

He eased to the bed, trying to avoid stepping in the shattered glass. On his hands and knees, he crawled across the bed to Brook who'd risen when he'd spoke but hadn't gotten one step before she'd fallen to the floor. She huddled now on the floor beside the bed with her arms over her head. Her tear-streaked face rose, and she grabbed at him.

"Are you okay?" What's happening? Who was that?"

"My brother," Jack said grimly. He kissed her cheek and pulled her up. "Get dressed, Brook; we have to go.

He reached for his discarded pants. She remained motionless, staring at him. "Brook, please, get dressed. He might come back." As he spoke, he yanked a dress from her closet and pushed it into her hands.

"We're safe, but you need to dress," he said in a calmer tone. He was scaring her badly. Her hands trembled in his.

She suddenly spun away, yanking her hands from his and vomited in the small trash can beside her door.

"Brook, sweetheart, take a deep breath and calm down." Worried for the baby now, he smoothed her hair and rubbed her back in small circles. She continued to retch, and his concern grew. *This stress couldn't be good for the baby.* A fresh wave of anger flushed his face and tightened his shoulders. His brother had tried to murder his pregnant wife. He'd shot her... in sudden fear he flicked on the light to examine her. Maybe that bullet had gone through the pack. She sobbed as he lifted her hair and pulled the garbage can from her. An angry looking bruise had formed on her shoulder, but the bullet hadn't broken the skin. He used the sheet to wipe the beans from her skin, then wiped her face.

He left her hugging the garbage can to finish dressing. Her pale, tear-streaked face and wide eyes followed him about the room. He pulled the dress he'd bought her in Paris over her head and slipped her shoes on her feet. She neither resisted nor helped. The once loose dress now fitted her breasts so snuggly he was afraid it might hurt but didn't want to take the time to fetch another. The homicidal grimace on his brother's face scared him to his toes. Edwin had looked desperate and insane. There was no telling what he would do, and Jack had no weapons. And when you didn't have a weapon and an enemy was after your ass— you ran.

"Jack," she said in a high-pitched voice when he pulled her upright and tried to put a sweater on her. She donned the sweater absently, repeating his name in a higher pitched voice.

Jack winced and hugged her tightly a moment. The desperation in her voice was too similar to the way she called out for him when they made love, but the difference rose the hairs on his arms. *His brother*, he thought again in rising horror.

"Shh, you're safe. We're okay."

"He shot me."

"Are you hurt?"

"He shot me," she said again and began to cry.

Jack snatched his pack from the floor and pulled her from the room and down the stairs. Her roommates huddled in a mass by the front door.

"Keep the door locked until the police arrive. I'm taking Brook to the doctor."

"Is she hurt." The woman who spoke reached for Brook.

"I'll take care of her. Stay away from the windows."

Jack pulled Brook outside, ignoring the questions and admonishments to stay and offers to call for an ambulance. Brook followed unresisting as he led her directly across the street and down a driveway, cutting through a backyard and onto a neighboring road. He headed to the hospital. There would be cabs there and telephones.

"Where are we going? What's going on?"
Brook asked in a quavering voice.

"Are you okay?" he stopped to hug her. She
still shook and gasped.

"No."

She slid to her knees, and he followed her
down to cradle her as she cried.

"Oh, God, Brook, I'm sorry. I'm not thinking
straight. Should I call an ambulance for you?"

"No." She peered over her shoulder and tried
to push herself up. "Are we safe here?"

"I want us off the street, and I need to call
and warn my father." Saying the words made
Jack's heart pound hard. Edwin might've already
killed him.

He swung Brook into his arms, grunting with
effort as he stood and began walking again. "We
need to get off this street."

"The police...."

Jack said nothing.

"Your brother," she said in a small voice.

Jack stopped and buried his face in her hair.
He took a few deep breaths and mumbled. "I
don't know what to do. He was going to kill us."

"Me. He couldn't have known you would be
there. He was going to kill me." Her voice rose
and thickened with tears. "I knew he didn't like
me, but..."

"I need to call my father. Edwin has gone
crazy."

"I can walk. Put me down, Jack."

Jack held her another minute, neither of

them speaking. He finally set her on her feet and kissed her cold lips.

"I'm so sorry, Brook. You should've been safe with us. I promise you, my father will love you. Something must've happened to Edwin. I never imagined..." he trailed off unable to finish the thought even in his head. He wanted to tell himself Edwin had done it for him, believing Brook a bad woman, but his brother had fired at him. Edwin had meant to kill them both.

"I'm sorry, Jack," she sniffled and wiped her face on the sleeve of her sweater. "We can call from my house."

"The police will be there now..."

She bit her lip and wiped her face again.

"I know I should report him, but he's my brother... I need to talk to my father first."

She nodded and took his hand. He hated the four-block walk to the hospital. Every car that passed them, he expected a hail of bullets to follow. Her cold hand trembled in his. He needed to get her somewhere safe and warm. With relief he spied a taxi.

"Grand central," he said.

"Your missus okay?" the cabby asked doubtfully.

"We just got some bad news," Jack said.

Brook cleared her throat and loosened her grip on Jack. "I'm fine, thank you."

"Not much traffic at this time of night. Trains run all night though," the cabby said. He continued to chatter until they reached their destination, apparently not caring that neither Jack nor Brook answered him.

"Well, good luck to you," the cabby said as he pulled up outside the terminal. "Hope whoever it is recovers."

Jack paid him and led Brook to the entrance. A soldier stopped him and searched his pack before letting them enter. Jack had forgotten the heightened security because of the war, but he was glad of it. His brother wouldn't be able to enter with a gun.

He bought two tickets to Pennsylvania and then searched for a phone. More soldiers patrolled in pairs, keeping an eye on the crowd. Jack got a few hard looks and was sure he'd have been stopped again if Brook hadn't accompanied him. She followed without speaking, but her distress was evident in her tear-streaked face and hard grasp on his hand. After a moments debate, Jack called Mr. Phips.

The phone rang eight times before a man answered.

"I need to speak with Mr. Phips; it's an emergency. Tell him Jack Pryor is calling and it's a matter of life and death."

"I'll wake him. Hold a moment," the man said.

Jack kissed Brook's cold fingers and glanced around him, half expecting his brother to show up and start shooting again despite the crowd and the guards.

"Am I dreaming?"

She shook her head, her beautiful blue eyes filling with tears. She hugged him close, resting her head on his shoulder.

"Jack?" Mr. Phips asked.

"I'm sorry to disturb you so late. I'm calling from New York. I just got home today. I don't know quite how to say this. It's going to be a shock."

"Are you well?"

"I'm worried for my father. I need you to go there and ensure he's alive. Edwin came here and tried to kill me."

"What?"

"He broke into my wife's room. I didn't realize it was him until I grabbed the knife from him, then he tried to shoot us. I don't know why, but I'm sure he meant to kill us."

Brook made a soft sound of distress and sagged against him. Jack tightened his grip on her.

"My wife is expecting and needs to rest. We're catching the six-a.m. train. Can you arrange for a car to pick us up when we arrive? I'm not sure what to say to my father. Will this shock kill him?"

"My dear boy..." Mr. Phips cleared his throat and blew his nose. "I shall go at once to your father's house and send for his physician. I'm unsure— say nothing until we speak. I'll come myself to retrieve you. Dear Lord. I thought

Edwin had been skimming, but this... I never suspected him capable of something so heinous. Have you spoken with the police?"

"No, I ran. I panicked. He shot Brook. I still can't believe this is happening."

"Does she need medical attention?"

"No." Jack squeezed the bridge of his nose. "Maybe. I don't know. The bullet didn't penetrate, but the shock in her condition..."

"I'm okay," Brook said but didn't release him.

Jack kissed her temple.

"I'll speak to the doctor. Give me the number of where you are, and I'll call you back in a few minutes. Jack—the police will have to be involved. I'll act as your solicitor and call and speak with them after I see to your father."

Jack gave Mr. Phips the number on the payphone.

"Wait there until I call back. You say your train leaves at six?"

"Yes."

"You should speak to the police before coming home, but I understand your hesitance."

Mr. Phips sniffed and blew his nose again. "Your father will be most upset. Most upset." He made a tsking noise and said, "I'll need to speak with Edwin. Perhaps he can turn himself in and seek professional help? I'll speak to Doctor Ames about admitting him. It's clear Edwin is very ill. The stress of running these companies is too much for him. I'll inform the police you're bringing Mrs. Pryor home to her doctor. Say nothing if they find you before you arrive home. Call my home. Mr. Randel can transfer messages and will know where to reach me."

Mr. Phips hung up, and Jack sat limply on nearby bench.

"Still feeling sick?"

She nodded against his shoulder. "Why would he want to kill me?"

"I don't know. Money, I suppose. Mr. Phips wrote me and told me he thought Edwin was mismanaging his businesses. He was worried Dad wasn't getting his mail. Jesus, this is going to kill him."

Sweat broke out on Jack's brow. His father could be dead already. Brook trembled against his side, and he was suddenly furious. He pushed away to see her face.

"I swear to god, Brook, I had no idea what kind of lunatic he was. I meant you to be safe and instead—" his fury choked him. Her scared, confused expression was breaking his heart. She'd trusted him, and he'd sent her into danger.

I didn't know." He hated the pale, pinched look on her face. "I didn't know," he said again louder, angry with himself now for not knowing, for not making sure she was cared for. *God, if I hadn't come home, Edwin would've murdered her.* Jack closed his eyes and pulled Brook to his shoulder again.

"Maybe he didn't mean to kill me," Brook said. "Maybe he meant to scare me away."

Jack said nothing.

"The shot didn't hurt me. Maybe it was blanks?"

He wished he could tell her Edwin had only meant to scare her, but blanks didn't make holes in walls. Whatever his intent had been when he'd entered, he'd intended to kill them both when he'd left. *And what had he intended? He'd carried a knife and tape.* Jack couldn't imagine a good reason any man would break into a woman's bedroom with those items, dressed as Edwin had been with his identity hidden and willing to use deadly force to escape.

"Maybe he really believed I'm a whore."

Her voice caught and cracked, and she rose her hands to cover her face. "I lived in a whorehouse in Pennsylvania. They were nice women like the ones in Paris, but maybe—"

"This isn't your fault. He's sick, Brook. And dangerous. Never trust him. We'll get him help, but I don't want him anywhere near you."

The phone rang, startling him. He jumped up to answer.

"Mr. Phips?"

"I spoke with Doctor Ames and he advises you keep your wife warm and still and if there's any sign of bleeding or cramps go at once to a hospital."

"My father?"

"I'm on my way there now. I debated calling, but if Edwin intended to harm him, he's already done so. Its best to wait for his doctor. Edwin can't reach home for hours yet."

"This is a nightmare," Jack said.

"We'll get him the help he needs. I'll call and leave a message with Randel when I have news."

"Thank you, Mr. Phips."

"Not at all, my dear boy."

Jack returned to sit beside Brook. "Mr. Phips is handling everything." He lifted a hand to feel Brook's brow, not liking how peaked she looked. His frown deepened when she began to cry and buried her face in his chest. He was seriously alarmed now. He'd seen her face tough situations without flinching. Of course, no one had been actively trying to kill her in her sleep before either. A battlefield was impersonal and while terrifying, not the same at all as murder.

He couldn't wrap his head around the idea that his brother had tried to kill him. He'd thought war was bad, but this was a nightmare.

"Dear God, he was like a father to me. I thought him cold, but I also thought he loved me..."

Brook took a deep hitching breath and sat straighter. The smile she gave was sickly, and the hand that she placed on his cheek shook. He snorted and pulled her head back to his chest. She was terrified and trying to comfort him.

"Shh," he whispered and rocked them, glaring at the men who paused to stare. Even after midnight Grand Central remained busy, mostly with men traveling alone although he spied a few families and couples. The room was brightly lit and the night warm, but he worried over his wife's shivering, wishing he'd thought to grab a blanket for her. He shrugged off his pack and rummaged one-handed, removing his dirty uniform jacket and draping it over her shoulders. The strong scent of beans drifted into the air, and he remembered she'd been shot. He couldn't seem to keep the thought in his head. Each time he remembered, it shocked him anew.

Edwin had shot his wife. What was he supposed to do now? He had no idea.

The phone rang, and he scrambled to his feet to grab it, apologizing brusquely as he shouldered a man out of his way.

He must have looked as harried as he felt because the man nodded and mumbled. "Quite alright," and headed for a nearby phone.

"Mr. Phips?"

"This is Randel Clemens, Mr. Phips' butler. Am I correct in assuming I'm speaking to Jack Pryor?"

"Yes, this is he." Jack's breath came hard and he wiped his sweating brow.

"I'm to inform you, your father took the news surprisingly well. He's angry and worried but in fine health and looking forward to speaking with you."

Jack let out his breath in a rush.

"Thank you for calling."

"The doctor has given your father a sedative and he won't be available to speak with you for some hours. I've called and arranged a car, and I'm to remind you that if your wife suffers from cramps or bleeding to get her immediately to a hospital. The doctor also recommends you keep her warm. I've taken the liberty of ordering hot tea and blankets, and the driver should arrive within the hour at the Forty-Eighth Street and Park

entrance.

"Thank you," Jack said again and wanted to smack himself for not thinking of hiring a car. He was obviously not thinking straight.

"Not at all. If there is anything else I can do, don't hesitate to call."

Randel hung up before Jack could thank him again. He returned and crouched before Brook, taking both her cold hands in his. "We've got a car coming, sweetheart. Are you well enough to travel?"

"I'm fine," she said in a shaky voice. "How's your father?"

"Well, the news didn't kill him outright...." She winced.

"He's a tough old bird. Maybe he knows something or expected..." Jack shrugged and stood, pulling her up with him. He grabbed his pack and slung an arm around her shoulders. "No. I know that's stupid. He'd never let Edwin run around if he knew he was this crazy. I just can't believe he shot at me." He clamped his lips together and shook his head. "Let's find that car.

Thwarted Again

Edwin pounded the steering wheel and cursed as he sped down route one. How was he going to explain this? He cursed again but slowed when a passing car laid on their horn. He couldn't afford to be pulled over. Jack would've called the police, and he needed to speak with his lawyer.

"Why didn't you just die in Europe? You ruin everything! It's my money! You have no right to it!"

Jack had taken everything from him, and now he'd call him a murderer. "But I didn't kill anyone," he said thoughtfully and slowed even more. "Who's to say he didn't shoot at me?"

He smiled as he contemplated the scenario he pictured in his head. His smile changed to a frown as he considered their father would assuredly believe Jack's version over his.

What he needed was an alibi and deny he was there at all. He could tell his father Jack was lying to discredit him and take his place.

He grimaced as he considered Sylvan's accounts, *but embezzling wasn't murder,* he assured himself. And while his father was sure to be angry over the theft of the funds, if he could prove he was nowhere near New York, no one outside the family would ever hear of the thefts, and Jack would be discredited in their father's eyes.

"And it wasn't even theft. Sylvan should've been mine all along." He repeated that a few times and realized he was cursing aloud when he lost his breath. He took a few deep breaths and had to resist the urge to scream curses again.

Even if his father believed Jack, there was nothing he could do to me, Edwin thought in satisfaction and increased his speed.

He'd go to Peggy. For enough money she'd lie for him, say he was with her. His smile widened. Peggy would say anything he wanted. And maybe he could beat Jack home. Maybe he hadn't called the police to protect the old man. The thought relieved him, and he relaxed slightly. Jack wouldn't want to upset their father, he was sure of that. It seemed likely he'd say nothing to anyone until he had a chance to speak with him, and it would take him much longer to catch a train and get home. He was sure to beat him there.

A new thought occurred to him, and he chortled. Brook had been frightened by his threat to call the police over their fake marriage.

It seemed likely she wouldn't let Jack turn him in if she thought her friends would suffer for it. Maybe he could intercept Jack and use that letter to keep him quiet, and their father need never know of their encounter in New York.

He'd have to break into his father's safe somehow. He frowned thoughtfully, then burst out laughing. "He has no idea where the letter is. I have time to steal it as long as he believes I have it."

Pleased with himself, he hummed as he drove.

"Maybe I could just smother the old man and blame Jack. It would be his word against mine." He considered this scenario as he drove. Would everyone believe the war had made Jack crazy?

His stomach rumbled, and he realized he was starving. He hadn't eaten a thing since speaking with the detective. He glanced at his watch and frowned thoughtfully. It would be hours before the train left. He had time to gas up, eat, and even take a small cat nap.

"I have all my bases covered," he assured himself as he slowed to exit the highway. "Even if he has called, it's my word against his." He shrugged his shoulders and pushed his doubts into the corner of his mind. He was an important man, he reminded himself. No one would believe Jack's lies.

Brook Meets Francis

Brook woke as the car slowed. For one moment she was blindingly happy to wake and feel her husband beside her until she remembered. Remembered terror made her stomach turn, and she sat slowly, both to keep her husband from waking and to hold back her nausea.

Pain shot from her hip to her shoulders and the bruise where Edwin had shot her throbbed with renewed vigor. The back seat was spacious but not big enough to stretch out fully, and her leg protested viscously as she tried to stretch it. She groaned softly as she rubbed her leg, making her shoulder throb harder.

Jack woke with a jerk and swore quietly.

"Sorry," he said and tried to wrap the blanket around her.

"I'm okay. Where are we?" The scenery outside the window gave her no clues. Early morning sun shone through the trees and the homes looked the same as those she'd spotted hours ago. They'd left the highway though and traveled down a two-lane road. She took the blanket from him although she was no longer chilled, and he craned to peer from the window.

"We've just reached Philadelphia and should reach Chester within thirty minutes," the driver said. "Shall I stop to let the lady rest?"

"I'm okay if you are," Brook said hurriedly.

Jack peered at her worriedly but nodded. "Drive on," he said, then softly to her," Are you sure? We can stop if you need a break. I don't know what I was thinking rushing off like that."

She turned to kiss him, meaning it to be a light kiss on the cheek, but he had other ideas. He moaned softly as he kissed her lips and kissed her deeply.

"I'm so sorry," he whispered when he broke from the kiss.

The pain in his voice tore her heart.

"It's not your fault," she said, willing him to believe it.

"Are you feeling better?"

"I'm fine."

"The leg hurting?"

She hastily dropped her hand from her thigh, and he sighed hard. "Brook, if you need to rest or anything at all... God this must be so horrifying. I'm so, so sorry."

"Please— I'm okay just a bit sore, but not sick anymore. I'm not hungry either," she added hurriedly when he opened his mouth.

He smiled ruefully and kissed her fingers.

"I can stop for tea if the missus needs a cuppa. There's a diner nearby that makes a fabulous breakfast," the driver offered.

"Thank you, but I'd rather not stop. Especially for eggs," she muttered, making Jack laugh.

The driver peered at her doubtfully in the rearview mirror, and she ducked her head, letting her hair swing forward to hide her blush. He'd been the soul of patience, stopping without complaint when she'd need to vomit and hovering with a thermos of tea and blankets.

"I really do feel better," she mumbled, and Jack stroked her hair.

"I'm so sorry," he said again.

"What will you say to your father?"

"I have no idea." He kissed the top of her head, then rested his cheek on hers.

They sat unspeaking with just the drone of the car engine and whir of the tires to fill the silence. The driver said nothing either, but the silence wasn't peaceful. Tension hummed in the air. Neither of them knew what to say.

"I'd meant for you to be safe with my family," Jack finally said. "I never dreamed I had enemies at home."

"I know." She hesitated, then blurted. "Do you think it was my fault? I swear I hardly even spoke with him. He just met me at the station and told me to go."

"I can't believe he sent you away. I'm not

doubting he did," he added hurriedly when she tensed, "but why would he?"

"He called me a whore. Said others had come and tried for your money. He said he knew we'd lied about being married and would have us all arrested, and he could, Jack."

"We are married." Jack kissed her temple and clasped her hands tighter.

"Lydia helped me so much. And Burns and Doctor Roberts; what if he turns them in?"

She felt him shrug.

"He can't prove a thing, and he wouldn't say anything even if could. His wife would kill him if he drags our name through the mud. Don't worry about that. Our marriage license is real." His voice trembled when he said. "Are you having doubts about us?"

"God no." She pulled away to see his face. "Are you?"

"Never," he said fervently and kissed her again. He smiled a more natural smile when he pulled away and smoothed her hair back. "I have no idea what others he was talking about. I swear to god, it's only been you."

"And the money?"

Jack winced. "My father is rich. My mom left me her business. Maybe..." he shook his head hard, and his expression tightened. "I really want to believe Edwin was protecting me, but I know that's a lie." He tucked her head against his chest again. "We'll sort it out. I swear to God, I'll make sure you're safe; that we're both safe.

Edwin is obviously sick. We'll get him help and ensure he can't hurt anyone."

"What's wrong with people that they do these awful things?"

"I don't know, sweetheart."

They were quiet for a few more minutes, then Jack craned his head to stare from the window. "We're almost home."

Brook tried not to appear as overwhelmed as she felt. His father would hate her, how could he not when she was disrupting his family like this? And maybe sending her away had been his idea. Maybe Jack was just as mistaken about his father as he'd been about his brother.

The car slowed, and she tried to straighten her hair and brushed futilely at her stained dress.

"You look beautiful," Jack murmured and she snorted.

Tea and vomit stained her dress, and she'd somehow managed to lose one of the buttons from her sweater. Her only consolation was Jack looked no better. His uniform was wrinkled and dirty and hung loosely on him. Stubble lined his jaws and his eyes were sunken, but they shone with love when he smiled at her.

"We'll be okay."

She nodded and gave up on her hair, letting it fall as it would and turned to gaze from the window. Trees lined the broad street and blocked the view of the large homes set well back from the road. The road wound and curved up a low hill and the homes became grander as they drove, hidden behind fences and landscaping.

She'd known his family was wealthy by the ring he'd given her but wasn't prepared for this level of opulence. *No wonder Edwin had sent me away,* she thought as the car halted before a gated drive. A man wearing blue livery swung open the gate and grinned broadly, calling loudly, "Welcome home, Master Jack."

Jack lifted his hand to wave but didn't open the window. "Thank you, Franz, it's good to be back."

Brook wondered if the man had heard him through the closed window. He smiled after them as if brisk greetings were normal. She shrugged and turned her attention to the house. She'd have time to make friends with the staff later.

Trees shaded both sides of the drive and allowed glimpses of extensive gardens and a wide stone porch. Brook's heart thudded as the car pulled up before the house. An older woman with gray hair and a tight smile emerged before the car came to a complete stop.

"Master Jack," she cried as she scurried down the broad steps. "Your father has been waiting." She reached for the door handle but let her hands drop and wrung them as if unsure what to do.

The driver exited the car and opened the door

Jack laughed as he stepped out and kissed her cheek. He turned from the flustered woman and offered Brook a hand. "Meet my wife, Brook. Brook, this is our housekeeper, Mrs. Schmidt." He peered around as if expecting to see someone and the smile faded from Mrs. Schmidt's face.

"Oh, you poor dear. You haven't heard, have you? Marie has passed. A tragic accident. I'm so sorry, Master Jack." Mrs. Schmidt patted him awkwardly and wiped at her eyes. She sniffed hard and straightened, saying briskly. "Shall I take your bags?"

A visible tremor shook Jack, and his eyes were bleak when he glanced at her. Whoever Marie had been it was clear her death hurt him.

"We've got it," Jack said. He turned to the driver. "Thank you. I'll be sure to give your company glowing recommendations."

As he spoke, Brook grabbed his pack and hugged it to her chest.

"I'll see to him," Mrs. Schmidt said and made a shooing motion. "Go speak to the mister. The house is in a twitter. He's sent most of the staff away, said they were annoying him with their pacing and worried looks, but we're all that concerned the doctor was called in the middle of the night, and he's been holed up with his lawyer since."

"I'll go to him directly." Jack tried to take his pack, but she clutched it tighter.

"Who is Marie?" Brook asked.

"The woman who raised me when my mother passed. She lived here my entire life. She was my mother's cousin and the kindest person." Jack rubbed his face and cleared his throat. "You'd have loved her. I loved her..."

"Oh, Jack," Brook said and tried to hug him.

He laughed sadly and took the pack from her. For a minute they embraced until Mrs. Schmidt cleared her throat.

Brook tried to take the pack back.

"Don't be silly," Jack said.

She frowned and clutched her sweater closed. Jack's expression softened, and he took her hand.

"It's just a house, Brook," he whispered as he led her inside. "They're just people, and you're the most beautiful woman I've ever seen.

She laughed ruefully and let her sweater fall open.

Their footsteps echoed on the marble foyer, and she gazed about, taking in the wooden paneling and crystal fixtures. Discreetly lighted art lined the walls interspersed with statues and potted plants. Despite the elegance it somehow had a homey feel. Maybe from the slightly shabby furniture she glimpsed through an open door they passed. It looked well-worn but clean and comfortable and reminded her of her father's study. A flicker of movement caught her eye and Brook wondered how many people lived in the house. Mrs. Schmidt had said all the other servants had left. She slowed, wondering if the occupant would come introduce themselves, but Jack tugged her hand.

"My mother's drawing room," he said but didn't stop. "Her room has the best view of the side gardens. It used to be my favorite room in the house. When Janice and I were little, we'd play on the patio while she worked at her desk in the adjoining office. I'll give you a tour later." He smiled tenderly at her. "I envision you sitting at her desk with our children playing in the garden. I'll be working across from you and be able to hear my family laughing. We'll be so happy here, Brook, I promise."

She tried to give him a reassuring smile, but by his pained grimace, failed. He released her hand to let her use both to grasp the rail, and she limped slowly up the stairs, having to pull herself up. The ride and tension had stiffened her leg, making each step an effort.

"We can redo a room downstairs until your leg heals or even put in an elevator," Jack said.

"This is quite a hike." Brook paused halfway up to catch her breath, resisting the urge to rub her aching leg. "I don't think I could manage it when I'm farther along."

He kissed her lightly, but it was the tender expression on his face that made her sigh and tear up.

He grinned and tweaked a strand of her hair. "We'll have to put in an elevator. I want lots of children."

She laughed, this time sincerely, and began climbing again. Another twenty or so steps remained to be climbed. They'd just reached the top when Mrs. Schmidt entered and called after them. "The mister has taken the blue rooms, Master Jack, and ordered the master suite readied for your use. Shall I send up tea, or perhaps ready a bath?"

Brook blushed hotly and released Jack's hand to clutch her sweater closed again. She was tempted to ask for that bath right now but had no clothes to change into and didn't want to miss Jack's reunion with his father. If his father didn't want her here either, it was best to know it and go at once.

The thought that he might convince Jack to send her way or that she might come between them made her stomach turn, and she had to take a few deep breaths to quell the rising nausea.

"Tea would be lovely," Jack called and changed direction, heading to the narrower corridor to the left, which the curve of the stairs had hidden.

They stood on a wide landing that overlooked the foyer two stories below them on one side with wide window seats on the far end that spilled sunlight across the hallway. Plump cushions looked inviting, and she was tempted to sit a minute but contented herself with admiring the view of a small interior courtyard. Somewhere there where stairs leading to a third story, she surmised because across from her were two rows of windows. And she assumed the room sizes were more traditional without the towering twenty-foot ceilings of these front rooms.

Jack let her look for a minute before pulling her forward. Chandeliers sparkled the length of the hallway. Brook had never been in a house as grand as this, and she took slow steps as she peered at the portraits lining the walls between the wide doorways, wondering if they were family portraits.

I haven't been home in years," Jack said as he led them down the long hallway. "It's nice to see my mom's room opened again though. Dad kept it closed up since she died. Don't worry, sweetheart, I swear my dad will like you."

She tried to smile back at him, but his smile was so strained she gave it up and just nodded. He grimaced and open his mouth as if he was going to speak but shut it and shook his head. The slight mummer of men's voices reached them, and she again tried to smooth her hair.

Jack taped once on a doorway and stepped into the room. Three older men waited inside the spacious bedroom. One lay in a bed. Another, dressed in a suit she thought cost more than she made in a year, turned from the wide windows, letting the blue silk curtains fall closed while the third rose from the chair he'd been seated in beside the bed.

"Jack," the old man in the bed cried out and held out a trembling hand. Tears filled his eyes, and he tried to rise. The other man pushed him back down as Jack released her hand to hug his father.

"Jack," his father whispered as he held him tightly.

"Dad, I'm so sorry to come home like this."

"Don't be ridiculous. I'm just happy you *are* home. And this must be Brook." He released Jack and held out a hand to her.

She shook it awkwardly.

"We're so happy to have you. This Edwin business..." His mouth tightened, and the happiness fled his face. "I'll handle Edwin." He clasped her hand in both of his a moment before releasing her.

"You'll rest here if you don't want to have a stroke," the other man disagreed.

Jack's father made an annoyed sound.

"I'm Mr. Phips, a friend of the family and Jack's solicitor," the well-dressed man said as he rounded the bed and offered his hand to Brook.

She shook it as he continued, "This is Doctor Ames, another friend of the family.

"He's a quack," Jack's father said irritably.

Doctor Ames laughed and waved a hand. "Fine. Don't listen. Kill your fool self." He turned from the bed and pursed his lips as his gaze raked Brook. "And you look like you could use a rest too."

"Yes, you should rest, my dear." Jack's father

said as he reached for a small bell beside his bed.

Mrs. Schmidt stuck her head inside the room from a doorway opposite the bed before he'd even replaced the bell on the table. It was clear she'd come up a back way and been lurking.

"Tea will be ready momentarily." Mrs. Schmidt bobbed her head and half curtsied.

"Escort Brook— I can call you Brook, can't I? and you must call me Francis or Dad."

"Brook is fine, Francis." She took Jack's hand, holding it in both of hers and gave him a beseeching glance. He pulled her into his side.

"I'll bring her to our room after we talk," Jack said to her relief and gave her a quick hug.

Doctor Ames waved her to his vacated seat.

Jack said, "Rest, sweetheart Your leg must be hurting you."

"I'll bring the tea at once," Mrs. Schmidt said.

"Doctor, if you could..." Jack trailed off, giving her an apologetic grimace.

She half laughed and shook her head. "I told you I was fine..."

"Doctor's make the worst patients," Doctor Ames said as he lifted Brook's hand and felt for her pulse. "Francis has told us you were attending medical school before the war. He gave her a friendly smile and dropped his hand. "Nice and steady."

Jack frowned and waved the doctor back. "She was shot. If you could check the wound?"

"Shot!" Francis exclaimed and turned to glare

at Phips as he threw back the covers.

"It's nothing," Brook said and tried to push Jack's hands from her sweater.

"It isn't nothing." Jack dropped his pack at his feet and used both hands to take her sweater.

Brook gave up trying to stop him and removed it.

"The bounder," Francis said in a combination of horror and indignation when Jack unzipped her dress and lowered the top to reveal the bruise.

Brook blushed and held the dress to cover her breasts as the doctor leaned closer and made a discontented noise. He sounded so like her father, she burst into tears.

"I'm okay," she said and tried to stop crying, pulling away and trying to do up her dress.

Eavesdroppers Seldom Hear Good

Edwin pressed his eye to the keyhole in time to see Doctor Ames pat Brook's hand and pluck the sweater from Jack.

He'd had to wait to enter this room until Mrs. Schmidt had returned to the kitchen where she belonged. He should've fired her when he'd gotten rid of Marie. The woman was getting above herself, listening at keyholes and being where she wasn't wanted. She'd almost caught him in Sylvie's study, his study now, he reminded himself, and he was glad he'd taken it over despite what was sure to be a scene from his father when he learned of it. Not only did it have easy access to the house, but it had easy access to his father's office— and safe. But first he needed to know what Jack had said. He ran to lock the hall door, then lowered himself to peer through the keyhole again.

Doctor Ames helped Brook don the sweater

as he said, "It's a bad bruise but without x-rays, I can't say if the bone is broken.

"It isn't," Brook said and sniffed.

Edwin fumed. If he'd been just a few minutes earlier he could've stopped them. But she wasn't hurt very badly at all. In fact, he was surprised he'd managed to hit her. He clenched the doorknob. Maybe she was lying, and his shot had gone nowhere near her.

The doctor patted her hand again and reached for his black bag that sat on the small table beside the bed, withdrew a wad of tissues, and handed them to Brook. While she blew her nose, he poured a glass of water and took out a small bottle.

"Take two, my dear. It's just a mild pain medicine. It's perfectly safe and won't harm the baby."

Sweat sprang to Edwin's brow, and he absently wiped it, thinking he might be sick. *She was pregnant? How could that be?* The sick feeling subsided as his anger grew. *She was probably lying about that too.* If she was pregnant, it wasn't Jack's child, he was certain of that, not with the way she lived with the whores.

Doctor Ames withdrew another bottle and placed it on the bedside. "Francis, you're to take this medicine in a timely manner. The shock hasn't been kind to your blood pressure."

"I'm perfectly all right," Francis said and scowled. He stood and reached for his dressing gown.

"Dad, do what the doctor says. I'll take care of Brook."

"I'm perfectly all right. It's just a bad bruise," Brook insisted.

Jack opened his pack and began emptying it to everyone's bemusement.

"What on earth are you doing?" Francis asked.

Jack withdrew a metal sculpture and placed it on the small table beside the bed. He rummaged again and took out another that he offered to Phips who hesitantly took it.

"I bought these for Brook. I'd intended them as a small reminder of our honeymoon in Paris, but they saved her life. See?" Jack took the sculpture from Phips and handed it to his father. "You can see the bullet. He meant to kill her, Dad. Those weren't warning shots or blanks. If she hadn't grabbed my pack, she and my unborn child would be dead right now. He crawled into her room with a knife. A knife!"

Edwin inadvertently turned the handle on the door, clenching the knob so tightly it hurt his hand, but no one appeared to notice the small sound. He forced himself to release it and took a few deep breaths. The pounding of blood in his ears blocked their next words.

His legs trembled badly as he lowered himself to peer through the keyhole again. He wished he'd bought enough bullets to shoot everyone in the room, but he'd used them all last night.

The doctor made tsking noises and felt Brook's pulse before reaching for Francis.

"Sit," he said gruffly and pushed him down into the bed.

"I've already spoken to the police. We're to report at our earliest convenience," Mr. Phips said. "I'd hoped he'd meant to scare her off..."

Edwin nodded and smiled, absently wiping his sweating brow on sleeve. He was about to enter and protest his innocence when Jack said, "I tried to tell myself that too." He squatted before his father and took his hands. "But he tried to shoot me too. More than once. We must do something about him. I'm sorry, Dad."

Francis patted his cheek. "I'll take care of it. I should've been more vigilant. I'd suspected he was stealing from your company..." Francis sighed hard and pinched the bridge of his nose. "I'd hoped he could pull himself out of the mess he was making." He dropped his hands and grabbed Jack's. "I swear I'd no idea he'd think murder the only way out. Agnes will be destroyed."

They were worried about Agnes? They believed Jack's lies and were worried about his damned wife? Rage suffused him, growing as the men continued to plot. They'd turn their backs and dismiss him as if he meant nothing. It was always Jack. It would always be Jack.

"We can arrange to commit him," Mr. Phips said. "Get him the help he needs. He can live out his years safely locked away, and his wife could continue as she is. No one need know. We could say the stress of running the business was too much, and he's retired for his health. Neither Jack nor Brook would even need to testify. Edwin will see this is in his own best interest."

"And the police will allow it?" Francis asked.

"The police don't yet know it was Edwin who fired the shots. If Jack say's nothing..." he cleared his throat and spoke directly to Brook. "I realize this is a lot to ask. The man did try to murder you and should be held accountable for it. If you'd like—"

"Whatever Jack wants is fine with me," Brook said without glancing up from Jack's pack she was repacking.

"Then, with Doctor Ames assistance, I shall prepare—"

A knock on the door interrupted them. Mrs. Schmidt entered from the main hallway and set the tea tray on the table before the windows.

Edwin ran from the room. Peggy would have to be bought off. He'd retrieve the money from his safe and arrange his alibi, and then let that bitch and his lying brother try to get rid of him. He'd ruin them; tell the world what a whore she was. They'd forgotten he knew their marriage was a sham. He'd make them pay for their lies. He'd fucking kill them both.

Brook made a soft sound of distress and slapped a hand to her mouth.

Jack released his father's hands to go to her but before he reached her, she'd jumped to her feet.

"I brought some sandwiches," Mrs. Schmidt said.

Jack laughed ruefully and turned to wave her away. "No eggs for Brook. Sweetheart, there's a bathroom right next door. Shall I come?"

Brook headed to the door whiteout speaking, holding his pack to her face, but waved him away. He hesitated and returned to his father.

"Brook can't bear the smell of eggs. Perhaps you could send up some toast and fruit?"

"I'm sorry," Mrs. Schmidt said as she replaced the plate of sandwiches on the tray. "I'd thought you might be hungry and might enjoy some egg salad.... I'll be sure to inform the staff."

"My wife is expecting—"

"My grandchild," Francis said excitedly, then glowered. "Ames, you must see to her. The stress... this can't be good. What was he thinking?

Jack waved the doctor back. "Brook's okay. She'll tell me if she needs a doctor. I'm more worried about you.

"Fiddle faddle." Francis waved his hand and glared at Doctor Ames. "I have plenty of life left in me. When I get my hands on him—"

❧❧❧

Edwin ran two doors down and into his room where he opened his safe and grabbed the money inside. He frowned as he eyed the thin stack of bills, but it would have to do until he'd got a chance to get more. Peggy would trust him to get it to her. His frown died to a feral grin, *and accidents happened.* If he could keep the police from being involved, he'd think of something to silence them all.

Water ran in the bathroom next door and he straightened. It had to be Brook. Anyone else would've used Francis bathroom, not his. Not even Agnes used his.

He laughed as he remembered he'd left a gift for Peggy hidden in the vanity, jewelry he'd stolen from his wife and meant to send to Peggy who showed her gratitude for such gifts by letting him draw blood.

"Fate," he said as he opened the adjoining door. He'd give her the jewelry and the money, but maybe Brook could be talked around or scared away. He still had the letter to threaten her with.

"Brook," he said in the kindest voice he could manage as he stepped into the room.

She dropped the small package she held and whirled to face him.

"I wasn't trying to hurt anyone just scare you away."

She nodded and took a slow step back, nudging the vanity drawer closed with her knee.

"I know the truth about your sham of a marriage, and how you really make your money." He held up his hand as she opened her mouth.

She snapped her mouth closed and took another slow step backward.

"But my brother loves you, and for his sake, I can accept you."

"Thank you," she whispered. Her gaze flicked from the knife he held to his face and she nodded and licked her lips, sliding Jack's pack over one arm, wearing it across her chest like a shield.

He glanced down, surprised he'd pulled the knife, he didn't remember doing so. He shrugged and tapped the handle of the knife on his palm, pursing his lips.

"This is just between us."

He smiled when she nodded again. He loved how afraid she was— how submissive.

"I have an alibi anyway." He picked up the package and slipped it into his pocket, and she took two quick steps away, grabbing the doorknob.

He rested a hip on the vanity. "Take one more step before were finished talking, and it will be your last."

Tears sprang to her eyes and trickled down her cheeks, and she removed her hand from the knob to place it beneath the pack on her stomach.

He frowned, not liking the reminder. "I bet it

isn't even Jack's. I know you worked at the whorehouse where I met Peg."

"Peggy Martin?"

He stood and glared. Fear and fury made his voice tremble. "You know her?"

He could see her deciding to lie. Of course she knew her, and by her reaction they were friends. Maybe good enough friends Peggy wouldn't lie for me. Of course, if Brook were already dead there would be no reason for Peggy to protect her. He hesitated caught by confusion. His logic seemed faulty somehow. He closed his eyes and rubbed his face hard, trying to gather his scattered thoughts.

The quiet creak of the door handle made his eyes spring open.

"You bitch!" he yelled and lunged after her.

"Help!" she screamed as he grabbed her by her hair.

"We're talking!" he shouted in a furious whisper and tried to drag her back into the bathroom.

A woman's cut off cry interrupted them.

"Brook," Jack shouted and raced for the door. She screamed again, and glass broke. He ran into the hall in time to see Brook scratch his brother's face. She slapped at his face and arms and screamed for help.

She'd turned the wrong way when she'd left

the room and had entered Edwin's bathroom. She and his brother stood on the landing five feet from his doorway. Jack didn't know if she'd turned the wrong way when she'd run from Edwin or had tried to get to the stairs, but it was clear a violent altercation had taken place. The vase that had sat on a small table was broken, likely the glass he'd heard break and her face was pale and strained.

"Let her go," Jack shouted and ran.

Edwin glanced over his shoulder. His face was contorted with fury, his eyes wild. Blood dripped across his forehead from Brook's scratches, and Jack could hear him pant from twenty-feet away. He slowed when he spied the knife Edwin held.

"Peggy will tell you I was nowhere near New York. She isn't your friend, but mine!"

Brook nodded frantically and clawed at the hand on her throat.

Edwin released her throat to grab her shoulders and shake her, pushing her hard against the rail that encircled the balcony overlooking the main floor.

"Yes. I'm sure she's a different Peggy," Brook said as her wide eyes begged Jack for help. She dropped her hands to hug his pack to her chest, turning her face away from both of them. Her hair swung forward to hide her expression, but Jack knew she was crying.

He slowed and held out his hands. "Edwin?"

Edwin grabbed Brook's throat again and

turned to yell over his shoulder at Jack, "Your wife is a whore. A whore Jack! I have proof."

Jack nodded and licked his dry lips, taking a slow step forward. "Okay, just let her go, and we can talk."

"Release her this instant," Francis snapped.

Edwin slumped and turned back to Brook. "Your goddamned friend," he said in tone of harsh disgust.

His expression darkened, and his lip lifted in a sneer. Jack began running again.

"Help," Brook cried and hunched away from the knife Edwin held. He laughed as he dropped the knife and grabbed her arms, grunting a bestial cry and heaved.

Jack screamed as Brook tumbled over the rail.

"You bounder!" Francis yelled breathlessly.

Jack knocked his brother away as Brook screamed again. The air seemed to be thick and slow his movements as he reached uselessly for his falling wife.

Brook!" his cry emerged as a wail. He knew he was too late. A fall from this height onto a marble floor would almost certainly be fatal. He closed his eyes as his hand grasped empty air.

Instead of the thump he'd been expecting, metal clanged, and she grunted and screamed a gasping cry. His eyes flew open, and he peered down.

His pack had caught on one of the decorative

scrolled curlicues that decorated the railing. She clutched the pack with both hands, kicking the air. Her terrified eyes locked on him.

Jack threw himself forward, the metal rail hard against his stomach. He grasped it with one hand and strained to reach her. "Grab my hand! Brook, grab my hand!"

Sweat burned Jack's eyes mixing with his tears.

"You fucker! Always taking what should be mine. Damn you, Damn you!" Edwin continued to curse as he tried to pull him away.

Jack released the rail to hit him without looking and stretched for Brook. She sobbed and lifted a trembling hand to him but screamed and grabbed the pack as a strap broke, leaving her dangling farther away. Edwin grabbed his legs as Brook screamed again.

"What's going on here," Agnes said.

Jack didn't spare a glance for his sister-in-law. He kicked backward, knocking Edwin loose, then turned and hit him as hard as he could.

"Damn you," Edwin cursed and tried to hit him back, but Phips and Frances grabbed his arms.

"Hold on, Brook. Please hold on!" Jack dropped to his stomach to reach through the railing. His fingertips grazed the edge of his pack. The muscles in his back and shoulder protested as he forced his arm farther, and he tried not to think of the pain she must be in with her wounded leg and shoulder. She wouldn't be able to hold on much longer.

The sound of a fight broke out behind him, but Jack couldn't spare any attention from his terrified wife.

"I can't," Brook sobbed as the strap of the pack parted with a sound like ripping paper.

Jack screamed and caught the trailing edge, yanking with all his might.

"Grab the rail!" Francis yelled. "Call for help!"

"What on earth is going on?" Agnes asked again. "Who is that woman, and what is happening?"

The weight suddenly left the pack, and he sobbed and let it fall as he bounded to his feet. Tears clouded his vision and the blood pounding in his ears muffled sounds as he reached over the rail for Brook who grasped the railing with a white-knuckled grip.

"Take my hand," he said and sobbed again when her hand closed on his. He pulled her up and fell backward, landing hard on the parquet floor with her on top of him.

"Jesus, are you okay? Doctor!" Jack called as he cradled his sobbing wife. He turned in time to see Edwin hit their father and push Phips away. Edwin laughed as he grabbed Agnes and shook her.

"Stop!" Agnes batted at his hands.

Edwin slapped her hard. "You ruin everything. I should've killed you years ago, you goddamned bitch."

Agnes cried out, struggling in his grasp as he yanked her away from the knot of men.

"Let her go, son," Francis said in a shaky voice.

Phips was trying to pull him to his feet while Doctor Ames hovered.

"See to Brook." Francis waved the doctor away.

"Brook," Edwin spat and shook Agnes again. "You aren't even a woman. To think, I squandered myself on you. I wasted my life on you. I should've killed you."

He laughed, the sound sending chills down Jack's spine. Doctor Ames peered over his shoulder and began to turn, his hand going into his black bag.

"Well, it isn't too late is it? The stairs are still here, aren't they? I wasted them on Marie, but if you think you'll lock me away and keep playing lady of the manor, think again!"

"Edwin, No," Jack cried out and tried to rise, knowing he'd be too late.

"Stop him!" Brook gasped out through her tears and pushed against his shoulder trying to rise.

Agnes seemed to sense her imminent danger. She screamed shrilly and stopped slapping at her husband to grasp his tie in both hands.

Edwin laughed as he pushed her hard. His laugh cut off mid cackle, and he grunted as he reached for her hands, but Agnes weight pulled him forward. He flailed as Agnes screamed and released him. The scream cut off abruptly, but Jack could hear her body thudding down the wide stairs.

For a moment, Edwin met Jack's eyes, his face furious. His eyes swung to Francis and his expression became bleak. He stopped trying to grasp the bannister and spread his arms.

Jack closed his eyes as his brother fell.

Epilogue

Five Months Later

Jack jumped to his feet as Doctor Ames exited the bedroom, rolling down his shirt sleeves. Francis rose to his feet and Mrs. Schmidt clasped her hands.

Doctor Ames grinned widely at Jack. Jack smiled shakily back. He'd been waiting in the hallway for hours. His father and the servants came and went, the quiet whoosh of the new elevator announcing their arrival.

Francis had ordered the stairs removed and an elevator installed where it'd been. The railing had been taken down and a wall put up. Two small couches and built in bookcases now filled what had once been the balcony.

Workmen had just finished installing the new wood paneling two weeks before and they'd done a fine job. The changes blended perfectly into the existing architecture. Jack doubted he'd ever forget the sight of his brother's face as he fell but maybe Brook would. And it was easier to walk the hall with the stairs gone. She seemed happy here and had made his mother's office her own and begun putting her mark on the rest of the house. And soon his children would run these halls and make memories they could all enjoy.

Doctor Ames said, "You have a fine son"—and offered his hand.

Jack shook it absently. "Can I see her?"

"Yes. Your wife is doing well."

"A toast to my grandson," Jack's father said, and Mrs. Schmidt laughed.

Jack rushed into his bedroom, the closing door cutting off the talk in the hallway.

Brook smiled at him, and his heart caught. She was exactly as he'd envisioned her so long ago. Sunlight haloed her hair, highlighting the auburn strands loose across her breast and gilded her check as she kissed the newborn she cradled in her arms. He tucked the red wool blanket about them and sat beside her, resting his hand on his son's back.

"Meet your son," she said in her musical voice as she held out the baby for his inspection.

He kissed her lips, then the baby's head and straightened the collar of her lacy robe as he pulled away.

"Jack Junior," she continued and lifted the baby to her cheek again

"We have a son." Emotion made his voice thick, and he had to clear his throat to continue.

"I'll telegraph your parents and send them tickets to come see us."

Her smile lit her beautiful eyes. "Maybe we can talk them into staying?"

Jack ran a finger along his son's cheek. "You're as beautiful as your mother," he whispered as he leaned to kiss the baby again. "How could your parents resist staying with him as enticement?" he asked as he straightened.

She laughed and slid her dressing gown open to settle their son to her breast. Jack watched with a contentment he'd never felt before as she fed their son and took the sleeping baby from her when he'd finished. The small warm weight in his hands made tears fall from his eyes. So many times he'd thought this day would never happen for him. To have such a loving wife, and now this beautiful boy... he was beyond lucky and knew it.

The death of his brother and sister-in-law might have frightened Brook away, but she'd been a rock. For months he'd worried the stress, or her injuries would cause her to miscarry, but here she was now, the picture of health and beauty. He and his father were still straightening out the mess Edwin had made of their finances but even with the losses they'd be fine. As far as the world knew their deaths had been another tragic accident. Doctor Ames and Phips had both given statements to that effect and none had doubted them, not even Mrs. Schmidt who'd arrived while Edwin fell.

It sometimes angered him that Marie had received no justice, but she wouldn't want little Jack to grow up with the stigma of a murderer in his family.

As if reading his mind, Brook said, "I'd hoped for a daughter we could name Marie, but he's perfect, isn't he?"

"He is, and maybe next time there'll be a girl?"

She winced, laughed, and rubbed her stomach.

He grinned. "But we need to have two daughters. Lydia and Marie Pryor."

She smiled the beautiful brilliant smile he loved and reached a hand to him. He kissed her fingertips. "We're going to be so happy, Brook."

"I'm already the happiest woman on Earth, Jack."

———————

The End

Upcoming Book by C. M. Conney

Hidden in Plain Sight

A Company L Novel

Can a suicidal woman and a desperate man rescue each other?

Henry Reynolds is a fighter willing to do just about anything to stay alive. When he's shot and left for dead on a battlefield in Belgium, he doesn't give up. Surrounded by the enemy, injured, freezing and lost in a Belgium forest. he's saved from certain death by a local who stumbles across him.

Anna Meas has given up. The cold woods call to her, and she'd meant that trip into the forest to be her last. But there's some things Henry won't do to stay alive and sacrificing an innocent woman to save his own skin is one of them, even if she wants to die....